Love and Purple Sea Serpents

Tani Miller

Love and Purple Sea Serpents

Tani Miller

ISBN 978-0-692-87807-1

ONE

So Damn Good-Lookin'

It has been said that a pretty face is a passport. But it's not, it's a visa, and it runs out fast.
Julie Burchill

On the first day of fall in the small town of Middleton, New Hampshire, a large brown delivery truck shuttered to an abrupt halt in front of Stella's Beauty Salon. The driver, Jimmy, reached for his cherry-cola, a free treat he had obligingly accepted from Casey the cashier at his last delivery. He stirred the dark red icy slush with its straw then took a sip. Suddenly—the truck lurched forward. His heart skipped a beat as the sticky cold drink sloshed onto his shirt. It felt like a minor impact.

Jimmy reached out the window and turned the side view mirror to see who had hit him. In the mirror's reflection he could see eighty-three-year-old Ida Mae Perkins backing up her old beat up sedan. He sighed, "Oh, man, not again." He hopped down from the truck and briefly surveyed his bumper for damage, cringing at the thought of the paperwork he would have to endure to explain yet another dent to his truck.

Jimmy made note not to walk between the two vehicles as Ida Mae aggressively wedged her big jalopy into the parallel parking spot behind his. As he stepped behind her car, it suddenly backfired, compelling him to leap back onto the sidewalk. He did a mental body scan to assure all of his body parts were still intact then cautiously approached Ida

Mae's open window. "Mrs. Perkins," he said with polite restraint, "you hit my truck again."

"Oh, dear," Ida Mae responded, peering up through her thick lenses, "did I do any damage?"

"No," Jimmy answered wearily. *Nothing new anyways,* he thought. "Are you okay?" he asked.

"Oh, yes, thank you," Ida Mae responded with a wide toothless grin. "I'll be more careful next time, Jimmy."

This was the third time Ida Mae had hit Jimmy's truck, but he was a compassionate fellow and didn't want to get the old bird in trouble. "Okay, Mrs. Perkins, thank you," said Jimmy, not convinced. *I have got to change my schedule,* he thought as he walked back to his truck, *Ida Mae shows up like clockwork.*

It was well known Tuesday was Jimmy's delivery day to the quaint little shops that lined Main Street, and not only by Ida Mae, several women in Stella's Beauty Salon were also taking notice. One of them, Dorothy Miller, cocooned in a leopard print cape, had risen from her chair to take a closer look through the large plate-glass window.

Before climbing back onto his truck, Jimmy stopped and carefully peeled off his cherry-cola soaked shirt. He squeezed out any remaining liquid. Fortunately he kept an extra shirt on his truck for days like this.

"Woo-ooo!" three young girls in a rusty red pickup hooted their approval as they drove by.

Jimmy smiled and waved back. He was of average height, but that was the only thing typical about him when it came to his physique. He was perfectly proportioned from his wide shoulders and sculpted pecs down to the sexy ripple of his abdomen. From behind, the view from Stella's window, one could get lost following the lines of his back and the curve of his firm buttocks.

"Oh, my," remarked Dorothy as she fanned off a hot flash with the latest gossip magazine. "Stella, throw me a towel," she called out to the salon owner, "I think Jimmy needs someone to dry him off."

Stella, winding another woman's hair onto gigantic blue curlers, laughed and shook her head. This happened every Tuesday, which not surprisingly, was also her busiest day. "Ida Mae must be up to her old tricks again," she chuckled.

"Tom Cruise," blurted a short, portly woman, her head covered in pink foils. She craned to take in the view.

"No, no," another lady argued, "Brad Pitt."

"He's got brown hair," Stella interjected, "Brad Pitt's a blonde."

"Yeah, Brad Pitt's a blonde," the lady in pink foils chimed.

"I don't care what color his hair is," stated Madge, a crusty-looking woman in her eighties, "I'd give him a go round any day."

"Oh, Madge," sighed the lady in blue curlers, "I highly doubt he would be interested in any of us."

"I could teach him a few things," Madge shot back with a naughty smile.

Everyone broke out in laughter.

Jimmy climbed into the truck and reached for his fresh shirt where it hung behind the driver's seat, still in its cleaner's sleeve. As he was buttoning it, he saw Ida Mae shuffle by and wave. He nodded back, unable to see her mischievous grin or the wink she cast up at Dorothy, still gawking through Stella's window. He stepped to the rear of the truck and began to sort through a stack of boxes for his deliveries. As always, his packages were neatly organized and he quickly found all eight. They were all small, nothing that would require the hand cart.

Before Jimmy stepped from the truck, he took a moment to check his reflection in a small mirror he had fastened to the overhead package bin. The same mirror his buddies back at the shop loved to tease him about. They had nicknamed him "The Stud." He didn't mind, he knew they were just jealous of his natural good looks. *Even if he wasn't so good-looking*, he thought, *I still have secret weapon number one: the uniform. Women can't resist the uniform*. His of course had been perfectly pressed, not like those other slackers back at the shop. Looking in the mirror, he ran his fingers through his thick dark brown hair. He gave his clean-shaven face a once over, checked his teeth, then flashed his signature smile. Satisfied with what he saw, he reached into the overhead bin where he kept his leather toiletry bag, one of the many gifts he had received along his route at Christmastime last year. Finding a bottle of Old Spice, another gift, he splashed some on. *Not too much,* he chuckled to himself, *can't lose the mystery*. Next he found the small plastic vial of breath freshener and after tightly squeezing his eyes shut, he spritzed. As usual, most of the overly concentrated spray missed its target. What did make it into his mouth caused him to wince. He was sure the awful taste rivaled that of his uncle's cheap whiskey. At the age of ten he had snuck a sip of it and to this day he could still not stand the sickly sweet taste or smell of hard liquor.

Ready or not ladies, here I come, Jimmy thought as he

picked up his packages and securely wedged them into the crook of his arm. He leapt energetically from the truck but not without having first filled his pants pocket with secret weapon number two: chocolate Hershey kisses. Along with their deliveries, Jimmy always gave every female customer a silver foil-wrapped chocolate kiss. Admittedly, secret weapon number two was not a purely selfless act, for it did not go unrewarded. In fact, the young deliveryman delighted in his own cleverness because the hugs, treats and real kisses that followed made him more than happy to oblige.

On the sidewalk, Jimmy paused for a moment and took a deep satisfying breath. His eyes surveyed his route on Main Street, or what he liked to refer to as "his domain." At the age of twenty-six, he was still a bachelor and there were lots of pretty, single women in this neck of the woods.

The rusty red pickup truck drove by and once again the girls hooted. Their pretty, youthful faces bright with laughter. "Lookin' good, Jimmy!" one of them called out.

Jimmy smiled broadly and waved back. *I should have a hat,* he thought. *Maybe a pirate hat, like Johnny Depp wore in the movie. No—a cowboy hat, then I could tip it and nod my head like John Wayne does in the old westerns on TV. Cowboys always make the women swoon.* His uniform came with a hat, but he refused to wear it. He thought it made him look like a dorky school kid. Worse—it messed up his hair.

Most everyone in the town of Middleton knew Jimmy. Not only because of his occupation; he was born and raised in the Middleton area. Growing up, he found the location to be the perfect jumping off spot for the outdoor activities he loved. With its White Mountains, lush forests and pristine lakes it provided some of the most stunning scenery in the country. Today was no exception. With fall engaging, the mid-morning air felt crisp and invigorating. It energized him and his legs moved quickly along the brick sidewalk. A kaleidoscope of newly fallen leaves seemed to dance and swirl along with him.

"Hi, Jimmy!" a pretty young woman named Cindy waved from across the tree-lined street; her short, red-and-white polka-dot skirt swished flirtatiously as she walked. Melanie, another stylish young woman walking with her quickly stiffened and averted her eyes towards the sidewalk. She held her breath as she always did when Jimmy came around.

"Hello, Cindy," Jimmy waved back. "Aren't the two of you looking gorgeous today!"

Cindy laughed and cheerfully grabbed Melanie's arm. "See, I told you he knows my name," she said, as if to settle a previous argument.

Melanie, her face now bright red from lack of air, gasped and took a deep breath.

"Oh, you are too silly," said Cindy, playfully taking hold of her arm. The two girls continued on their way as girlish laughter bubbled up between them.

Jimmy often had this effect on women. Even though admittedly he may not be ready to settle down, he still considered himself one of the good guys and he genuinely liked women. He was polite and even though he used flattery without reserve, it was always tempered with respect. *And let's face it,* he thought with a chuckle, *it doesn't hurt to be so damn good-lookin'*.

Jimmy's first delivery was to The Big Pink Donut Shop. Like most of the businesses on Main Street, The Big

Pink Donut occupied the first floor of a restored two story brick-faced building. The buildings were all built in the sixties and their architecture could only be described as simple and basic. It was the various details such as interesting hardware, awnings, decorative wood trim, window displays and flowers that set them apart and gave each building its own personality. Many of their owners also lived in the apartment space on the second floor. The Big Pink Donut's attributes included a pink and white candy-striped awning and pink flowers spilling out of a rustic window box. Through the plate-glass window, fresh pastries easily beckoned customers in as they walked past. Not to mention the realistic looking replica of a giant pink frosted donut suspended from a horizontal pole above the awning.

Following the morning rush, Marjorie, the owner, a plump woman with auburn hair twisted into a loosening bun, was busy restocking the doughnut trays. She was assisted by her daughter, Tammy. Recently, twenty-one-year-old Tammy had returned from college where she had received a degree in fashion design. She was temporarily helping out at the bakery while she decided where next to take her career. However, Marjorie had other plans. She had decided it was time to find her only unmarried daughter an eligible suitor. Seeing Jimmy come in, she seized the opportunity. She gave Tammy a discreet nudge and nodded toward the counter. Tammy looked up and immediately froze in her tracks. A bit of an oddball and painfully shy, Tammy had always had a huge crush on Jimmy. That morning, anticipating his deliveries, she had picked out her favorite vintage dress to wear—a lime green and pink frock with a full skirt and mother-of-pearl buttons. The dress was in perfect condition and she had carefully pressed the original grosgrain ribbon belt, trimming it of any lose threads.

She had even found a matching pair of pink rhinestone reading glasses in her extensive accessory collection. She wore them even though they made her lose her balance.

"Mmmm—mmm," said Jimmy as he took in the sweet smell of pastries commingled with the aroma of freshly brewed coffee. "Smells good in here," he commented as he placed two chocolate kisses and a small package atop the glass display case. His mouth watered as he scanned the sugary confections. As always, the case was filled with fanciful cupcakes. Today's assortment was exceptional. There were red velvet cupcakes with buttercream icing, carrot cupcakes with a cream cheese swirl and toasted coconut, and banana nut cupcakes topped with candied pecans, just to name a few. There was also a fresh tray of The Big Pink Donut's signature brownies bulging with chunks of dark chocolate and walnuts.

Marjorie, realizing Tammy had still not budged, wiped her sugar-laden fingers on her apron and picked up the package along with the chocolate kisses. "Thank you, Jimmy," she said with a smile, "it's always a pleasure to see you. You remember my daughter, Tammy, don't you?"

Tammy pushed her pink rhinestone glasses up on her nose and somehow managed an awkward smile.

"Of course," Jimmy responded, smiling back at her.

"Would you like a cookie?" Marjorie asked, nudging her daughter again, this time with more conviction. "The chocolate chips are fresh out of the oven."

Tammy, instead of taking the cue, made a bee-line to the far end of the counter and nervously began refilling the glass sugar containers. Marjorie frowned and gave her a reprimanding look.

"Sure," said Jimmy.

Marjorie reached into a glass pedestal dish on the counter with a napkin and carefully selected a cookie. Everyone knew Marjorie's chocolate chip cookies were to die for; they had a melt-in-your-mouth quality and were one of her best sellers. She also knew they were Jimmy's favorite. She handed the cookie to him and smiled proudly as he quickly devoured it.

"That was dee-licious," said Jimmy, flashing a grin at Tammy.

Tammy, caught off guard, accidentally overfilled a container and sugar poured out onto the shiny pink Formica countertop. Embarrassed, she readjusted her now crooked rhinestone glasses and managed another awkward smile.

Marjorie rolled her eyes.

"Beautiful dress you have on, Tammy," Jimmy complimented.

"Thank you," she replied, a spark showing through her shyness. "It's vintage 1950's," she added, surprising both Jimmy and her mother. "I found it in a thrift shop in Vermont," she continued, her voice rising in excitement. "Its tag says 'Made in Paris.' I couldn't believe it when I found it." Realizing she was beginning to ramble, Tammy quickly reigned herself in and diverted her attention to cleaning up the sugar. *What a nerd,* she thought to herself. But she really couldn't help it; she was a freak for vintage.

"Cool," Jimmy nodded, impressed.

Marjorie rolled her eyes again. "Can you set a spell, Jimmy?" she asked. "Have some coffee?" She picked up a white coffee cup and shot a stern look at Tammy.

"Wish I could Marjorie, but a man's gotta work," Jimmy responded. "Have a nice day," he called back as he headed out the door.

"You, too," Marjorie replied, watching him go.

"Bye, Jimmy!" Tammy perked at the last minute but she was too late; Jimmy was already out the door. Up on tip-toes she leaned as far over the counter as she could to catch one last glimpse of him as he went.

Marjorie frowned then gave Tammy's arm a snap-out-of-it whack.

"*MOTHER!*"

Jimmy's next stop was Bartlett's General Store. A large free-standing building, *its* personality was shaped by the old reclaimed barn wood Mr. Green, the owner, had integrated into the exterior. On its wide front porch, fresh produce reflected the upcoming fall season. Apples had ripened early this year and there were barrels full from local orchards of sweet Red Delicious, crisp Cortlands and tart McIntosh. Displayed on hay bales were pumpkins of assorted sizes and an old farm table offered odd shaped gourds and colorful dried corn tied with raffia.

Inside, Jimmy dropped off two boxes and a chocolate kiss for Mrs. Green. She treated him to a chunk of homemade peanut-butter fudge and gave him an apple to tuck into his pocket. "For later," she added with a wink. "Can't have our Jimmy going hungry."

"Thank you," he replied. *Now if only someone would give me a corned beef sandwich*, he thought to himself as he left. Treats were common on his deliveries, although he truly did appreciate the kindness.

As he approached his third stop, the Calico Quilt and Fabric Shop, he looked at his watch. *Right on schedule*, he thought with satisfaction.

The Calico had the best selection of fabrics and notions in the area. Table after table had endless choices of fabrics: denims, chambray, cotton, tulle, wool, flannel, and much, much, more. If you could not find what you were looking for, Emmy Harris, the owner, would order it for you. In a small town like Middleton, she knew service was especially important. Inside, the popular store was bustling with female customers of all ages. On this day, they were having a sale on Celtic plaids and they had just received their first shipment of holiday fabrics.

Ding, ding, ding, the doorbells chimed as Jimmy entered the Calico. An excited, "Jimmy's here!" rippled through the store. Within moments, he found himself engulfed in a bevy of eager women looking for *their kiss.* And not necessarily a chocolate kiss. After all, not only were there daughters yet to be married in this town, there were also quite a few feisty widows.

Mrs. Chadwick, a woman in a golfing outfit edged in. "My daughter, Erin, will be in town this weekend. I would love for you to meet her."

Before he could respond, Trish Norton, the local librarian, invited him to a party she was throwing the next weekend. She was gazing dreamily up at him and over-blinking her baby blues.

"Such strong arms," admired Mrs. Robins as she squeezed his tanned bicep, her mature cleavage spilling out over her red scoop-neck top. "I could sure use some help around the house," she hinted with a wink.

A vision of vultures on a fresh kill suddenly flashed in Jimmy's mind. Beginning to feel boxed in, he nervously laughed and set a delivery package on the checkout counter.

He forgot about the chocolate kiss; he was more concerned about finding a clear path to the door. He stepped to the right of Mrs. Robins but another woman stood in his way. After several foiled attempts to leave, he soon found himself cornered between the bolts of seersuckers and chambrays. Several of the women were actually advancing toward him with their lips puckered up.

Emmy emerged from the back room and quickly realized Jimmy's predicament. She could see Jimmy's only chance for escape was for her to escort him to the door. "Okay ladies, step aside," she announced. "You know Jimmy is on a time schedule." She stuffed her tape measure into one of the many pockets of her blue work apron, then, amongst groans of disappointment, she began to shuttle Jimmy 'commando style' toward the door.

"Thank you, Mrs. Harris," said Jimmy, following closely.

Just moments from a successful getaway, a tall robust woman stepped into the aisle and blocked them. It was Hilda Brunner, a large imposing woman, gripping a bolt of navy blue flannel. As was Hilda's style, no matter what time of year it was, she wore her silver hair pulled tightly back in a low bun under a tilted dark fedora. Her gray pinstripe suit which she made herself (McCall vintage pattern #7973), was tailored to perfection. Its oversize shoulder pads emphasized her already broad shoulders. All of which only added to her ability to intimidate. "Hello, Jimmy," she said in her thick German accent, "I hear you are giving out kisses today."

"Huh, yes," Jimmy stammered and fumbled in his pocket for a chocolate.

Hilda leaned forward and jutted her chin, offering him

her left cheek.

Jimmy cringed and took a step back. Behind him near the counter, several other women had nervously huddled together. All of them knew Hilda and her dominating personality.

Emmy, at the age of sixty-six was much shorter than Hilda but robust in her own right. She stepped protectively in front of Jimmy and purposely planted her bobby-socked sneakers on the floor. “Step aside,” she said, looking menacingly up at Hilda.

An audible gasp came from the huddle of women. *No one* had ever challenged Hilda before.

Hilda squinted back at Emmy then firmly planted her size 13 black penny-loafers.

Emmy, still holding her ground, warned, “Back down Hilda or I’ll have to cancel that special order of yours. It won’t be easy finding Scottish wool in this town.”

For a moment, time froze and the huddle of women held its collective breath.

Hilda straightened up and took pause, her eyes still locked with Emmy’s. Finally, she grudgingly stepped aside only to reveal scrawny Ida Mae Perkins. Her eyes were squeezed shut and her lips were expectantly pursed. Jimmy, eyes-wide, quietly slipped past her and fled out the door.

“Oh, don’t you just love a man in uniform,” sighed Linda Lou Johnston as she watched him go. She was wearing a cute, blue-and-white floral dress (Butterick pattern #5488).

Cling—clang—clink. The bells jangled on the antique brass-hinged door of Middleton’s Old and New Bookstore announcing Jimmy’s arrival. His nerves had settled quickly following the Calico and his confidence was renewed.

The atmosphere of the bookstore was the exact opposite of what Jimmy had left behind at the Calico; it was comforting and quiet. But not because there were no customers, in fact, there were plenty of them. With row upon row of well-stocked bookshelves, it was a haven for those seeking the touch and smell of a real book, anxious to open new doors with each turn of a page. Though most of the books in the store were used, they were always clean and well organized. There was no hint of mustiness here as often found in old bookstores. Around every corner, artfully arranged book displays beckoned readers in search of new adventures, enrichment and inspiration.

In the many quiet nooks of the bookstore you could find *the regulars* occupying their favorite oversized armchairs, their books illuminated by colorful stained glass lamps. Unlike the women at the Calico, *their* emotions were unspoken. They were evident only if one took a closer look and analyzed their facial expressions or their body language. Like retired Colonel Richard Wilson. His jaw was set like stone as he sternly gripped his unlit pipe between his lips. He was scrutinizing a recent book written by a war correspondent he had considered completely out of touch. On the front, *he* had known a very different war. Or take Jane Bell. Deeply engrossed in her latest mystery novel, she was biting her fingernails as she turned each page with trepidation. In another corner, Wendy Maher, a self-described hopeless romantic, was suppressing quiet giggles and twirling her hair with her finger as she lingered on a page of a love story set in the days of castles and knights.

Near the front door of the store, natural light from the large glass window flooded onto a table full of new arrivals.

Of late, as was common this time of year, cookbooks were flying out the door as fast as they arrived. This table was usually the first stop for anyone that entered the store, but not Jimmy, *he* was on a mission. And not just to make his delivery—her name was Kate.

Jimmy spotted Kate, the owner of the store, immediately. He thought she looked pretty-as-a-picture in her soft blue pullover with her long brown hair femininely clipped back. Besides the fact that Jimmy found her attractive, he also thought her to be genuine and easy to talk to. He didn't get the sense that she wanted something from him like he often experienced with other women. He fixed his eyes on the counter where she stood, immersed in thought as she looked through some papers. He approached quietly and carefully placed two foil-wrapped chocolate kisses directly in front of her.

Kate, seeing the chocolates, looked up to find Jimmy grinning, awaiting her reaction. She tilted her head and smiled, "Now I know you give these to all the ladies on your route."

"Yes," responded Jimmy, "but only you get two."

"Thank you," said Kate, accepting the chocolates. "How's it going today?"

"Let's just say I made it out of the Calico alive."

Kate shrugged, "Hey, handsome has its price."

"Yeah right," he responded, lingering for a moment in her dark brown eyes.

Clink—clank. The front door opened and Jimmy snapped back into reality. He set a package on the counter and spun around to leave. "See ya."

"See ya," said Kate. *Silly kid*, she thought, shaking her

head as she resumed her work.

"Oomph."

Kate looked up. Jimmy had run smack into Ed, her husband, who had just entered the store. The balance of Jimmy's packages had gone air-born.

A tall, slender man, Ed towered over Jimmy. Although unruffled by the collision, he was clearly aware of the chocolate offerings to his wife of twenty-five years. He looked sternly down at Jimmy over the wire rims of his glasses and said, "James."

Jimmy's words stumbled, "Oh . . . uh . . . hi, Mr. Harrison." He quickly gathered his packages and headed for the door. "Uh . . . have a nice day."

Clank—clank.

Just outside the door, Jimmy ran into another person. This time it was Annie, Kate's friend. She knelt down and tried to help him pick up his once again scattered packages only to find herself bewildered by his unintelligible mumbling.

Annie entered the bookstore. She was dressed in her usual jeans and sneakers. Preferring a feminine touch, she was wearing a soft aqua plaid shirt over a white tank top with a hint of lace at its neckline. She always leaned toward casual—but neat. Far from being a fashion diva, comfort and common sense had long ago overridden trends for both Annie *and* Kate. Her light-colored hair was pulled back in a loosely secured ponytail. A few tendrils had fallen down and were tucked behind her ears. On her back she carried a small backpack. In her hand she toted a blue satchel; it appeared to be heavy. "What's gotten into Jimmy?" she asked as she approached Kate and Ed still standing at the counter.

Kate raised her eyebrows and looked directly at Ed.

"What?" Ed frowned back, "I did nothing."

"Really?" asked Kate.

Ed looked at her with sad eyes, "I'm hurt that you would accuse me of something so . . . so . . . uncivilized."

Annie grinned. She enjoyed the banter that always seemed to surface when they were together. She looked toward Kate for the next pitch. Best friends since childhood, she appreciated that when Kate married Ed it had added a whole new dimension to their relationship. They never made her feel like she was a third wheel. Plus, he was really smart yet still capable of extreme goofiness. Annie felt right at home.

"Yeah, yeah, cry me a river," Kate responded.

Annie laughed and looked back at Ed.

Ed staggered and pretended to take an arrow to his chest. Recovering, he said, "Gee, Kate, last night I was the man of your dreams."

Annie giggled and looked back at Kate.

Kate blushed and let out a chuckle.

Ed smiled wryly knowing he had won *this* round.

Seeing the banter was over, Annie carefully set down her blue satchel. She winced as she rubbed her shoulder.

"What's that?" asked Kate.

"Camera equipment," Annie responded, still rubbing her shoulder. "The new lens weighs a ton."

"You okay?" asked Kate.

"Yep," said Annie.

Kate turned her attention back to Ed. She noticed he was now holding a small stack of books. "What ya got there cowboy?" she asked.

"Kate," he answered, "you just won't believe what I found."

"Let me guess, books?" Kate responded.

"Darn," said Annie, "I had that one."

"No, really," said Ed as he set the books on the counter. "Look at the mint condition of these. This one is nearly fifty years old."

"Nice," said Kate, looking them over carefully. "Where did you get them?"

"Flea market," Annie piped with a grin.

Ed and Kate looked at her and chuckled. No big surprise, Ed was always at the flea market.

"We should make a nice profit on these," Kate commented. "What is this one," she asked, picking up a small tattered pamphlet, "an old Boy Scout Manual?"

"Oh, I'm keeping that one," he declared, grinning like he'd found the golden egg.

"Still trying to earn your badges?" Kate asked.

"Maybe," Ed shrugged. "And," he said as he placed an old paperback book on the counter, "*this* one's for you."

Kate gently picked up the book and examined it. She could see the cover was in *very* rough shape and many of the pages had been earmarked or torn. This surprised Kate because Ed was so particular about the condition of the books he bought to resell. "What is this?" she asked. "It looks like an old travelogue."

"Open it to page 53," Ed beamed. "Trust me; this is *way* better than chocolate kisses."

"Oh, wow," said Kate. "It's an old picture of the lodge."

Annie leaned in to see for herself. "It almost looks the

same as it does today."

"Look in the lower right-hand corner," said Ed, now wearing a big confident grin.

Kate and Annie took a closer look at the picture. *"I can't believe it!"* said Kate with surprise. *"Look, Annie—it's us!"*

"No way," said Annie, carefully taking the book.

"See," said Kate, pointing to four small girls walking along the edge of the lake. "There's you, me, Nance and Jordan. We must have been eleven or twelve years old in this picture."

"That's crazy," said Annie, handing the book back to Kate.

"And listen to this," said Kate, reading directly from the open page. "Buckskin Lake and Lodge are nestled into a pristine forest known for its outstanding beauty. The lodge can only be accessed by an antique white ferry named "The Swan," both of which are operated by the Kingsley family. A favorite hike for visitors is up Great Spirit Mountain where an elaborate carving of an Indian Chief looks out across the land. Legend holds that following a full moon if you touch the shield on the raised hand of the Indian carving it will bring you peace, courage and protection from evil."

"Dang," Annie smiled, "if they only knew."

"This is great," said Kate, turning to Ed. "Thank you, sweetheart. We'll have to show this to Nance and Jordan."

Cling—clang—clink. The bookstore door opened again. This time it was Dr. Judy Conrad, the local retired psychologist, and not to mention, a bit of a celebrity. Middleton was Judy's hometown and there were many committees here that considered themselves lucky to have

Judy on their board. Not only had her successful career made her wealthy and influential, she was also well-traveled and a supporter of the arts. With a quick wit and a no-nonsense decision-making style, Judy was a blessing to the small laid-back town. As always, she was sharply dressed with an artsy flair. Her silver-gray hair was precisely cut into a smart-looking bob.

Judy walked directly up to the counter. Peering over the rims of her multicolored glasses, she stated, "I'll have a decaf cappuccino."

Ed chuckled.

"Judy," Kate replied as she had many times before, "you *know* we don't have a coffee bar."

"Humph," Judy responded. "And you call this a bookstore?" She shifted toward the recent arrivals table. "So what's new?"

Ed took the travelogue from Kate and followed her. "Judy—you won't believe this."

Annie laughed and turned to Kate, "Are you ready to go?"

"Yes," Kate replied emphatically, stacking her papers into a neat pile. "Do you have everything you need for the trip?"

"Uh-huh," Annie replied.

Suspicious, Kate inquired further. "Did you pack without a list again?"

"Yes," Annie grinned.

Kate grimaced. "Did you remember your meds?"

"Yep," Annie replied proudly.

Still unconvinced, Kate asked her if she remembered floss. Annie always forgot floss when she didn't make a list."

"Rats," Annie declared. She looked upward, once more reviewing her mental list.

Ed, still beaming over the book, rejoined them. "Are you guys ready to go?"

"All set," said Kate.

"Let me just speak to Judy before we go," said Annie. She headed down "The Classics" aisle where Judy had gone. The connection between Judy and Annie ran deep. In fact, if it had not been for Judy's intervention, Annie might not have survived a childhood trauma. Well, not just Judy, there was also the old scar faced Indian and the actions of another child—Kate, desperate to save her best friend.

Kate turned her attention back to Ed.

Ed handed the old travelogue back to her. "I take it this has earned me some points?" he asserted more than asked. Looking briefly around, he seized the moment and pulled Kate close.

"Of course," Kate answered with a smile.

"Are you sure you want to leave a handsome fellow such as myself to his own devises for two weeks?" he asked.

Kate laughed, "You'll survive."

"*Ooo-kay*," he warned.

She reached into the pocket of his jacket in search of the keys to the old blue Suburban parked out front, the trusty transport for her and Annie's trip.

"Wrong pocket," Ed quipped.

Kate looked at him slyly and pulled her hand out of the *wrong pocket*—along with the keys.

Ed shrugged innocently. "I filled the tank and I checked the air in the tires—just so you know."

"Thank you," said Kate. "These . . . are for you," she

said handing him her stack of papers, "some things that need to be done while I'm gone. Nothing complicated, just a few internet orders to fill. Do you have the store keys?"

Ed checked his pants pocket and replied, "Yes."

"Don't forget to turn out the lights when you leave."

"No problem," Ed nodded.

"There's plenty of food in the fridge," Kate reminded, throwing her purse over her shoulder. "Now," she placed her hands firmly on Ed's shoulders, searching his eyes, "we talked about the green stuff in the bottle next to the sink, remember?"

"Yes," Ed answered, slowly recalling this fact.

"What is it for?" asked Kate.

"Ummm . . . I'm thinking, I'm thinking," Ed contemplated, tapping his chin.

"*Dishwashing,*" said Kate. "And don't forget to feed the dog."

"What dog?"

"Very funny," said Kate. She gave him a quick kiss goodbye. "I'll call you when we get to the cabin."

"Bye, Judy," Kate waved as she and Annie headed out the door. "See you out at the lake."

"Okay," Judy answered, her eyes glued to her book of interest.

* * * * *

Annie threw her small backpack into the back of the Suburban then carefully placed her satchel full of camera equipment on the floor board beneath her seat. Soon they were off on the short drive to Kate's house where they were to pick up some last minute provisions for their trip. They had really been looking forward to spending time together with two full weeks of fun and relaxation at Kate's cabin on Buckskin Lake.

Now, both in their mid-forties, Kate and Annie had been best friends since they met at the lake as children. Their friendship had sustained them through many difficult times and it was important to keep their bond strong. The year before had been an exceptionally difficult one and they were not able to have their time at the cabin to indulge in what they jokingly referred to as their favorite sport: "jammie hangin'." The only official rule of jammie hangin' was to lounge around in pajamas whenever possible, preferably accessorized with a glass of wine or a really good cup of coffee.

Annie had been diagnosed with breast cancer and most of the previous year had been dedicated to her treatments, so *this* year was especially important to them. So special, that when two other girlfriends from their early years at the lake asked to join them, they hesitated. Although they were both great girls and normally a lot of fun, each of them had recently had their heart's broken—not the best scenario for a fun-filled vacation. First, there was Nance. Her best quality was her ability to see the good in everyone. Unfortunately, that same quality made her quick to fall in love and ignore the red flags. Her most recent breakup had left her teetering between reality and denial. Then, there was Jordan. The way her three year relationship had ended five months earlier had left her full of anger. A beautiful girl, she easily attracted many suitors but only long enough for them to realize there was a target on their back and her quiver was fully loaded with arrows. No man stood a chance with her.

After agreeing to the reunion, Kate and Annie had made a pact to keep the weeks full of fun activities and positive conversation. But they were about to find out it was much easier said than done.

Kate's Suburban headed north on Middleton's Main Avenue. The dark green leaves of the Princeton Elms that lined the street were just beginning to show a tinge of yellow. Light traffic moved at an easy pace. The small but still bustling town of Middleton had yet to be discovered and the town folk liked it that way. They also supported a thriving art and music community and at least one famous author seeking privacy lived nearby. The survival of the many small family owned businesses in Middleton was imperative, but equally important was a quiet place to sit and just enjoy the beauty of a spring day. A lot of care and planning went into insuring just that. The crown jewel of Middleton was a beautiful public park in the center of town. It offered comfortable benches thoughtfully placed amidst the greenery surrounding a small lake. Tall trees and open breezeways made it a perfect lunch spot for friendly folks in a town where almost everyone knew each other. A large white gazebo gracing the edge of the lake was set among spectacular hundred-year-old oak trees. On weekends, the town frequently hosted musical events in the evenings. Strings of tiny sparkling lights and old time carriage lamps gave the park a magical look. Traffic was strategically routed away from this area to insure an enjoyable experience and a safe environment for people to walk. Bicycles were a welcome and respected form of transportation in *all* parts of Middleton.

At the second traffic light, one of only three in the town of Middleton, Kate turned the Suburban west onto the road that would eventually take them to her home. As they turned the corner, Annie noted, "I see Jimmy's recovered."

She pointed to the Ice Cream Hut where Jimmy, leaning on the counter, was enjoying a milkshake and flirting with pretty Haley Thompson, the server.

* * * * *

"We should be dancin'—ye-aah."

Jordan opened one eye and looked at her friend Nance. She was sitting in the chair next to her at Ronald Reagan National Airport, awaiting their departure to New Hampshire. Nance had her music headphones in and was quietly bobbing to the beat of the Bee-Gees. Every once in a while she'd blurt out a word or two, oblivious to how loud she was. Jordan sighed; it was not like she was going to get any sleep anyway, not in an airport bustling with a million strangers.

BEEP—BEEP—BEEP. A transport vehicle went by. The vacant tired faces of the passengers stared back at Jordan. She felt like she was looking in a mirror. She and Nance had been traveling since 5:00 a.m. that morning and without a doubt they were definitely starting to get on each other's nerves. Well, Nance at least, was getting on *hers*; Nance was far too nice to get angry about anything. But all morning she had listened to Nance talk about Randall, the pilot she had been dating and it was making Jordan *absolutely* crazy. *The guy had treated her like a jerk*, she thought, *but to hear Nance talk about him, you would have thought he was the perfect gentleman*. Jordan knew the truth. She had been there for all the lonely nights and tear-filled phone calls. Randall had not called for three months now, yet it was obvious to Jordan, Nance was checking out every pilot that walked by—searching. Like clockwork, every half hour, Jordan watched Nance check her cell phone for messages that were never there. She wanted to grab her friend and shake her into reality.

BEEP—BEEP—BEEP. Another transport vehicle carrying another group of stressed out strangers went by. Jordan winced. The impersonal onslaught of terminal noise was endless. A nice-looking man in a grey suit headed toward the empty seat next to her and she quickly threw her purse on it. "Sorry," she said and he blankly moved on. She sighed again and looked back at Nance. On the surface, Nance was still her bubbly old self, but they had been close since childhood and it was easy for Jordan to see the effect the past few months had had on her friend. For one, unruly bangs had replaced her normally cute hairstyle. Also, she wasn't wearing any makeup. It's not that she needed to wear makeup or ever wore much of it for she was blessed with beautiful fine-pored skin. But, Nance, *loved* makeup; it was an art to her and in her early years she had wanted to become a cosmetologist. That dream never materialized; instead, she married and helped her husband to achieve *his* dream of becoming a doctor. Unfortunately, a few years ago he asked her for a divorce. He never really gave her a good reason why, which only left her confused. To her credit, Nance said she had no regrets, plus she had two beautiful children.

So after twenty years of marriage, with trepidation, Nance re-entered the dating scene. But she was quite naïve' about men and had always worn her heart on her sleeve. When she met someone she liked she would immediately do what she knew best—take care of him. After quite a few rough bumps and rejections, she was ecstatic when she met Randall. She was sure the handsome pilot was *the one*. In the beginning, he showered her with flowers and affection, the latter being something she was in dire need of. Even though he traveled a lot, they maintained their connection with frequent phone calls and text messages. However, about six months into the relationship, his personality changed and he began to pull away. He never really said it was over, he just stopped calling and did not respond to her attempts to get in touch with him. Now, three months later, and although in her heart she knew it was over, Nance was still hanging on to any thread of hope it was not.

"Ye-aah." Nance crooned.

Jordan glanced back at Nance and saw she was un-wrapping a candy bar, her third today and it wasn't even noon. That was another reason she knew Nance was unhappy, sweets were her *go to* escape in times of trouble. It was hard to tell if she had gained any weight because she was wearing sloppy oversize clothes. It did not matter to Jordan how Nance dressed, she loved her friend unconditionally, but she knew this was a sign of deeper trouble. Nance just didn't seem to care anymore. It all irked Jordan to no end. *Why wasn't Nance angry?*

Jordan regretted she had snapped at Nance earlier that morning, but from the onset she had disagreed with how Randall treated Nance. She felt he was taking advantage of her kindness. Vocalizing her opinion had only strained their relationship and their conversations had become shorter and shorter. But the truth at the time was, they were *both* in relationships that were crumbling. This getaway to Kate's cabin would be good for both of them. She leaned back in the uncomfortable terminal chair and closed her eyes. She tried to envision being back at the lake—it had been so long.

BEEP—BEEP—BEEP. Jordan bolted upright. She groaned, reached for her purse and found a container of aspirin. She quickly popped one, draining the balance of her bottled water.

A short pudgy man ran by waving red, white and blue pompoms. He was wearing nothing more than *really* short jean cut-offs. If he wanted a reaction to his bizarre behavior from fellow travelers he did not get it. *Why would he*, thought Jordan, *it's an airport for God's sake. One gets immune to such oddities*. She remembered when she flew as a child how well-dressed her parents had been. It always felt like a special occasion with her dad in a nice suit and her mother in a smart two-piece. *Everything has changed*, she thought, saddened by this reality. Her attention was diverted by a pretty, young woman in four-inch heels as she strutted stiffly by. *Ouch,* Jordan winced, watching the woman continue on her way. When she passed a group of young pilots, Jordan saw her smile at them flirtatiously. *And yet, everything stays the same.*

Surges of people continued to ebb and flow as multitudes of planes arrived and departed. A frazzled looking tour guide followed by twenty or so Japanese tourists went by. BEEP—BEEP—BEEP. Another transport vehicle inched its way past.

Jordan looked at her watch. *Forty-five minutes till board time*, she noted. She closed her eyes again and her thoughts began to drift to her own defunct relationship. *Rodney Piedmont*, she thought, *the man's man—the guy every woman wanted to date. Why wouldn't they? In all appearances he was the perfect catch.* Not only was Rodney born into money, everything he touched turned to gold. Through his prestigious public relations company he had acquired many influential contacts, not to mention high-ranking friends in Washington. He was highly-educated, well-traveled, and excelled at many sports. In the upscale neighborhood where he had built his mansion, he was considered their most eligible bachelor and of course was invited to every party. He exuded confidence and his dark blue eyes could pierce you with their focus, making you feel as if you were the only person in the room. He also had a knack for remembering names and other significant things about people he had met. “Where’s that beautiful new baby of yours?” he would ask or, “Congratulations on your promotion!” or some other endearing question or comment. But if you scratched Rodney’s surface, if you dug deeper, you would hear the real truth and it would go something like this: “Don’t make your answers too long though because it’s really all about me.” Everything Rodney did was self-motivated and he was an expert at making sure no one found out; he would give *just* enough. To most people that would be fine, but to a girlfriend, it was a lonely, frustrating life. Unfortunately, before Jordan had realized it was all just for show, it was too late; she had fallen in love, caught up in the fairy tale herself.

Appearances were very important to Rodney. In fact, Jordan began to feel the pressure to be perfect, too. Like the immaculately manicured neighborhood Rodney lived in, so was he. He was always impeccably groomed, not a hair out of place. His clothing and shoes were all designer and only the finest of suits would do. So as the world revolved around *him*, slowly but surely, Jordan changed herself to fit into his world. Her interests took a back seat and there was never time to do the things *she* liked to do. At first, it did not seem to matter because their life was full of activities. There were charity events, parties, award ceremonies and so on.

In the beginning, Rodney seemed attentive enough, but she soon began to notice there were never any deep conversations. Inquiries about her day were quickly cut off by the detailed accounts of *his* accomplishments as he boasted about his business acumen, his connections and his conquests. It was not like Jordan needed emotional support; she had always been quite independent. But this was the person she had given the number one spot in her life to, wasn't he supposed to care? He was not a giver in the bedroom either; he was insatiable and would get angry if she refused to have sex with him. It didn't matter how she felt.

Something bumped hard against the back of Jordan's chair bringing her back to the moment. When it bumped three more times she turned around to find a little, blonde tousle-haired boy bouncing hard against the back of the chair behind hers. His oblivious mother sitting across from him was enjoying a conversation on her cell phone. Jordan gave the boy the evil eye. He gave it back. She frowned and turned back around only to have the bumping resume. She turned and gave the boy the evil eye again, this time with more conviction. The little boy withdrew in alarm but within moments the annoying bumps began again. This went on for several minutes until finally the mother, still on her cell phone, came over and took him by the hand. "I'm sorry," said the mother sweetly, "boys will be boys."

BEEP—BEEP—BEEP.

Jordan tried to close out her surroundings as her thoughts drifted back to Rodney. They had dated for about three years, but then came the night that changed everything for her. It was a night that would haunt her for the rest of her life. It happened on the day of her father's eightieth birthday party. John lived at the Pinewoods Assisted Living Facility a couple of miles from Jordan's home. A sweetheart of a man, they had always been close. When he had a heart attack at the age of seventy-eight, the decision was made that he should no longer be living alone. Jordan had insisted he move in with her, but he had refused. He was an independent old guy and he did not want to be a burden to her. She argued but finally agreed and was happy when she found a facility near her home that had an excellent reputation. Jordan visited almost daily; she took him out to lunch regularly and often participated in festivities at the home.

Early on the day of John's birthday, Jordan had decorated the recreation room at the home in anticipation of her father's big night. Old friends were invited as well as new friends he had made at the facility. She was doubly excited because Rodney had agreed to go with her, something he rarely did. In fact, in the three years they dated he had only seen her father two times.

At six o'clock that night, Rodney had showed up at Jordan's apartment as expected, but she soon found out he had other plans for their evening. She had noticed he looked a bit overdressed for her father's party. He was wearing a dark blue sports coat and a crisp white shirt open at the collar. His diamond and gold cuff-links gleamed back at her when he entered the door. "Guess what, darling," he had said excitedly, "I've got reservations for Louie's!"

Caught off guard, Jordan had blinked back at him. Louie's was the most glamorous and popular restaurant in the area and known as the place to see and be seen. Rodney had been trying for months to get reservations. Her words had stumbled, "But . . . but, tonight is dad's birthday party."

"You see your father practically every day," Rodney had responded rather coldly. "Do you know how hard it is to get reservations at Louie's?"

"But it's my dad's eightieth," she had protested.

"Please . . . do this for me," he begged as he slipped his arm around her shoulder. "Just this once."

Jordan's mind froze. It was stuck somewhere between frustration and confusion. And it was never, "Just this once."

Turning to face her directly, Rodney had gently gripped both her arms and looked deep into her eyes. "We can go to your father's birthday party straight from dinner." he assured her. "What time does the party start?"

"Like—now," she had answered, looking at her watch.

"We can be in and out of the restaurant by quarter to eight," he had promised.

Jordan had hesitated. She could not believe he was doing this. But she had looked into his pleading eyes and remembered thinking, *Even if it wasn't important to her, it was important to him.* Through her numbness, she had heard herself ask, "Quarter to eight?"

"No later," Rodney had raised his hand and sworn.

"Okay. I'll call the home and let them know I'll be late," Jordan had agreed. "I'll ask them to wait for me to cut the cake. I want to be there for that, okay?"

"No problem," Rodney had responded.

Somewhat dazed, Jordan had picked up her purse and her father's gift.

"Uh . . . is that what you're wearing?" Rodney had asked.

Jordan had looked down at her black capris and white

tank top, “I . . . I guess not. I’ll just be a minute.”

“Why don’t you wear that sexy little blue number you had on the other night,” Rodney had called out after her.

As usual, what was important to Jordan had taken a back seat to what was important to Rodney. At Louie’s, among the loud chatter and live Jazz music, she had pretended to enjoy herself. As she feared, the night lingered much later than planned as Rodney hobnobbed with the other tables. At eight o’clock he invited another couple to join them at their table for a drink. Jordan had attempted to make polite conversation but could only think about her father. It was close to nine o’clock before they finally left the restaurant. At 9:29, Rodney’s black Jaguar had pulled into the parking lot of the Pinewood. Jordan could see all the lights in the recreation room were already out. Sadness had waved over her. She had missed her father’s birthday party.

In hopes of speaking to John and hand-delivering his birthday gift, Jordan had slipped quietly in the door and down the hall to his room. She peeked in and could see he was fast asleep, a birthday hat clutched in his hand. The card she had given him earlier in the day stood next to her picture on the nightstand. He looked peaceful and she had decided not to wake him. She set his gift on top of his dresser and decided to pick him up first thing in the morning and take him out to breakfast. They would go to the diner in his old neighborhood where he could see more of his old friends; he would enjoy that.

That night, alone in her bed, the little sleep she got had been fitful. About 6 a.m. the phone had rung, it was Betsy, the head nurse at the Pinewood. She gently informed Jordan that John had quietly passed away during the night. Jordan was beside herself with guilt and grief. She had felt anger, too. Not only at Rodney for being the selfish bastard that he was, but also at herself for not standing her ground with him. She could not believe she had become such a wuss. She remembered thinking, *If this is love, I want out*. But this was nothing new, she had wanted out for some time now, albeit in reality, she knew she just couldn't do it. There had been an ongoing war waging between her mind and her heart and her heart was winning. This only compounded the frustration she had already felt in the relationship. Since she was incapable of initializing the split, somehow she needed to make him do the leaving. So one night she came up with a plan; a plan that she knew would end the relationship and make *him* go away.

"Stayin' alive, stayin' alive," Nance sang—completely off key.

Back in the moment and the chaos of the airport terminal, Jordan suddenly felt weary. She looked at her watch. *Thirty minutes*. She reached over and touched Nance's arm. "Nance," she said loudly, "thirty minutes. I'm going to buy water, do you want one?"

Nance removed an earphone, "What?"

"Thirty minutes to board time. Do you want water? I'm going to the bookstand."

"No thanks, but can you please get me a couple candy bars? Any kind."

"No. You've already had three this morning," Jordan protested.

"Please," Nance smiled.

"Okay," Jordan reluctantly agreed, knowing she'd already upset her friend at least once today. She got up from her chair and stretched briefly. She wore a stylish black jogging suit over her fit and shapely figure. With beautiful features and sleek dark hair, she had always been a head-turner and nothing had changed with age. The eyes of several men followed her as she wove her way toward the bookstand.

"When did you get to be so mean?" Nance had asked her earlier that morning after Jordan had coldly reacted to a man offering help with her tangled seatbelt.

Jordan had thought about Nance's comment later; she had not always been so jaded against the opposite sex, it had begun five years earlier when her husband of fifteen years had asked for a divorce. She had asked him, "Is there someone else?" He had said, "No," but then remarried only six months later. Desperately needing direction and to channel her emotions, Jordan had thrown herself into her work and built a successful interior design company. She was determined from that point forward to be the captain of her ship. She was doing quite well for herself, then, she met Rodney. She had hoped he would be the icing on the cake, but that was not to be. *And Wow*, she thought now, *how quickly I relinquished my new-found independence.*

At the airport bookstand, Jordan picked up three candy bars, water from the cooler and then took a moment to peruse the paperbacks. A rugged-looking guy in a plaid shirt and jeans came over and picked up a novel. Her guard was up in full force and he felt uncomfortably close so she moved on to the magazine rack. A tabloid headline caught her eye, it read, "Sexiest Man Alive." She picked it up and flipped through the glossy pages of handsome men with buff bodies and shiny white teeth. She wondered what criteria the magazine used to make their decision. *Was it purely based on looks? Did they do good things? What? What makes a man sexy?*

"Travel much?" a man's voice questioned.

Jordan jumped. The man in the plaid shirt was standing next to her again. She plopped the magazine back on the rack, shot an angry look at him then proceeded to the checkout counter.

The man discreetly sniffed his armpits.

Back in her chair next to Nance, Jordan's thoughts went back to her plan to end her relationship with Rodney. It had worked perfectly, just as she had hoped. Only she had not expected the pain that followed. And it didn't make letting go any easier that Rodney was so damn good-looking.

TWO
Old Friends, Old Dogs and Old Trucks

She is a friend of mind. She gather me, man.
The pieces I am,
she gather them and give them back to me
in all the right order.
It's good you know, when you got a woman who
is a friend of your mind.
Toni Morrison

As the Suburban passed the bright white church steeple, it signified the edge of the town of Middleton. From there, Kate and Annie drove past picturesque red barns and lush pastures where fat black-and-white dairy cows grazed contentedly. The cowbells they wore around their necks clanked melodiously as they walked through the thick grass. Kate stopped at Campbell's Co-op, a roadside farm stand, to buy plump blueberries, ripe tomatoes, assorted field-fresh vegetables, honey and eggs for their trip. As they continued on their way, on several occasions she pulled over so Annie could take a photo. Photography was Annie's passion and she saw endless opportunities for pictures.

Kate loved living out in the country, but to her and her husband Ed, it was not just about connecting to nature. At first, on a superficial level, you might not get the connection between the two of them. Kate was an avid outdoors person and a rock climber, while Ed was book smart and unassuming. Get to know them and one would find a commitment on a much deeper level. Both of their families had farmed the surrounding area for many generations and they both felt a strong devotion to family, to heritage, and to each other.

Kate and Ed lived in an immaculate two story home that had been passed down to Kate through many generations. The spacious house, built in the nineteenth century, stood alone on a hill overlooking the farmlands that separated it from Middleton. The surrounding hundred acres, also a family legacy, included its own apple orchard. Though no longer a cash crop, the orchard still provided plenty of apples each year. On a clear day from the house's wide wraparound porch, you could see the town's white steeple piercing the sky in the distance. With comfy chairs and a swing, it was a frequent gathering spot for friends and family.

Inside, the home was a showplace, certainly comparable to any magazine shoot. Most of the beautiful antique furniture in the house was original and Kate took special care of it just like she did the friends and family she adored. Photos of loved ones, and books—lots and lots of books lined the shelves on one wall in the family room. She felt strongly all of these things were to be cherished. She passed this on to her daughter, Emma, along with the sturdy foundation of a good education. At the age of forty-six, Kate, already a grandmother, looked forward to enriching her granddaughter's life as well. It was a picture-perfect time in Kate's life and she reveled in the fulfilling rewards of a close, loving family.

Kate's gift for creating a beautiful home was only exceeded by her natural talent in the kitchen. Any visit, planned or unplanned, was greeted by fresh-baked goodies such as banana bread, blueberry muffins, apple pie or cookies, depending on what ingredients were available in season, or more important, organic. The latter was one more reason Kate loved living here; she knew exactly where the food she bought was coming from.

Born to nurture, Kate had found in Annie someone who not only needed to feel cared about, but one who also marveled at her skills as a homemaker. This gave Kate yet another opportunity to share and pass on what she had learned from her mother.

Annie's childhood was nearly the opposite of Kate's. She had grown up in an often violent home until the divorce of her parents at the age of twelve. Although by adulthood, Annie had overcome most of the setbacks a child experiences coming from such a destructive environment, she still had a tendency to get off track. Blown by the winds of emotion and bad memories, Annie's thoughts could at times tangle like tumbleweeds. She would become confused when faced with a dilemma, unsure of what to do. Kate had a way of reaching in and getting to the heart of the imposing problem. She could look at a situation objectively and from all angles. This also meant she did not always agree with Annie's point of view, something that Annie learned to greatly appreciate. Annie called her "The Truth Seeker."

There were plenty of roads that sidetracked Annie while she was searching for her true life. Some of the roads she chose, namely the men she allowed into her life and the years she cared for her parents when they became disabled with age. Other roads were unavoidable, like her battle with breast cancer and her divorce from a man she had deeply loved. Their marriage had crumbled under the financial and emotional strain that came with *his* cancer.

Following her divorce and for the next fourteen years, Annie cared for her parents. Her mother was confined to a wheelchair due to a succession of strokes and her father had advanced Alzheimer's disease. Her father was known as a "walker," a term used to describe Alzheimer patients that will walk off if given a chance. Since he looked normal and was always neatly dressed, unaware visitors would often aid in his escapes. Between them, her parents were forced to move from eighteen different nursing homes. But as difficult as those times were, Annie found caring for her parents to be one of the most rewarding times of her life.

After the death of her parents, Annie's financial obligations began to ease and she was looking forward to doing some of the things she had always wanted to do. She loved nature and wanted to travel and photograph wildlife, but that was not yet to be. During the years Annie cared for her parents she often neglected her own health and had not had a mammogram in more than five years. At the age of forty-three she was not concerned, even though both her mother and her grandmother had had breast cancer. After all, she was much younger than either of them when they were diagnosed; each of them had been in their sixties, so she was completely shocked when she received *her* breast cancer diagnosis. However, like any life experience, she found if one keeps an open mind, one never knows what surprises are in store.

Terrified about the upcoming first visit with her oncologist, Annie was worried that her nervousness would compromise her ability to communicate and to ask important questions. Her answer came in a book that suggested the use of spontaneous drawing to identify her true feelings. The day before her appointment, she quickly penciled four small drawings. She was completely unprepared for the results. The first drawing depicted her kneeling at a grave. The headstone read "RIP Cancer." She was placing flowers on the grave and saying the words, "I'm sorry." She knew exactly what the drawing signified; she felt she had somehow caused her own cancer. In the second drawing, she had a suitcase in hand and cash sticking out of her pocket. She wore a heart on her sleeve and the sun shined brightly above with the year written on it. Annie interpreted this drawing to mean it was finally time for *her* since her finances were improving and she could start to travel. The heart on her sleeve meant she was also open to love. Life looked promising, and besides, she did not *feel* sick. The third drawing showed Annie sick in bed. She was bald and hooked up to an IV bag with a skull and crossbones drawn on it. Beside her was a night stand stacked with bills and on the floor was a bucket for the obvious. On the wall was a clock ticking away with the word "LIFE," written on it. She was repeating the word, "Stupid," over and over. In reality, from what Annie knew of chemotherapy, this drawing revealed what she felt she was facing and a decision to accept it as a treatment would be a major mistake. Her final drawing depicted the aftermath of chemotherapy. She had drawn a picture of herself as an old woman trudging along with a cane. She was weighted down by a backpack full of bills. There were two headstones now, one marked "Hopes," the other marked "Dreams." In the corner, an hourglass again with the word "LIFE," on it, was quickly running out of sand. She was saying the words, "On my way to work." This drawing greatly clarified to Annie what she thought chemotherapy would do to her and to her life.

Even though the drawings were crude, Annie took them to her first visit with her oncologist. When her doctor asked her if she had any questions, she hesitantly handed her the drawings. The doctor was a bit surprised as no one had ever done this before. But the fact was, Annie's drawings had revealed a wealth of fears and concerns that helped to open a dialog between her doctor and herself.

Between surgeries, chemotherapy and radiation, Annie's treatments enveloped the better part of a year. It was a physical and emotional roller coaster as one day the news would be good, the next day the news would be bad. After she completed chemotherapy and radiation, subsequent tests revealed more problems and when her body woke up from the chemically induced menopause, a hysterectomy followed. Finally when it was all behind her, she was inspired to write and illustrate a book that best described her journey with the difficult yet humorous moments that came with her chemotherapy and hair loss. Like the time she pulled her head scarf too tight and it gave her an instant eye lift. Or the absurdity of using a lint roller on her head to catch ever-loosening bits of remaining hair. There were many inspiring moments, too, like the glow on a friend's face who had been given the opportunity to help. It had been just a simple task, lifting a bag of garden soil into her car, but it had taught Annie how important it was to let loved ones contribute. After all, *they* were going through a difficult time, too. In the same spirit as her book, she then designed a successful line of greeting cards for those going through cancer treatment. Some of the cards were funny, some were edgy, while others were sentiments that helped her to survive such a difficult time.

Whereas cancer had given Annie a vehicle for success, Kate had kept the wheels on the track. Throughout all of the treatments, she was there for Annie. She drove her to doctor visits, cooked healthy meals and frequently spent the night.

Later when an unscrupulous professional took advantage of Annie's budding new career, it was Kate who pulled her through. All it took was one well-written letter to sever an unethical contract. Letter composing was another of Kate's attributes and she was often called into service by those who knew. Now, Annie was finally enjoying both the good health and the financial rewards she had hoped for.

There were the obvious differences between Kate and Annie. Education, family, and domestic abilities to name a few. In addition, Kate's passion was climbing mountains. Annie loved the sea. Annie loved rustic. Kate loved antiques. And when Kate saw reality, Annie saw what could be. Each brought something different to the table and both women were enriched by the relationship. There was no judgment here. No matter what was going on in Kate's life, she always made Annie feel a part of it. Although not related by blood, they were sisters in the truest sense of the word.

"Wow, look at your apple trees," commented Annie as they pulled up and parked in front of Kate's house. Their dark trunks, gnarled and bent, reminded Annie of the trees in the Wizard of Oz movie, waiting to slap your hand if you reached for their fruit.

"The Cortlands should be ready to pick any day now," said Kate.

"I hope we're making applesauce this year," said Annie.

"Of course," Kate answered, "and apple pie, and apple turnovers, and apple crisps . . . ."

Up on the porch, Blue, Kate's golden retriever, rose slowly from his comfy bed to greet them. In the old days he would have been overcome with excitement and knocked you to the ground. Kate bent down and nuzzled his face. "Good boy," she said, leaning back just far enough to avoid a predictable lick.

"Hello, Blue," said Annie, greeting him next. He leaned heavily into her hand as she gently scratched the back of his neck. She kneeled and with her arm around him turned to take in the view. A soft breeze coming up from the valley wisped across her face. "I'll make my bed right next to yours," she said softly to Blue. A big wet lick crossed her face. "Ew," Annie cringed. "*Someone* needs to brush his teeth."

Inside the house, Annie immediately gravitated toward the basket of goodies on the kitchen counter. "Mine," she stated, wrapping her arms protectively around it. That morning, Kate had filled the basket with fresh-baked muffins and cookies. Annie inhaled deeply and grinned, "I smell chocolate chip cookies."

Kate laughed, "It wouldn't be a jammie hang without chocolate chip cookies. Not one that I would want to be at."

"Me, neither," Annie agreed.

"I'm going to change and get my bag," said Kate as she headed down the wide sun-washed hallway. "Have a cookie if you want one."

"If you say so," Annie grinned, having already plucked one off a plate on the counter. *Mmm, that's different*, she thought, savoring its flavor. *Is that bacon*?

"Don't eat the ones on the plate," Kate called out. "Those are for Blue."

Annie froze for a moment, shrugged, and ate it anyways.

In her bedroom, Kate took off her earrings; they were intricately carved hoops given to her by her grandmother. She safely stowed them in an antique box on her dresser. She changed into a cream-colored Henley and released her dark hair from its clip. As she loosely braided it, she called out to Annie, "Did you bring a warm jacket? You never know what the weather's going to do up there."

"Darn!" Annie frowned.

Kate chuckled and shook her head. "Don't worry, I keep an extra one in the car," she said as she instinctively stuffed some extra pairs of socks into her duffle bag.

"Thanks," said Annie, indulging now in one of the chocolate chip cookies from the basket. She drifted into the dining room. Kate was very innovative when it came to decorating and Annie started looking around to see what was new. "You put away the milk glass," she observed, speaking loud enough for Kate to hear. She was standing in front of the hutch where a pretty set of blue-and-white china was now displayed. "This is my favorite pattern of all your dishes," she added.

"Mine, too," Kate responded.

Annie's gaze shifted to the family photographs on the wall. She always lingered at the photo of Kate's parents. It had been taken on their wedding anniversary and the couple was happily locked arm-in-arm. A big sheet cake on the table below them read "Happy Fiftieth." This photo always had the same effect on Annie; it made her reflect about her own parents. *Their* portrait was tucked away in a box under her bed. A commissioned painting, it had been torn in half by her mother during a fit of rage. Her eyes lowered in sadness as she thought of the anguish her mother must have felt in that moment. Oddly, although Annie vividly remembered the portrait when it was intact, in this moment she could not remember if she had both pieces. She surmised it didn't matter and she had no desire to open the box for the answer.

Back in the kitchen, Kate began loading a small cooler with milk, butter and various meats and cheeses for the trip. Annie leaned on the counter and noticed some new photographs lying there. "Wow, who are these guys?" she asked, flipping through the small stack.

"Those pictures are from my last climbing trip," Kate answered.

"I'll take one of each," Annie joked as she admired the young buff men surrounding Kate in the photos.

"You could have gone with us," Kate reminded.

"Oh, no, that's way out of my league," Annie responded. "Apparently you're forgetting my lack of depth of field. Gee, Kate," she mused, "how far across is that crevasse?"

Kate chuckled. As an avid rock climber and mountaineer she had numerous peaks checked off her list. She was very independent and she never gave up what she loved when she and Ed married. This was just one more quality about Kate that Annie admired. She had seen time and time again girlfriends who gave up on their dreams, their hobbies and their friends once they married. To his credit, Ed was quite supportive when it came to Kate's pursuit of climbing, even if it meant her trekking off for weeks on end with her male climbing buddies. He seemed completely secure in his relationship with Kate, although unbeknownst to her, he had given more than one overly-firm handshake.

Kate slung her duffle bag over her shoulder and picked up the cooler. Annie grabbed the goodie basket and followed her. As they stepped onto the porch, Blue, who had been observing them through the screen door, wagged his tail, sensing a road trip. "Not today, Blue," Kate said. He sighed loudly in disapproval then plopped heavily back down on his bed.

Kate loaded the cooler and her backpack into the Suburban then she and Annie, still clinging to the basket, headed toward the old gray barn behind the house. Long ago, Ed had converted the barn into a workshop where he spent many hours tinkering. Like Kate, he had a passion for old things and he always had several refurbishing projects in the works. Flea markets and old farms were his mecca. His current project was an old antique truck that Kate had recently bought.

"*It's beautiful*," said Annie, impressed by her first view of the truck's new paint. I *love* the color," she added, admiring the deep red glossy finish.

"Thanks," said Kate as she retrieved her climbing gear from a hook on the wall. "It's pretty much finished. I can't wait to start driving it."

"Ed is doing such a great job," Annie expressed, checking out the shiny gold lettering beginning to take form on the door panel. It would soon read "Middleton's Old and New Bookstore."

"It's amazing what a new paint job can do," said Kate as they exited the barn. She loaded the climbing gear into the back of the Suburban while Annie placed the more delicate cargo on the floor behind her seat, a.k.a. the basket of goodies.

They had an enjoyable drive ahead of them. A half-hour drive to the airport in Manchester to pick up Nance and Jordan, then backtrack another hour and twenty minutes to the lake. With good weather and road conditions like today they should reach their destination by three o'clock. Though they both agreed, regardless of the weather, any drive's a pleasure when you're in good company.

As the Suburban occasionally bumped along the road up Montgomery Ridge, Annie reflected on the day that she and Kate had driven this same road to Joe Montgomery's farm to pay for the old truck. It had been a beautiful day very much like this one and had reaffirmed why neither of them ever wanted to live anywhere else. As they had come over Montgomery Ridge, the view had opened up to a landscape of lush farmlands, glistening lakes and picturesque apple orchards. Beyond the farmlands, one could see wave upon wave of green rolling hills leading up to the distant rise of the majestic White Mountains. The natural qualities of the area created boundless opportunities for hiking and adventure, a love both Kate and Annie shared. They had descended the ridge into an area known as Pleasant Valley. There, the many fields of grain that lined the road had received plenty of rain this year so everything was thriving and bursting in ripeness. Every homestead along the way, no matter how big or how small, had a productive vegetable garden. Their rewards were eagerly shared or traded with their neighbors. The larger farms had "honest pay" vegetable stands where one could count on a variety of vegetables fresh from the fields. Joe's family owned and managed much of the land in this area, thus the name, Montgomery Ridge.

Kate had always wanted an antique truck like the one Joe was selling and to Annie it was one more perfect way to define Kate's grass-roots style. When Joe had finally decided to sell the old truck, Kate was thrilled; she had admired it for years and she knew Joe had taken excellent care of it. If there was one thing Joe knew for sure it was engines, as was the way with most men in the area. At any county fair, one would find a plethora of them powwowed around anything that ticked, whirred, throttled or chugged.

As they had turned onto the long dirt road that led up to the farmhouse where Joe and his wife Laura lived, Blue, who was along for the ride, had become very excited. This was familiar territory for him. The golden wheat swaying in the field with its scents of the wild was an irresistible calling to a dog that did not know he was old.

When they had come to a stop in front of the house, Laura, who was hanging laundry on the line, had greeted them. Her pretty blue-and-white gingham dress had fluttered femininely in the breeze as she approached.

Kate had called out, "Is it okay if Blue is loose?"

"Of course," Laura had said.

Kate already knew the answer but wanted to be polite. She had opened the Suburban's door and Blue had launched himself out like a rocket. He briefly greeted Laura, licked her hand several times then turned and bounded off into the tall grass. He had kept Kate abreast of his whereabouts with excited *aarphs* and leaps of delight as woodchucks scattered and small flocks of birds fluttered into the air.

"It's so good to see you," Laura had said, giving each of the girls a hug. "Come," she motioned, "I have a fresh pitcher of ice tea made." Annie and Kate had followed Laura up the steps onto the porch of the modest farmhouse. Laura motioned for them to sit and they had settled into two white wicker chairs plump with floral cushions. They were definitely thirsty and Laura made exquisite ice tea. She claimed it was the water, water that came straight from their well. Montgomery farm like others in the area was organic; no pesticides went into the ground there.

On a small wicker table next to her chair, Annie had noticed a tray full of colorful beads and shells. There were also delicate pieces of blue and green sea glass. In the center of the tray was an intricate necklace beginning to take form. "Is this one of your designs, Laura?" she had asked.

"Yes," Laura had replied, appreciating Annie's interest. She handed her and Kate each a tall glass of tea poured from a glistening pitcher full of ice and lemon slices. "It's a custom order."

"It's beautiful," Annie had expressed, admiring the multi-strand necklace of turquoise and deep red and gold beads taking form.

"Yes, really beautiful," Kate had added as she leaned forward to take a closer look. "Is that carnelian?"

"It is," Laura had answered, delighted to share in this knowledge.

"I love the earrings you made for me," Kate had said, touching her earlobe instinctively. "I wear them all the time."

"I wear mine all the time, too," Annie had said. "See?" She turned her head and revealed small gold hoops, each with a carefully chosen turquoise bead.

"It was a pleasure," Laura had responded, pulling her light-colored hair back and securing it in a soft knot. Delicate blue sea glass and pearl earrings, another of her creations, dangled from her ears. A few loose strands of hair fell and softly framed her face. Having always been a pretty woman, age seemed to be having the reverse effect on Laura. She had taken good care of herself and now in her late sixties she still sported the figure of a woman in her thirties. Her rosy cheeks, clear complexion and perfect teeth would make any model envious. Though it was more than Laura's looks that made her beautiful; there was a naturalness and serenity about her. One got the sense that here was a woman truly happy with her life and the woman she had become.

"I'll let Joe know you are here," Laura had said as she walked over to the edge of the porch and released a small yellow flag, signaling Joe. It was a good distance, but one could see Joe on his tractor out in the north field. He had waved in response then brought his tractor to an abrupt halt. Soon his pickup truck had lurched onto the dirt road that led up to the house and puffs of fine grey dust plumed out behind him.

"You should see how fast he moves when the red flag goes up," Laura had said, grinning as she filled two other tall glasses with tea. She spooned a heaping teaspoon of sugar into one of the glasses and stirred.

"What does the red flag mean?" Annie had asked.

Laura had winked and gave a mischievous smile.

"Ohhh," Kate had chuckled.

"You mean like . . . lunch is ready?" Annie had asked.

"No, Annie," Kate had said, shaking her head.

"No?" Annie had looked at her then back at Laura. "An important phone call?"

"Annie," Kate had said, raising her eyebrows in disbelief.

Annie had looked at her, blinked, and then again looked back at Laura. She still had not gotten it.

"*Annie,*" Kate had said, clapping her hands and clasping her fingers together in some sort of signal.

"Ohhhh," Annie had laughed, her face pinking up.

Laura had looked at Kate inquisitively.

"'Clan of the Cave Bear,'" Kate had explained, rolling her eyes.

"Ohhhh," Laura had laughed, remembering the novel she, too, had read many years ago.

As Joe's truck had eased to a halt in front of the farmhouse, Blue had emerged from the field with a small stick in his mouth. His coat was full of small stickers, leaves and various other hitchhikers. He had quickly trotted over to his potential new play pal.

"Hello, Blue. How are you today?" Joe had asked. He playfully wrestled the stick away and tossed it. Blue had eagerly bounded after it then found a grassy spot in the yard where he settled in to gnaw.

Politely removing his cap, Joe had wiped his brow with the red bandana he kept tucked in the back pocket of his jeans. Stepping up onto the porch he greeted the girls as Laura handed him a glass of cold tea. "Thank you, sweetheart," Joe had said, taking the glass and quickly emptying it. "Ahhhh, that was good," he complimented, flashing a grin that could make any girl swoon.

Joe had always been a quietly charismatic and handsome man. One could not help but notice how his farmer's tan and neatly trimmed silver hair perfectly complimented the brilliant blue of his eyes. It was a consensus that for a man in his late sixties, he still had plenty of swagger. Like Laura, he was in excellent shape for his age and his tall nicely proportioned body moved with an ease and confidence that could only be described as sexy.

Laura picked up Jester, the calico porch cat who had been patiently awaiting her affection. She settled onto the wicker loveseat with him and Jester had purred so loud it was audible to everyone.

"Are you ready to get your truck?" Joe had asked Kate.

"I'm ready," Kate had responded, hopping up from the chair. "I've only been waiting for . . . let me think . . . 30 years."

Joe had grinned. "It's in the barn," he said. "Let's go."

Joe had known Kate since she was a child and knew she was a good kid. When she was a teenager she frequently helped on his farm. There were always oddball chores to be done and animals to be fed. On occasion, with permission from Kate's father, Joe would allow her to drive the truck around the property, well before she had a driver's license. He noticed she was always very careful to avoid any mishaps so he knew his trusty old truck was going to a good home. That was important to Joe. Up here a man gets attached to these things—old trucks and such. To the dismay of many a wife, every homestead had its own prized collection of old vehicles in various states of deterioration. One could find them either rusting away in an old barn, or worse, stacked up in the yard. Old parts were a commodity in this area, although often they ended up in fantastical whirligigs that dotted the landscape. This of course tended to fascinate the men, too.

Blue, still in the yard, had been enthusiastically scratching his back with all fours in the air. Kate called to him and he quickly sprang to his feet. He had run to her side and nudged her hand for praise. As Joe, Kate and Annie began the walk to the barn Blue had eagerly trotted out ahead, not as fast as he used to be but every bit as determined.

"Watch out for Stinker," Laura had called out after them. Stinker was the big ornery barn cat who had a strong dislike for dogs. Blue had had several encounters with him in the past, the last one resulting in a painful scratch on his nose.

As they walked, Annie remembered thinking about how nice it was to be around Joe and Laura. They were such a loving couple. Again, she had briefly reflected on her own childhood, but the thought only lasted for a moment for on such a beautiful day her mind soon shifted to the scenery coming to life around her. She had stopped momentarily, mesmerized by the way the wind—ever so light, was moving across the field like gentle waves. She tilted her face upward and smiled. *Mare's tails,* she thought at the sight of thin wispy clouds sweeping across the sky.

At the barn, Joe had swung open one of the large red doors. Inside, the truck was parked where Joe had left it the week before. Even though the engine was relatively new, Joe had given it a spin, just to make sure there were no problems.

Kate knew the truck well and was aware the body had a few minor issues that her husband could easily remedy. For its age, the interior of the truck was in excellent shape except for two small holes in the head liner. Joe, given the right opportunity, liked to joke the holes were from Laura's high heels. This comment was always made in Laura's presence and it was always followed by a whack to whatever body part of his was closest to her.

As they had approached the truck, they could see that Blue, already in the truck bed, had his nose pressed up against the rear window of the cab. His tail was wagging energetically. When they looked inside they found Momma Cat, another of the feline barn residents, nursing her new litter of kittens.

"Aww, look Kate," Annie had said, "kittens." She remembered looking longingly at the five wiggling black-and-white newborns.

"Annie," Kate had said firmly, "step away from the truck." She could see Annie was already picking one, possibly two out for herself. "You can't travel if you have kittens," she reminded.

Annie had nodded sadly in agreement, "*All right*."

Joe had then reached in the open window and gently rubbed Momma Cat on the head. "There you are old girl. We were wondering where you moved your litter to. I'll get Laura," he had said. "We'll take the litter up to the house."

As they turned to go, Kate had called to Blue. He was still glued to the rear window, looking in.

"Blue. Come," Kate had repeated firmly.

Blue gave Kate one of his signature whines in response then had reluctantly jumped down off the back of the truck. Unfortunately, he had not noticed the angry green eyes or the twitching tail hidden below. Stinker, the barn cat, had been waiting. Suddenly, all fifteen pounds of spiked grey fur and claws let out an ear-piercing scream! Blue bolted for the barn door nearly knocking Annie to the ground.

Joe chuckled at the sight and in his unruffled drawl had said, "Stinker don't take kindly to dogs."

THREE
Polished by the Sea

Our truest life is when we are in dreams awake.
Henry David Thoreau

At the time Joe sold Kate the truck, he and Laura had been married nearly forty years, but life had not always been perfect for them. The two bullet holes in the tailgate of the old pickup truck attested to that. There was a particularly rough patch five years into their marriage and around the time their first child, Lindy, turned three. No one knows for sure what put the marriage on a bad path that year. Some folks said it was because the drought had been as hard on families as it had been on the crops. While others said it was the pretty, young barmaid, Lila Jean. Lila Jean worked down at Clancy's bar where Joe was spending more and more time drinking. She had always given Joe special attention and the more Joe drank the more he confided his troubles to her. But whatever ailments Joe had he was cured of them the night Laura took her shotgun and unloaded two bullets into the rear of his truck. It had been easy to find where it was parked in what had become its *usual spot* outside Clancy's. Fortunately, the truck was empty, although everyone knew if Laura wanted to shoot Joe she could have; she was a crack shot with a rifle.

The next day, Lila Jean hurriedly picked up her final paycheck at Clancy's and bee-lined it to the bus station. Noticing Laura's green truck parked at the corner, Lila Jean glared at it in one last defiant moment. She could not see the face of the silhouette in the truck, but when she saw the early morning sunlight glint off the shotgun barrel it was all she needed to scurry onto the bus. "Take me back to the big city," she said furiously to the driver, "it's safer there."

Watching the bus pull away, Laura's shoulders dropped as her anger turned to sadness. She let out a deep sigh then set the gun down on the seat and closed her eyes for a brief moment. She reached up for the rear view mirror, angled it and looked tiredly back at the woman reflected there. *Who is this person?* she silently questioned, brushing her uncombed hair away from her face. *I don't even know myself anymore.* Her mind filled with confusion and fear. *I need to get away*, she thought. *But where will I go?* She had more than just herself to be concerned about; there was also her daughter, Lindy.

Laura laid her head back and tried to remember a time in her life when she was truly happy. Her thoughts went back to when she was a child and every year her parents took her on summer vacations to the coast. How soothing the sights and sounds of the sea had been to her. She remembered how much she loved combing the beach for small bits of sea glass and shells. These very memories now filled dust-covered glass jars in her attic. *I'll go to the coast*, she decided. She could clear her mind there and figure out what to do. She would use the small amount of savings they had in a coffee can on the shelf in the kitchen. "Savings for a rainy day," as some called it. Well it was *storming* now, if only in her head.

Laura managed to slip in and out of the old farmhouse before Joe had a chance to find her. He was well into regretting his foolishness and had been looking all over town for her since the incident the night before. Yes, he had gravitated toward the pretty, young Lila Jean. Her attention did a lot to ease the stress he was under and even more for his suffering ego. Now he was glad it never went further than a few good laughs. Odd thing was, Lila Jean was exactly the way Laura used to be. She always seemed cheerful and happy to see him. She had big dreams for her life and she was excited about the future. Laura had changed.

But Joe knew he was not completely guilt free either, and in reality, he loved Laura with all his heart. It was obvious things were not right between them. He could only hope it was not too late to change the direction their marriage was heading.

Before leaving the farmhouse, Laura called her parents, Bob and Irene. She let them know what had happened and where they could find her. Her plan was to rent one of the beachfront cottages in Sandcastle, a small town on the coast where her parents had taken her as a child. She was scared and she had never ventured that far on her own so it pleased her greatly when her parents offered to come and stay with her. That way they could watch after Lindy and give Laura some much-needed time to herself.

The night before, prior to going to Clancy's, Laura had left Lindy in the trusted care of her best friend, Jenna. Time was of the essence now and she sped quickly down the dirt road leading to Jenna's house. The sun was coming into full view and golden shafts of sunlight were quickly spreading across the fields of grain. Tom, Jenna's husband, deep in the field on his tractor, hesitantly waved as she passed by. He was Joe's good friend and likely knew what had happened. Situated on a small rise above their farm, the house, a two story grey-and-white with a metal roof was a welcoming sight.

Jenna, still in her robe, met Laura at the screen door with a sympathetic hug. "I've made fresh coffee," she whispered as they stepped into the kitchen. "The baby and

Lindy are still sleeping."

"I can't stay," Laura responded.

"Can't stay? What do you mean?" asked Jenna, her face flooding with concern. She followed Laura into the spare bedroom where Lindy slept, a fluff of blonde curls under a quilt of pink and blue.

Laura quickly packed Lindy's overnight bag and threw it over her shoulder. "I'm leaving. I'm going to the coast," she said as she gently bundled and picked up Lindy.

"The coast? Where will you stay?" asked Jenna. "What should we tell Joe? He's looking all over town for you." Her concerns grew as Laura moved quickly out the front door and down the steps to the truck. She watched nervously as Laura settled Lindy, now half awake, into the car seat. "Are you sure this is what you want to do?" she asked, her eyes searching for answers in Laura's.

"Yes . . . no . . . I don't know," Laura shook her head, confusion and tears brimming in her eyes. "All I know is I can't stay." She kissed Jenna goodbye on the cheek. "I'll call you when I get settled."

"*Wait.* When are you coming back?" Jenna asked. She felt a surge of fear—this was all happening so fast. She knew how Laura felt; they had had many long talks. Even before Lila Jean she had feared something like this would happen. Like Laura, she, too, had long sublimated her own dreams to follow that of her husband's. But women around here did not leave their husbands, no matter if they were happy or not. Now, she could not bear the thought of losing her best friend.

"I don't know, Jenna," Laura answered as she climbed into the driver's seat. "I just need some time to myself—to sort things out."

"Just . . . give me a minute," said Jenna, gesturing with her hand. She ran back into the kitchen then quickly returned. "Here," she said, handing Laura a small brown bag through the passenger window. "Sandwiches . . . for the road."

"Isn't this Tom's lunch?" asked Laura, accepting the bag.

"I'll make another," said Jenna, managing a shaky smile. "Is there anything else you want me to do?"

"Yes," Laura responded, aware of both the love she felt for her best friend and the distress her leaving was causing. She reached out and touched Jenna's arm. "Please . . . don't worry."

* * * * *

When Laura arrived in Sandcastle her parents were already there. They had rented one of the small, white clapboard cottages nestled in a cove at the water's edge. Though her emotions were spinning out of control, Laura immediately felt a comforting sense of the familiar.

The first few weeks were the roughest for Laura and she spent many days just sitting on the shore staring out to sea. It is well known the sea is a master of many moods and everyday Laura's emotions changed with it. Some days she felt anger, as the sea pounded relentlessly on the rocks and storms raged across the horizon. On others, she felt depressed and gloomy, like the gray overcast days that seemed to go on forever, accentuating her own sense of doom.

It was no secret that Bob and Irene had contacted Joe to let him know Laura and Lindy were okay. After all, they loved Joe and they had high hopes this story would have a happy ending. They knew their daughter Laura well enough to suggest to Joe that he give her a little time. He reluctantly agreed and threw himself into fixing up the old farmhouse. *For when Laura comes home*, he told himself.

A full month had gone by before Laura's emotional fog began to lift. One morning, after a particularly stormy night, the skies cleared abruptly. Laura awoke feeling different, too. Peacefulness was setting in. Peacefulness that only days by the sea could have given her. She lingered in bed for a moment and watched the gentle breeze billow the sheers in her bedroom. Morning light fell softly across the weathered wood floor. *Perhaps with peace will come clarity*, she hoped, rising.

Laura peeked out the window and saw the early morning sun was just beginning to glint through lavender and gold tinted clouds. She picked up a piece of sea glass from her nightstand and held it to the light, admiring its soft blue color. *Sea glass,* she suddenly realized, *there would be great pickings after a storm like last night!*

She opened her armoire and quickly searched for her *new* favorite dress, a white linen shift with pin-tucking and abalone shell buttons. Not only had her time by the sea revitalized her, her style of dressing had changed here, too. She now embraced the comfort of linen dresses, flowing cotton skirts and peasant blouses. She loved the way the natural fibers moved as she strolled along the shore. In addition, she often found no need for shoes.

Everyone in the house was still sleeping so Laura quietly slipped out the screen door. She grabbed her collecting basket from a wicker chair and headed down to the beach. She felt more aware of her surroundings this morning than on previous days spent mostly enveloped in her thoughts. As she walked barefoot in the warm sand, she breathed deeply and noticed how fresh and salty the air smelled. Rays of sunlight sparkled on the gently moving waves as they lapped lazily along the shore. She genuinely smiled for the first time in months as she watched several small sandpipers dart out in front of her, their tiny yellow legs a blur. Nearby, Ring-billed Gulls fluttering over the water were having lively conversations with each other as they contended for a breakfast of small fish.

As Laura continued to walk, she thought about Joe and how she missed the closeness they had shared in the early years of their relationship. She remembered the times they spent here on this very beach. He even proposed to her here. It had been the perfect ending to the perfect day. They had promised each other that every year they would come back here and for the first few years of their marriage they did. Unfortunately, that changed like everything else. Laura knew she still loved Joe, even though what Joe had done was wrong and inexcusable. But she also knew that *she* had not been perfect either. She, too, had changed. Full of creativity as a young girl, Laura had had dreams of pursuing some sort of career in art. There was nary any form of art that did not come naturally to her. Joe on the other hand, was much more reserved and traditional in his ways. He definitely did not like change. He came from a family of *hands in the dirt* farmers and the women rarely worked outside the home. In order to please Joe, Laura put aside her dreams and the art she loved. She quit spending time with her friends, too; the same friends that had enriched and inspired her, friends that brought laughter and funny stories to share. In her own words, she had become boring and increasingly distant. Her normally upbeat spirit just did not seem to soar anymore. When Lindy was born, it was truly a blessing. She felt alive again as motherhood temporarily revitalized her. But the drought soon followed bringing crop failures and financial troubles, a strong recipe for disaster to a marriage already in jeopardy. Being married to a man of such charm and rugged good looks did not help either. The flirtatious smiles and lingering looks from other women did not go unnoticed. Jealousy rooted in low self-esteem often took a seat at the dinner table. Frustration of a life with dreams left unfulfilled and a lack of appreciation by *both* parties salted the wounds of despair.

Laura walked thoughtfully for a while longer along the shore. Finding many beautiful pieces of sea glass and shells she carefully placed them into her straw basket. As the sun rose higher in the sky, she sat down in the sand and watched a small sailboat skip across the pale blue horizon. She truly felt at ease for the first time since she had arrived. Soon, Laura's body fell under the spell of the rhythmic sounds of the waves and she lay back in the soft sand and closed her eyes. She fell asleep and began to dream. The dream started out as a fine summer day, very much like today. She was walking along the shore and came upon an exquisite piece of aqua-colored sea glass lying in the sand. She picked it up to admire the color, but it revealed much, much more. A vignette began to play across its small surface of a day she and Joe had walked along the beach. The sun was setting in glorious layers of orange and pink as they strolled along hand-in-hand, happily recounting their day. Unbeknownst to her, Joe had secretly placed a ring box in her collection basket. When she finally noticed it, he had opened the box, knelt on one knee and sweetly proposed to her. Laura was so caught up in the moment she excitedly embraced him and they both fell to the sand laughing. Laura smiled at the memory and carefully placed the exquisite piece of aqua-colored glass into her basket.

As the dream continued, another piece of sea glass caught Laura's eye as it sparkled in the sun. This time it was a brilliant blue piece. *So rare*, she thought as she eagerly picked it up and brushed away the sand. To her pleasant surprise, another vignette danced across the smooth surface of the small sea jewel. This time it was of her wedding day. The following spring after Joe had proposed, they married on a hillside covered with wildflowers as hundreds of white butterflies flitted around them. It was magical. Loved ones and close friends surrounded them as they joyfully kissed for the first time as husband and wife. Laura very carefully placed the rare blue piece of glass in her basket and continued to walk.

Soon, another piece of sea glass shone brightly in the sunlight. Laura picked up a delicate green piece and watched affectionately as a vignette of the day Joe blindfolded her and surprised her with their new home. Joe knew how much Laura loved the old farmhouse, and for a while, it looked as if it was beyond their reach. But Joe would have done anything to make Laura happy and somehow he made it happen. Laura placed the delicate green piece of sea glass gently into her basket.

Yet another piece of sea glass appeared as Laura strolled in her dream. This time it was a white piece, barely visible against the sand. She picked it up and tenderly watched as Joe sat crying at her bedside. It was shortly after the birth of Lindy and Joe was overcome with emotion. His face was buried in his hands; he was terrified about being a father.

Laura lovingly reassured Joe, her heart bursting with love for him. And Joe proved her right. As she placed the white piece of sea glass in her basket, Laura thought about how he had grown to be an excellent father. He was patient and supportive, attentive and loving.

Still dreaming, Laura set the basket down in the sand for a moment as she expectantly looked around for the next piece of sea glass. She wondered with anticipation what story it would have to tell. Suddenly, the wind began to blow and she cowered as lightening cracked and the skies turned black and threatening. Gentle waves quickly turned monstrous, crashing on the shore like fists pounding drums of war. She watched in horror as a big wave came out of nowhere, grabbed her basket and began to sweep it out to sea. "No!" Laura screamed. She ran toward it and threw herself into the turbulent sea, desperate to save her precious sea glass. Waves crashed around her as she thrashed frantically, only to watch in agony as the basket drifted further and further away. Finally, exhausted and defeated, Laura made her way back to the shore and collapsed. She began to weep inconsolably. Laura's beautiful dream had quickly turned into a nightmare.

Then, just as quickly as the storm had appeared in her dream, the skies cleared and the sun's rays once again beamed through the clouds. Laura, still stunned and feeling the pain of her loss, wiped away her tears and rose from the sand. There, lying on its side at the edge of the water was her basket. She ran hopefully to it, but as she dropped to her knees she thought, *Surely the sea glass will be gone*. Ever so carefully she turned the basket upright. Her treasures were still there! But somehow, they were different. As she gently lifted them from the basket, she could see the sea glass and shells had intertwined and connected to form a beautiful necklace. She held it up in the sunlight, admiring its beauty. *This was not ordinary sea glass*, she thought, each piece now had new meaning to her. They represented hope. They represented family and commitment. *I will wear you forever*, she thought and tenderly placed the necklace around her neck.

Laura awoke from her dream with a jolt. Her hand immediately felt for the necklace, but of course, none was there. Inspired, she excitedly jumped to her feet, grabbed her basket and ran all the way back to the cottage.

"*Good morning*," she chirped as she scurried through the screen door of the cottage. Her parents and Lindy were sitting at the kitchen table. She stopped momentarily and gave Lindy a big kiss on her head then continued on to her bedroom.

Bob and Irene looked at each other, confused. They rose from the table and with Lindy in tow followed Laura to her room. After so many days of anguish and sadness, her parents were relieved to see her so happy and greatly interested as to what had brought about the sudden change. They silently watched from the doorway as Laura proceeded to carefully pour the contents of an old mason jar out onto the bed. She spread the collection of colorful beads, polished stones, seashells and sea glass over her white comforter then took a step back and eyed them with intent.

Lindy, caught up in her mother's excitement, hovered near the bed. She pulled at Laura's dress. "What you doing, Mommy?" she asked.

Laura bent down, cradled Lindy's face, and said, "I'm making something *very* special."

"What, Mommy?" Lindy insisted, eyes bright with

curiosity.

"You'll see," Laura replied as she began to rummage through the top of her closet. She pulled down an old, flowered cookie tin. Her mother, a consummate sewer, never went anywhere without it. She opened it and searched past the odd buttons and spools until she found a package of silk embroidery thread. Next, she reached for the white wicker tray that sat on the small table by the window. She placed a handful of thoughtfully selected shells and sea glass on it. When she had laid them out on the tray in a design as close to what she could remember from her dream, she once again searched the bed for two very special polished stones. When she found them, she turned to her father and asked if he could drill tiny holes in them. He adjusted his glasses and looked at the stones then back at the earnest eyes of the daughter he loved so much. Without a word he took the stones from Laura's hand and trotted off to find his toolbox. Fifteen minutes later when he returned, Laura was adeptly hand-knotting the chosen seashells and pieces of glass into an intricate necklace.

"Perfect timing," Laura said as she took the stones from her father. Immersed in her work, she did not notice when Irene quietly disappeared and motioned for Bob and Lindy to come with her. An hour later, when the necklace was complete, Laura lifted it up and admired it in the light now gleaming through her bedroom window. She was very pleased with her work and she tied the beautiful necklace around her neck. When she emerged from the bedroom, her face aglow, her mother was just putting lunch on the table.

"Oh, Laura, it's gorgeous!" Irene raved upon seeing the necklace for the first time.

Her father, tilting his bifocals, proudly admired the

workmanship.

"Bootiful, Mommy!" Lindy beamed, causing them all to laugh.

After lunch, Laura sat on the porch with Lindy and fashioned a bracelet to match her necklace. Then Lindy gleefully chose her own beads and watched with great interest as Laura crafted a tiny bracelet for her wrist. As she worked, endless jewelry designs began flooding Laura's mind and she quickly penciled ideas onto paper while they were fresh.

Later that week while looking through a selection of dresses at her favorite boutique, *Vera's by the Sea*, the proprietor, dressed in a flowing blue floral dress, came over and admired her necklace.

"Dahling, where did you buy this necklace?" Vera inquired in her European accent.

"I made it," Laura answered, grinning with pride, "and this bracelet, too."

"They are *absolutely* stunning," Vera raved. "I *must* buy some for my customers. They are the perfect accessories for my clothing line. When can you bring them?"

Laura, stuttering at first, offered to bring her collection by next week.

"That would be purrfect," Vera responded and floated away.

"Thank you," said Laura. She was momentarily frozen as she comprehended what had just happened. Then the wheels started to turn. "Have a nice day," she called out as she headed out the door and rushed home to begin work on *her collection*.

* * * * *

Back on the farm, Joe looked nervously at his reflection in the mirror as he combed his neatly trimmed hair. It had been three months since Laura left and finally she had agreed to see him. He closed his worn leather suitcase where it lay on the bed and latched the buckles securely. He walked from room to room in the house to make sure it was presentable, having high hopes that Laura and Lindy would be coming home with him. He lingered for a moment in the doorway of an unused bedroom that just two months ago was full of old storage boxes. As a surprise for Laura, Joe had cleaned the room out and turned it into an art studio. The previously dingy walls now boasted a fresh coat of creamy butter-yellow paint. The old torn curtains had been replaced, now crisp white organza sheers graced the large sash windows. From a mail-order catalogue, he had purchased a painter's easel and a wooden stool which he carefully placed near one of the windows for plenty of natural light. In the attic, he searched and found Laura's paints and brushes in a dusty box. The brushes now stood in tall, gleaming mason jars on a table next to the easel. A rose floral settee and a gilded mirror along one wall perfectly reflected Laura's rosebushes that were blooming vigorously outside the window.

Joe wanted everything perfect for Laura but more than anything else, he wanted her to be happy. In the quiet living room he paused and took one last look around. Then, he picked up his suitcase and closed the front door behind him.

As Joe began the long drive to the coast, he thought about the mistakes he had made in their marriage. Admittedly he was old school and believed a wife's place was at home, so when Laura wanted to go to a nearby college and take an art class he had protested. The truth was he was afraid if Laura got a higher education she would leave him. After all, he was just a farmer with barely a formal education that ended at the age of fifteen.

The remorseful thoughts continued as Joe drove. *I never even complemented her on how pretty she always looked or how nice the house was kept. Not to mention how delicious her meals were,* he ruminated. The latter causing his mind to drift since he had been living on peanut butter sandwiches. He sure missed Laura's pot roast. When Laura begged to get away and go to the shore, he would never take the time. The farm always needed this or needed that. He remembered telling her there was no time for such frivolousness. Sometimes it would even make her cry. The miles and the regrets seemed to go on forever. When Joe finally arrived at the shore, his hands were trembling as he pulled the keys from the ignition of the truck.

Irene, seeing him arrive, came to the door of the cottage and gave a quiet wave then pointed toward the beach where he should look for Laura. He nodded and waved back. From where he stood he could see Laura in the distance sitting on the shore. He picked up the bouquet of flowers he had bought at a roadside stand and took a deep breath. As he walked he could not help but look out at the sea. The water was mesmerizing as it sparkled like a field of diamonds under a brilliant sun and deep blue sky. Voluptuous white clouds were billowing like tall ships across the horizon.

As Joe walked, a steady soft breeze pressed invitingly against his skin. His thoughts turned back to Laura. She was still sitting on the sand ahead, staring out to sea. She knew he was coming today yet he noticed she had not looked his way or risen to meet him. *Lord, please let this go well*, he silently prayed as he continued to walk toward her. Immersed in his worrisome thoughts, he nodded politely as he passed a barefoot young woman walking along the edge of the water.

"Joe!"

Surprised to hear his name spoken by a stranger, Joe turned around. Before him stood a strikingly beautiful woman dressed in a white peasant blouse and a flowing skirt. Long wavy hair wisped in the breeze and fell femininely on her tanned shoulders. Her clear blue eyes and her smile were as welcoming as the warmth of the sun. It was Laura.

Joe stuttered Laura's name. There were so many things that needed to be said, but in this moment, he found himself speechless. He fought the urge to pull Laura into his arms, unsure of himself or how she might react.

Laura could tell he was very nervous. "Are those for me?" she asked, nodding toward the flowers.

"Oh, uh, yes," Joe stammered again and handed the flowers to her.

"Thank you," she said. "They're beautiful."

"Laura," Joe began, "I just want you to know how sorry I am for hurting you."

"I know," Laura responded softly. She could see the honesty in his eyes. She gently placed her hand on his arm. "Walk with me?"

"Yes . . . of course," Joe answered.

They walked quietly for a while along the shore. Soon, Joe started to relax as his body began to absorb the many soothing gifts the seashore has to offer. It was Laura who broke the silence, "I'm sorry about the bullet holes in the truck."

Joe chuckled. "I like 'em," he said, "adds character."

They smiled at each other then continued walking. Joe watched as Laura stopped and picked up a vibrant pink scallop shell peeking through the sand. *She looks so peaceful,* he thought. *It's obvious how much she loves it here. I should have never taken this away from her . . . I never should have taken this away from myself,* he realized.

Joe reached out and touched Laura's arm. She stopped and turned to face him and he gently brushed her hair away from her face. "You look amazing, Laura," he said.

"Thank you," she responded, blushing.

"This necklace you are wearing . . . it's beautiful. Did you make it?" Joe asked.

"Yes," Laura grinned then added proudly, "I've been selling my work to the local boutiques."

"That's wonderful!" Joe responded. "Although I'm not surprised; you're so talented."

"Thank you," said Laura.

Still admiring the necklace, Joe asked curiously, "Where is this stone from? Did you find it here at the sea?"

Laura looked at the small polished stone then back up at Joe. With a gleam in her eyes she said, "It's from our farm . . . our home."

Joe's eyes teared as his emotions overcame him. He swept Laura up into his arms and kissed her. In that moment, love once again took Laura by the hand. There was no anger left, the days by the sea had washed it all away and brought the clarity she had hoped for.

"Daddy, Daddy!" Lindy cried with delight as she ran through the cottage gate. Bob and Irene, watching from the doorway, waved and watched as Lindy gleefully ran toward her parents. Barefoot and wearing a pink striped pinafore, her blonde curls bounced with each excited step. She was running as fast as her little feet could go when she suddenly tripped and fell face down into the soft sand. Joe and Laura rushed to her expecting to console her tears, but instead, Lindy was laughing when she raised her sand-covered face. Joe and Laura began to laugh, too, enveloping her in their arms.

Joe, Laura and Lindy played for a while on the shore—wading in the warm water, building sandcastles and watching blue-green fiddler crabs as they darted in and out of holes. Joe noticed Lindy had learned so many new things here. She knew the names of all of the birds, most of the shells, and even the little wiggling fish that accumulated in shallow pools. She even understood about the tides and how they were affected by the moon. Seeing the world afresh through his young daughter's eyes was all the inspiration Joe needed to ask if she would like to visit again next year. Lindy's head bobbed excitedly up and down with approval.

Later when the breeze had stilled and the water lapped calmly on the shore, Joe and Laura sat down and watched as Lindy avidly searched for her own collection of sea glass and shells. The sun, now low on the horizon, its bright glow transitioning to a softer light of serene pastels.

Laura looked down at her feet and moved the sand with her toes. "Did you really mean what you said, Joe," she asked, "about visiting here next year?"

"Definitely. Things are picking up on the farm," Joe responded. "In fact, Laura, I've been thinking about making an offer on a beach cottage."

"Really?" Laura beamed.

"Really," Joe answered, pulling her close.

Just then, Irene called out from the cottage gate to let them know dinner would be ready soon. Joe was instantly on his feet.

Laura arose and brushed the sand from her skirt. “Are you hungry?” she asked as she slipped her hand in his.

“*Very,*” Joe responded, “but please, anything but peanut butter.”

From that day forward, Joe and Laura connected in a deeper way than ever before. As the years went by, their differences only made them stronger. Laura’s easygoing attitude helped Joe learn not to sweat the small stuff while Joe’s courage and self-confidence helped Laura to conquer her fears and brave new challenges. Now in their sixties, they were enjoying a lifetime of love in its truest form, unconditional and altruistic, built on a solid foundation of appreciation and respect.

FOUR
Here We Are . . . But Where is That?

Weather forecast for tonight: dark,
continued dark overnight,
with widely scattered light by morning.
George Carlin

As Kate parked the Suburban next to the curb at the airport in Manchester, she reminded Annie to try to keep things positive with Jordan and Nance.

Inside, the baggage claim area was bustling. Waves of new arrivals were staking their claims next to the baggage carousels. On tippy-toes, Kate and Annie craned their necks to look for their friends.

Annie pointed and waved. "There's Jordan." She called to her, "*Jordan!*"

Jordan raised her arm in the air and waved back. She navigated the ever-shifting sea of people and joined them. They all embraced.

"*Wow, you look great*," complimented Annie.

"Thank you, Annie," Jordan grinned, "so do you. How are you?"

"*Wonderful,*" Annie answered.

"That's terrific," Jordan responded.

"How was the trip?" asked Kate.

"The trip? Well, the flight was fine," Jordan answered, "but Nance nearly drove me crazy."

"Nance? What happened?" Kate asked. "You guys are best buds."

Jordan shrugged and shook her head, "One word–Randall."

"Oh. Still not over it, huh?" asked Kate. She had suspected this.

"Nope," Jordan answered. "She actually still has hope it will work out. When she admitted that, I lost my temper. Nance retaliated by slapping on her headphones and not speaking to me."

"Where *is* Nance?" asked Annie, looking about the still bustling baggage area.

"She stopped in the gift shop," answered Jordan. "She's probably buying more candy bars. I've lost count of how many she's had today."

"Oh, no, not good," said Kate.

"Tell me about it," said Jordan.

"*Hello, everybody!*" Nance called out cheerfully. Her hands were full of candy bars. She was alternately dropping and picking them up as she scurried their way.

"And there she is," said Jordan, "the pied piper of candy bars."

Annie and Kate recognized the bubbly voice, but they did not immediately recognize Nance. Normally she would be stylishly dressed and sporting a cute haircut. The person they saw coming their way was disheveled looking and wearing clothes at least two sizes too big.

"*It's so good to see you guys*," Nance gushed. She gave Kate and Annie each a big hug.

"We're *so* happy to see you," said Kate. "How are you?"

Nance smiled and pushed her long bangs from her eyes. "Okay," she responded, her voice trembling a little.

"Awww," Kate said, giving her a shoulder squeeze. "Listen, we're going to have a *great* time out at the lake."

"That's right," added Annie, patting Nance on the shoulder.

"Geez, Nance, why don't you just page him?" Jordan snapped. "I'm sure he'll answer to Captain Jack Ass."

Nance spun around, her brow crinkled in defense. "When did you get to be so mean?" she asked for the second time that day.

"You're drowning yourself in candy bars! It's been three months since he's called—*get over it!*" said Jordan, obviously at the end of her rope.

"You know your attitude isn't so great either," countered Nance angrily, completely out of character. "Ever since Rodney dumped you, you treat all men like dirt!"

"Rodney didn't dump me! I dumped . . . ," Jordan lashed back.

"*OKAY!*" Kate intervened. "Need I remind you of the importance of this time together? Annie's just beat cancer for God's sake! Let's just relax and try to have a good time."

"Oh, gosh, of course," said Nance, regretting her behavior.

"Yes, I'm sorry," Jordan apologized, feeling like a petulant school girl. "I've been a little on edge lately," she admitted.

"A little?" Nance blurted. A laugh quickly followed; even she knew she was incapable of holding on to anger. She reached out to embrace everyone in a group hug, "I love you guys!" With this, the air quickly cleared of emotional shrapnel. There was plenty of love and a long history of friendship between the four of them.

"And yea," Jordan pumped her hands in the air, "Annie, you are truly looking great! What a scare that was."

"Thank you," Annie smiled broadly. "I feel great. Listen, thanks for all your phone calls and cards, *both* of you. It meant so much to me."

"And how is Ben?" asked Nance with a smile. She was referring to the new man in Annie's life. "And *when* do we get to meet him?"

"He's wonderful," Annie responded, her face lighting up. "Hopefully you'll get a chance to meet him soon."

"He sounds like a wonderful catch," said Nance.

"*I*," said Annie, "am my own best catch."

"High five on that, Annie," said Jordan.

Annie grinned and returned the gesture.

Kate smiled. She was pleased. That was the first time she had heard Annie say that. She knew childhood had not exactly handed Annie the keys to make such a statement. Her confidence had been hard won.

A bell rang and a warning light blinked as the luggage carousel began to turn. "That should be our bags," said Nance.

"I'll get them," said Jordan.

Uh, oh, thought Nance, watching her go.

Jordan headed over to the crowded carousel and jockeyed into position. Past experience had taught her baggage retrieval was pure business. It required her complete attention and the accomplishment of three pre-set goals:

> Goal number one: Get as close to the carousel as possible. Do this quickly as others will be trying to do the same.
>
> Goal number two: Clear an arms-length of area around you. This can be accomplished by poking your elbows out and taking side-to-side steps.
>
> Goal number three: Focus and try not to make a fool

out of yourself.

Nance's luggage came around first. Jordan successfully retrieved the bright blue bag from the carousel then repositioned herself. When *her* large red bag came around she grabbed the handle, but somehow it managed to flip and wedge precariously on the conveyer belt. A man quickly stepped forward to assist her, but Jordan refused his help. "I got it," she said coldly, not even looking up. She kept her eye on the bag as it slowly drifted away on the creaking conveyer belt.

In a couple of minutes her still wedged suitcase came back around. This time when she grabbed the handle it pulled her clumsily along, causing her to hop over several obstacles before she finally had to let it go again. Alarmed, the same man, now fearing for Jordan's safety, reached in again to help. Jordan stated even more loudly, "I GOT IT."

"*Okay,*" the perplexed man stepped back, surrendering with his hands in the air and taking the full brunt of a glare from Jordan.

With both pieces of their luggage finally secured, Jordan straightened up and took a second to regain her composure. She called into play Goal number four: If you make a fool of yourself, pretend it didn't happen. She smoothed her jogging suit, held her head up and stiffly rolled their suitcases back to where Kate, Annie and Nance were still standing. They had watched the scene unfold with their mouths' agape.

"Taking no prisoners I see," said Kate. "Shall we go?"

"Yes please," Annie piped.

They put the luggage in the back of Kate's Suburban then piled in to begin the drive to the lake. Conversation flowed easily and the mood turned merry as they laughed and plotted their days to come. It was like old times again when as children, every day at the lake had been an opportunity for new adventure. In the front seat, Kate and Annie smiled at each other—things were beginning to look up.

Once inside the rolling hills of the forest, the view of rustic farms and cornfields changed. Now the scenery was a mix of tall deciduous and coniferous hardwoods. Traffic was light. In a few weeks, the road, famous for its gorgeous and inspiring fall color would be mobbed with leaf peepers.

An hour into the drive, Jordan and Nance both began to doze in the back seat. It may have been due to the sweet woodsy air, or perhaps the car ride. More likely it was due to the fact they had been up since three that morning. Whatever it was that lulled them to sleep, there was unquestionable comfort in being among good friends.

Kate and Annie drove along quietly for a long while, but as they came around a large bend in the road, Annie suddenly yelled, *"STOP!"*

Kate brought the Suburban to an abrupt halt causing Jordan and Nance to toss precariously forward in their seats. They both grunted as the seatbelts caught, nearly knocking the wind out of them.

Annie grabbed her camera from her satchel and leapt from the car.

Kate took a deep breath. Her heart was beating a mile a minute. She shook her head when she realized what the fuss was about.

Recovering, Nance and Jordan turned around and watched Annie slowly back-track then quietly inch her way up to a fence post where a small yellow bird was perched.

"Is . . . she . . . ," Jordan began.

"Yep," Kate answered before Jordan could finish. Annie was taking a picture of a bird. This was nothing new to her.

Jordan groaned and plopped back in her seat.

After taking several photos, Annie hurried back to the truck and hopped in. "Okay," she said, buckling her seatbelt.

Silence.

"What?" Annie asked, aware of the looks coming her way.

Kate put the Suburban in gear and the drive resumed, though Jordan and Nance were reluctant to doze off again. Soon they turned onto the tree-canopied road that led to the ferry landing for the Buckskin Lodge. Although the lodge was not on an island, the owners still maintained access to the area via the beautiful white vintage wood boat christened "The Swan." The same boat spoken about in the old travelogue Ed had picked up at the flea market. Like the lodge, it was still operated by the Kingsley family. They felt the limited access helped to contribute to the serenity and beauty of the area. There was a private road that allowed service vehicles and deliveries. From the lodge, vans transported guests to recreational areas and were on hand in case of an emergency. Otherwise, electric golf carts and bicycles were the only other modes of transportation around the lodge and cabin area.

Once they parked, there was not much for the girls to carry from the Suburban. Kate was up there several times a year and kept the cabin well stocked with basics. Almost anything else one might need, if not too exotic, could be picked up at the small general store the lodge owners maintained.

Colby, one of the many strapping young men that worked at the Buckskin, was on the dock talking to a group of visitors waiting to board the boat. He looked more like a surfer than a lodge employee with his long blonde ponytail and tanned skin. Lean, yet muscular, he wreaked energy as he excitedly spoke about the amenities of the area. Another young man, Tim, was loading one of the delivery vans with luggage to be delivered to the lodge and cabins.

"Hi, Tim," greeted Kate. She and the girls handed over their larger pieces of luggage and the cooler. "Thank you. Just drop them on the porch as usual."

"Yes, ma'am," responded Tim.

Walking toward the dock, Kate grumbled, "Ma'am. I hate it when that happens."

"Yeah, the nerve," Annie agreed. "We're far too young to be referred to as ma'am."

As they approached the landing, another large white van pulled in and came to an abrupt halt. The side door flew open and three brawny men exited noisily, each one seemingly larger than the one before. Kate, having climbed in the Alps multiple times, quickly discerned they were Swedish by their accents. Approximately in their mid-thirties, they were characteristically tall, athletic and very blonde.

"Move, Olaf. I need to stretch," bellowed another man from inside the van.

Olaf, stockier and mid-fortyish, clumsily stumbled out the door. "Hey! Watch who you are pushing, Karl." He glared back into the van and menacingly flexed his large arm muscle.

"Ooooo . . . I'm scared Olaf," teased Karl as he stepped out and began to stretch. Karl, also mid-fortyish, was by far the biggest and most intimidating of all. He easily stood

6'4 and with his muscular build he undoubtedly topped the 200 pound mark.

Olaf was still fussing when Karl suddenly became aware that Kate, Annie, Jordan and Nance had stopped to watch the commotion unfold. He gave Olaf a sharp heads-up elbow.

"*Hey,*" protested Olaf, caught off guard by the painful jab.

"Olaf," Karl said quietly, pulling off the knit cap he was wearing. He nodded and smiled politely at the women. Olaf, also wearing a knit cap, quickly followed his lead.

Kate, Nance and Annie smiled and nodded back. Jordan offered nothing more than a contemptuously raised eyebrow. To make it worse, stepping from the driver's side of the van was someone Jordan never thought she'd see again, the man who had tried to help her with the luggage at the airport. Her eyes narrowed as she looked at him with suspicion. He looked back at her just as warily.

"Oh, great," said Jordan.

"Don't you know who he is?" Annie asked her.

"No," Jordan responded flatly.

"It's Grant. Grant Kingsley," said Annie. "His parents owned the lodge."

"Didn't you recognize him at the airport?" asked Kate.

"No," answered Jordan. "And if he's looking for an apology he can forget it."

"Look how handsome he is," Nance noted. "You know, he always had a huge crush on you, Jordan."

Jordan frowned at Nance. "And?"

Nance sighed.

Grant handed Colby the keys to the van and walked

down to The Swan. There, he proceeded to help the small group of passengers onto the boat for the twenty minute ride to the lodge. As she boarded, Kate, a frequent visitor and having known Grant since childhood, greeted him then motioned behind her, "You remember Nance, don't you?"

"Nance, great to see you!" he grinned.

Nance's face flushed bright pink. "Hi," she said shyly.

Annie stepped up next and quietly smiled up at him. Having been too sick to come last year, she wondered if he had noticed her absence.

"Annie . . . come here," Grant quickly reassured her with a bear-hug. He held her out at arm's length. "You're doing well?" he asked.

"Yes. Very," she grinned. "Thanks for asking."

Jordan came along next and stopped at the edge of the gangplank. He recognized the same irritated look on her face from when he saw her at the airport. Taking no chances he took a step backwards with his hands raised, giving her room to pass. Jordan grimaced at him as she boarded the boat.

Kate and Annie grabbed an open bench in the front while Nance and Jordan headed to the long bench that stretched across the back of The Swan. As the Swedes piled onto the boat one-by-one, they, too made their way to the back and filled the bench on either side of Jordan and Nance. Aware of the amorous looks coming their way, Nance pushed her bangs out of her eyes and smiled nervously. Jordan just looked like she wanted to kill something. Annie, watching the scene unfold, snapped a quick picture then turned back around, suppressing her giggles.

"Hello, Mr. Lewis! Good to see you!" expressed Grant, as he helped a frail old man onto the boat.

"Good to see you, too, Grant," Mr. Lewis responded, managing a weak smile.

"What brings you to the lake, Mr. Lewis?" asked Grant.

"Unfinished business," Mr. Lewis stated.

Carefully holding Mr. Lewis' thin arm, Grant navigated him toward the bench seat directly behind the captain's chair. The old man breathed a sigh of relief then affectionately ran his hand across the well-preserved wood. "I love this old boat," he said. "I can see you've been taking good care of her, Grant."

"Yes sir, Mr. Lewis," Grant assured him, "just like you taught me to do."

Mr. Lewis nodded his head and smiled.

"Would you like to drive her today?" asked Grant, hoping to raise Mr. Lewis' spirits.

"*Boy would I,*" said Mr. Lewis, perking up at the thought.

Overhearing their conversation, many of the other passengers looked at each other nervously, but not Kate and Annie. They knew who Mr. Lewis was; he had been the captain of The Swan for more than 50 years until he retired only two years earlier. But now he was in his eighties and appeared to be in poor health, so it was easy to understand the nervous looks of the other passengers.

Grant started the engine and let it run for a few minutes until it began a steady purr. He released the dock lines then shifted the boat into gear and steered her safely away from the dock. Soon, all eyes were upon Mr. Lewis as he shakily rose to his feet and steadied himself behind the wheel.

"The water's moving fast today," Mr. Lewis observed

as he gripped the wheel with hands crippled by arthritis. "We should stick close to the left bank."

Grant nodded, "Good idea, Mr. Lewis."

The wary passengers were all ears as they shifted their eyes toward the left bank.

"Watch that log on the right, Mr. Lewis," Grant said with more than enough time to spare. The nervous passengers lurched simultaneously to the right for a look.

"I saw it Grant, thanks," said Mr. Lewis as the boat easily coasted to the left of the log.

After a few tricky maneuvers, the passengers relaxed, realizing they were in no danger. This old guy knew how to handle the boat. Grant took a seat on the bench behind where Mr. Lewis stood.

Annie excitedly pointed to a family of otters cavorting on the shore and snapped a few pictures. Eventually, even she settled in just to enjoy the gentle scenery of the river as it glided by.

Jordan however, was more intrigued by the interaction between Grant and the old man. Something miraculous was happening with Mr. Lewis. She watched as he firmly held his position at the steering wheel. Slowly his small stooped shoulders began to straighten and his pale skin brightened as color began to come back into his cheeks. On occasion, he made a comment to Grant about the water or the boat but never once did he take his eyes off the course. One could tell he took his job very seriously and the task was revitalizing him.

Jordan's observant eyes turned toward Grant. Once again, she suspiciously eyed him. *That's Grant?* she questioned to herself. *He sure isn't the gawky, skinny kid I remember.* She had to admit, *This Grant is gorgeous.* Anger flared and she quickly looked away, *Yeah, red flag number 356.*

Except for the low rumble of the motor, The Swan, like its namesake, glided effortlessly along, a ripple of dark water fanning out behind her. Jordan's attention shifted, honestly captivated by the scenery. *It is so beautiful here*, she thought. But as she began to relax, her eyes again drifted over to Grant where he sat behind Mr. Lewis. Her mind drifted, too. He was sure easy to look at with his sandy-blonde hair and tan muscular arms, much taller than she remembered. And how could you *not* notice his beautiful blue-green eyes? Suddenly aware of her thoughts, Jordan scolded herself and for the next few minutes purposefully looked anywhere but at Grant. She looked off to the left, she looked off to the right and she even counted the stripes on the awning covering the boat. When she inadvertently looked directly at Olaf, she was appalled to find him grinning back at her. Alarms went off in her head. *Avert the eyes! Avert the eyes!*

But eventually, Jordan just could not help herself and her eyes began to trace the rivets along the deck up to the base of the captain's chair. She slowly raised her eyes to where Grant's hand was touching the bottom of the steering wheel. *Strong masculine hands, another tough guy*, she thought, indifferently. *Wait—his hand is touching the bottom of the steering wheel.* Suddenly she realized that Mr. Lewis was not steering the boat—*Grant* was. He was just letting Mr. Lewis *think* he was the one doing the driving. It touched her. *That is so sweet*, she thought. *Whoa girl—let's not get carried away!*

When the river merged with the lake, the Buckskin Lodge came into view. But if one did not know it was there, and if the afternoon sun was not reflecting off the big plate-glass windows, one's eyes might not immediately see the building. Built in the classic "Parkitecture" style of the early nineteen-hundreds, the lodge was designed to blend into its natural surroundings. Set among a lush forest of firs and hardwoods, it perched above Buckskin Lake, a pristine and natural migration passageway for birds. The area surrounding the lodge was a nature lover's dream, a place of uncommon beauty that allowed wildlife to thrive. Behind the lodge, stately mountains appeared to rise abruptly. Considered to be one of the best climbing areas in the Northeast, the quick access from the Buckskin Lodge lured climbers from all over.

Small cabins began to appear along the shoreline. Some were privately owned, grand-fathered in from earlier days, while others were rentals managed by the lodge. Most visitors were seasonal, but a few people lived here year-round. Though the winters were harsh, it made the spring rebound ever more precious and rewarding. Rental canoes, kayaks and several small boats were lined up along the shore and dock, ready for easy access to the lake known for legendary trout fishing. For Kate, it was quieter here this time of year. Besides the fact that the lodge would soon be closed for the winter, the summer months were a time of children and activities, while autumn was a time of rest and renewal.

As The Swan approached the landing, Mr. Lewis took a seat and Grant took over the controls. At just the right moment he swung the boat around and expertly docked her, a feat Kate had seen him preform many times before. "Show off," she discreetly teased from behind where she sat.

Grant grinned over his shoulder, "Sometimes I get lucky."

"I wouldn't put that on your resume," Kate quipped.

Grant chuckled. "Good point."

When the boat was secured, passengers rose from their seats and gathered their belongings. As they began to go ashore, Jordan watched as Grant first assisted Mr. Lewis off the boat. She noticed the old man seemed much more agile and confident in his movements than when he had first boarded. Kate and Annie were up next and gladly accepted Grant's courteously extended hand for support. They both thanked him as they stepped onto the dock.

"You're quite welcome, girls," Grant responded. "Enjoy your stay. Don't hesitate to call if you need anything."

As the boat emptied, the Swedes stood back and politely let Jordan and Nance exit ahead of them. For whatever reason, Jordan, while happy to no longer be a part of a human sandwich, ignored Grant and refused to take his hand as she exited. Not paying attention, she clumsily tripped off the gangplank and awkwardly caught herself. Kate and Annie, confounded by Jordan's all-but-gracious debarkation, could only assume whatever had happened between her and Rodney had *really* pissed her off.

"Now you have a wonderful day," Grant said as he watched Jordan march off.

"Way to go, Grace," Kate quietly teased Jordan. Annie and Nance chuckled.

Olaf, exiting The Swan next, grinned at Grant, "Oooo, not so good with the ladies . . . I teach."

"*That's just great*," Grant responded, a dismal look on his face.

Even though there were golf carts available for portage to the cabins and the lodge, Kate and Annie always opted for the short walk to the cabin. It was their way of shedding the outside world and transitioning to the slower pace of the lake. As they walked along the shady path, birds flitted and chirped as they scavenged for their afternoon meal while several tiny chipmunks scampered up ahead. Freshly fallen leaves and pine twigs crackled under the girls' feet, releasing their woodsy scent into the air. Unfortunately, Jordan, still locked into her attitude, and Nance, checking her cell phone for reception, failed to appreciate their surroundings.

When they arrived at the cabin, they found on the porch next to their luggage a large bouquet of flowers and a bottle of wine. Annie quickly plucked the card from the flowers and opened it. She read it out loud, "To all the girls, have a wonderful time! Ben."

"That's so sweet," commented Kate, opening the cabin door. "You know it's not easy getting a bouquet of flowers out here."

Annie picked up the bottle of wine. "Merlot," she smiled, "my favorite."

"I'll take that," said Jordan, snatching the bottle. She strode past everyone into the cabin. Nance and Annie shrugged at each other and followed her inside.

Annie was grinning ear-to-ear as she placed the bouquet on the kitchen table. It was such a pleasure to have a generous, thoughtful man in her life. That had not always been the case. With self-esteem had come wiser choices. With cancer she had realized how precious time was and the *significance* of those choices. In a cabinet she found a white ceramic pitcher. She filled it with water then began to thoughtfully arrange the flowers as Kate unpacked the cooler. Jordan and Nance carried in their luggage from the porch then simultaneously collapsed on the sofa.

"You guys must be exhausted," said Kate. "Can I make you some coffee?"

"Sure," Jordan responded. Sitting back up, she looked around the cabin. "This is *so* nice," she complimented. "I can see you've added a lot of personal touches."

"Thank you," said Kate.

The original log cabin built by Kate's father and grandfather had only consisted of two bedrooms and a combined kitchen and living area. Through the years, Kate's father and her husband, Ed, had added two more small bedrooms to meet the needs of their growing family. They were lucky to have had many summers when the whole family could enjoy the cabin, including Kate's grandparents. In the cozy living room, a cream-colored sofa and two oversize chairs snuggled up to a stone fireplace. Handcrafted wood lamps, family photos, books and colorful quilts completed the inviting interior. On one wall was an oil painting of the lake done by Kate's grandmother, one of many on display. Next to it hung her grandfather's original snowshoes.

"You know, better yet," Kate suggested, "why don't we freshen up and head down to the lodge for an early dinner?"

"Sounds good to me," said Nance.

Jordan, too, agreed. "Where do you want us?" she asked, picking up her luggage.

Nance and Jordan followed Kate down the short hallway to their bedrooms. Minimally decorated, each room had its own charm with decorative wrought iron headboards, down comforters, side tables and a small dresser.

As Nance closed the door to her room, she caught her

reflection in the full-length mirror that hung on the back. Her shoulders slumped. She was frequently disappointed with what she saw in the mirror and today she felt she looked especially old and tired. She pushed her annoying bangs out of her face, plopped down on the bed and dumped her purse out. She searched among the empty candy wrappers, chocolate bars and miscellaneous contents of her purse until she found her cell phone. She checked it to see if she had missed any calls or messages, still hopeful she would hear from Randall.

No calls, she saw, disappointed.

Maybe a message, she hoped.

No messages.

Probably no signal here, Nance thought, still hanging on to a grain of optimism. She sighed then refilled the scattered contents into her purse. Lifting her luggage onto the bed she opened it and frowned at what it revealed. *When did I become such a fan of stretch pants and tee shirts*, she wondered, *I used to have such a cute wardrobe*. None of her clothes fit these days; they were either too small or too big. Lately, she had resigned herself to 'One Size Fits All' purgatory. She remembered she had a nice new pair of dark blue jeans along. She found them in the bottom of her suitcase and pulled them on only to realize what she already feared, she could not button them. It was just an inch or two but she winced because they were *new* inches that were not there when she bought the jeans a month earlier. *Darn it! They must have shrunk when I washed them*, she thought. Then she noticed the price tag was still hanging on them. She sighed again, took the jeans off and neatly folded them. She placed them back in the bottom of her suitcase. Defeated, she reached for her standard pair of stretch pants in a dark color and pulled them on.

"*Oh, man*," moaned Annie from her room across the hall. "Kate, do you have any extra socks along?"

"In my duffle bag," Kate answered from the kitchen.

"Thanks."

"We'll be on the porch," Kate called out as she and Nance headed out the door. Annie soon joined them followed by Jordan who appeared looking quite chic in white jeans, a black tank and a distressed blue denim jacket.

"Oooo, white after Labor Day," teased Nance.

"Look who's talking fashion queen," said Jordan.

Nance looked down at her outfit. "What? I'm comfortable."

"Is that the same shirt you had on?" asked Jordan.

"No," Nance answered, "that one was tan, this one is taupe. I think I'm stuck in neutrals."

"In more ways than one," chided Jordan.

"That's okay," said Annie in Nance's defense, "some of us float to our own boat."

"March to our own drummer," corrected Kate.

"Exactly," Annie concurred.

During the ten minute walk to the lodge, although unspoken between them, something began to stir in both Nance and Jordan. Something about this place, something familiar, something good. They had so many wonderful childhood memories here.

When they reached the lodge they found the lobby bustling with people signing up for various activities. Every morning, vans transported people to hiking and climbing areas or to landings for whitewater raft trips and river floats. Other popular excursions included wildlife viewing and photo expeditions. There were also people signing up for boat and bicycle rentals. Annie, an avid fisherman, had already secured one of the small motor boats for the morning. There were several exciting *new* additions to the lodge activities since Kate had been there in the summer: four canvas-top rental Jeeps. Annie was thrilled to find out Kate had reserved one for later in the week. The lodge also had a gift shop, a small gym, a well-stocked newsstand and an indoor climbing wall.

From the lobby, a wide staircase led up to a central gathering area, a spacious room with heavy wood beams that revealed the rustic architecture of the lodge. On one wall was a large fireplace cobbled with the smooth rocks that lined the local river beds. Through the years, the fireplace had warmed many icy fingers and toes after a day of adventure. Comfortable leather sofas and chairs anchored by geometrical tribal-style rugs were placed strategically around the room, creating many private nooks for visitors to congregate. Original Indian blankets hung on the wall along with large paintings of various animals, inhabitants of the surrounding area. One painting was of a great black bear, another was of a regal ten-point buck, while still another was of a moose, his magnificent antlers in their full glory. Indian artifacts and pottery were artfully displayed inside large glass cases. These drew the interest of visitors and historians alike.

However, the most striking art was not inside the lodge, it was the ever-changing view of the lake through the wall of large glass windows facing the west. Just outside, a deck that ran the length of the building was a favorite place for visitors to hang out in the evening. Besides being a spectacular spot to watch sunsets, it was common for animals to be spotted on the distant shore of the lake. On most evenings, amidst quiet rumblings of conversation, clicking cameras and scanning binoculars, people mulled about and listened intently as the resident field guide answered their questions. And one never knew whom one might meet at the Buckskin Lodge. The area with its pristine woods and moderate to challenging landscapes drew everything from hardcore adventurer seekers to birdwatchers.

There were two dining choices inside the lodge. One was the Old Tyme Diner. Its menu offered grass-fed burgers, home-style cooking and ice cream. The other was the Mountain View Bistro. It was known for its superb meals and excellent service. The girls opted for the relaxed atmosphere of the Bistro. Kate figured the extra T.L.C. wouldn't hurt either.

The Bistro lived up to its reputation and as the girls enjoyed a sumptuous meal they shared a bottle of wine and chatted about old times. The sun setting outside the window was the *piece de resistance* as it splayed rays of golden light from behind plumes of lilac and mauve clouds. "God light," as Annie had heard it described.

After dinner, they lingered at the table, enjoying the lack of a schedule and a second bottle of merlot. Annie reached in her purse, pulled out some old photos and began to pass them around. They were pictures of them taken here at the lodge when they were children.

"These are great," Nance laughed, flipping through a small stack. "You and your camera, Annie."

"I remember taking this photo," said Jordan. She was looking at one where Nance was putting big rollers in Annie's hair. "You fixed all our hair and put makeup on us that day. That was hilarious," she chuckled. "Until we got in trouble with my mother for using her cosmetics."

"Oh!" said Nance excitedly. "I've been meaning to tell you my daughter, Sophie, has decided to become a cosmetologist. She wants to open her own salon someday."

"Wow, that's great Nance," Kate responded. "Isn't that what you always wanted to do? You should get your own degree and join her."

"Ohhh, that was a long time ago," said Nance. She looked back at the picture Jordan had shared, a hint of sadness in her eyes.

Annie held up a picture of Kate and Jordan rock climbing. They were crazy good at the sport even at that young age and quite competitive. She passed the photo to Jordan and asked, "Are you still climbing?"

"No, not lately," Jordan responded, her eyes lowered and she twirled her glass of wine. "Life with Rodney was pretty much all about Rodney."

"Oh," Annie responded.

"This looks familiar," said Nance, picking up a photo of Kate and Jordan diving into the lake. "Dare I ask if there will be a race out to the lake float this year?"

"*That's right*," Jordan remembered, "you owe me another match, Kate."

"Anytime," Kate smiled.

Other photos passed hands. There was one of Annie holding up a big fish, one of Kate swinging out over the lake on a rope, and one of Nance wearing her favorite summer accessory: a purple sea serpent life preserver.

"This is my favorite one," said Annie. It was of the four of them huddled around a fire. They were roasting hotdogs at the end of what had likely been an adventurous day.

Their youthful faces illuminated by the glow.

"Oh, look at this one," gushed Nance. She turned the photo around for all to see. There they all stood, four devoted friends, their arms wrapped around each other's shoulders. Every one of them had a bandage on at least one of their knees.

"That could have been any day back then," commented Kate with a smile. "We were so close."

"Who took that picture, Annie?" Jordan asked.

"I think it was Mr. Lewis," Annie answered. "Remember?" she chuckled. "He used to call us the 'Scraped Knee Gang.' Although I'm not sure he remembered us on the boat today. It's only been a few years since he retired, have we changed that much?"

"I don't know," Nance frowned. "It isn't looks I'm worried about." She looked over at Jordan, "Do you think we still have what it takes?"

Jordan's eyebrow rose, "To do what?"

"You know, hiking, climbing . . . ."

"Oh, I got what it takes," Jordan responded. "Then again," she hesitated, "I threw my back out last year and for two weeks I walked around with my butt jacked up like a bird."

"What were you doing?" asked Kate.

"Vacuuming."

"Oh," they all commiserated.

"All I can say is, at this point in my life, if it ain't self-propelled, self-cleaning or self-defrosting, I ain't buying it." Jordan stated.

"Amen to that sister," said Nance, raising her wine glass.

"Amen," they all agreed, clinking their wine glasses

together.

"Oh, crap," said Jordan, noticing a tiny speck of red wine on her jeans. "Merlot and white jeans, what was I thinking?" She dipped her paper napkin into her water glass and applied it to the spot only to watch in horror as it quickly doubled in size.

Looking over, Kate suggested she find their waitress, Ellie. Club soda should do the trick.

Jordan agreed and found Ellie on the other side of the dining room. She asked her if she had any club soda and pointed toward her thigh.

"Oh, my," Ellie responded. "Yes, of course. Follow me."

They stepped inside the kitchen door. There, another waitress, Brin, joined in the effort to remove the spot with a bottle of club soda and a fresh paper napkin. She, too, became confused when the spot only seemed to get worse.

Ellie suddenly realized, "It's the napkin! It's black and the ink is coming off on your jeans!"

"Oh, great," Jordan frowned.

"What about soap?" suggested Brin.

"That might work," Ellie agreed then quickly scurried away. She came back with two cloths, one with soap on it, the other dampened with plain water. After another diligent effort, it was obvious nothing was working and the tiny speck now loomed to the size of a silver dollar.

"What about bleach?" asked yet another waitress joining in. "The jeans *are* white."

Brin nodded, "That's a good idea."

"But, then I have to take my pants off," said Jordan, none too happy with *this* suggestion.

"We'll put you in the storage closet. We can give you a tablecloth to wrap around yourself," said Ellie. "You wouldn't want that stain to set."

"No," Jordan reluctantly agreed.

"We'll watch the door and make sure no one comes in," promised Ellie.

"Okay," Jordan sighed.

Meanwhile, back at the table, twenty minutes had gone by and the girls were beginning to wonder where Jordan was. Kate arose from the table and peaked inside the kitchen door where she spotted Ellie rushing about. She asked if she knew where Jordan had gone.

Ellie cringed, obviously having forgotten about Jordan in the storage closet. "Yes, in there," she pointed. "Sorry," she smiled sheepishly, whizzing past with a tray of food.

Confused, Kate hesitantly knocked on the door. "Jordan, are you in there?"

"Come in."

Kate opened the door to the small room and found Jordan leaning against a storage shelf. A white tablecloth was tied around her waist and she was holding a half empty wine goblet.

"Can I interest you in a glass of Chardonnay?" Jordan asked dryly.

"Huh . . . how does one go from having a tiny spot on her jeans to being half-naked in a storage room?" Kate inquired.

"It's a long story," Jordan responded. "Can you see if you can find my pants?"

"Sure," said Kate. "I'll go see if I can find your pants. Perfectly normal," she mumbled, closing the door behind her.

Why me? Jordan thought, shaking her head in disbelief. *Well, I guess it can't get any worse than this*. She set her wine glass down and began to readjust the tablecloth around her waist. Suddenly, the door burst open. It was Grant, carrying a case of wine on his shoulder. Jordan quickly covered herself but not before he got a good glimpse of her sexy, white lace underwear.

"Oh . . . sorry," said Grant, averting his eyes. He set the heavy box down on a shelf. "Uh . . . what are you doing in here," he asked, respectfully keeping his back toward her.

Jordan, flustered and embarrassed, blurted, "Who uses black paper napkins in a restaurant? They nearly ruined my white jeans!"

Grant turned and looked at her, baffled by the statement. He wasn't sure how to respond.

"*Yes, that's right*—white after Labor Day," Jordan added angrily.

The storage room door opened again. This time it was Kate holding Jordan's jeans. There was an awkward moment before Grant, still at a loss for words, bee-lined it out the door.

"And the magic continues," said Kate.

As Jordan quickly wiggled into her jeans even *she* couldn't help but giggle.

* * * * *

Back at the cabin, the girls donned their pajamas and they each claimed an Adirondack chair on the porch. Kate, an expert in the art of jammie hangin', brought out an armful of cozy quilts then disappeared again only to return a few minutes later with a tray full of sugar, cream and steaming hot cups of coffee. She also brought out a bottle of Bailey's Irish Cream Liqueur, for anyone interested. *Everyone* was interested.

It was a beautiful night and from the cabin porch the girls could see the lake glowing under the light of a pale moon. The silhouetted trees swayed gently in the cool night air as an owl hooted somewhere in the distance. *Who-who-whooo.*

A second owl, this one closer, responded, *Who-who-whooo. Who-who-whooo.*

"I love it when they do that," said Annie, "talk back and forth."

"I do, too," said Kate.

After a few more calls the owls stopped hooting and were followed by complete silence.

"It's so peaceful," Jordan commented, gazing out at the moon. "I don't know why I stopped coming here. After my parents sold their cabin I could have taken one of the rentals, but neither my ex-husband nor Rodney liked anything remotely considered roughing it."

"Ed really doesn't either," said Kate, "but it never stopped me from coming here. I would be miserable if I could not have this in my life."

"So would I," Annie agreed. "It centers me."

"Besides," added Kate, "you can hardly call this roughing it."

"That's true," Jordan chuckled.

"Maybe we should just keep this our little secret," Kate winked. She glanced over at Nance who had not joined in on the conversation. In fact, she had barely said a word since they had arrived back at the cabin. She was bundled up in her quilt and looking wistfully out at the lake. "Nance, are you okay?" Kate asked.

"Yes," Nance responded softly. "I was just thinking about Randall."

"*Oh, please*," Jordan's eyes rolled.

Kate gave Jordan a reprimanding look then turned back to Nance. "It just takes time, Nance," she said.

"Don't get her started," Jordan warned.

"Well what if I never meet anybody else?" Nance said woefully. Her face flushed as she verged on tears.

"You will," said Kate.

"And I hate the way I look," Nance blurted. "Who's ever going to want me looking like this?"

"Looking like what?" Kate asked, surprised by the comment.

"I know I've really let myself go," Nance continued. "I don't even know how much weight I've gained; I'm afraid to get on a scale and get myself *really* depressed. I'd probably break the damn thing anyway."

"Now you're just being ridiculous," said Kate. "First of all," she firmly reassured her, "you're beautiful, you're smart, you're funny. Any man would be lucky to have you in his life."

"*Yeah right*," Nance responded, tugging the quilt further up around her shoulders.

"I'll tell you what makes you special to me, Nance," said Annie. Nance looked tearfully her way. "When I was going through my cancer treatments, you always had a kind word to say or came up with something absurdly funny and made me laugh. You have no idea how important that was to me during such a difficult time. But, you don't just do things like that for me," Annie continued, "you do that for everybody you meet. You are the kindest, sweetest person I know. That's what really makes you beautiful, Nance. *That's* what defines you."

"And just so you know," Jordan added, regretting her initial reaction, "not every man likes a skinny woman. There are entire cultures that prefer their women with fuller figures."

"Oh, okay," Nance scoffed, "so now I have to move to another country."

"No," Kate intervened, "but you do need to be healthy, Nance. You shouldn't be eating so much sugar and junk food."

Nance sighed. "I know. My blood pressure has been really high lately."

"Are you on medication?" asked Kate.

"No . . . not yet," Nance replied.

"Well, that's good," said Kate. "You know, none of us are saints when it comes to eating, especially on vacation. You just have to diversify a bit."

"You mean like M&M's instead of Clark bars?" asked Nance, managing a half smile.

"No, like fruits and low-fat yogurt," Kate responded.

Nance sniffled, regaining her composure. "You're right."

"I can help you with that when we get back home, Nance," offered Jordan.

Nance nodded back. "I'm . . . I'm also worried I won't be able to keep up with you guys. My energy level and stamina are not what they used to be."

"You will," the girls reassured her, reaching out.

"There's no pressure to perform here," said Kate.

"Okay," said Nance.

After a quiet moment, Annie asked, "Nance, besides

Randall, is there anyone else you're interested in?"

Kate and Jordan cringed. Obviously *not* the best timing for that question.

Nance considered, dabbing at her eyes with her napkin, "Well, there is this attorney named Brian."

"Oh? What is he like?" asked Annie, encouraged.

"I'm not sure," Nance responded, "but one of his colleagues told me he is known as 'the whiner' in court."

"*The whiner,*" Jordan reacted. "Why would you want to go out with anyone known as the whiner?"

"*I don't know,*" Nance responded, her defenses going up again. "He seems like a decent guy."

"So in court," Kate surmised, "he would be like . . . *Your Hon-norrr*," using her best whiney voice.

They all laughed.

"Or, when you're on a date, it would be like . . . I *hate* this restaurant!" Annie joined in.

Laughter again.

"Or, when he wants to get you in bed . . . *Hon-ney,*" Jordan jested.

"Or, when . . . ," Kate began again.

"*Okay!*" said Nance, no longer able to resist laughing. "Since when did you guys become comedians?"

"Well," said Jordan, still chuckling, "*this* comedian needs a good night's sleep; I'm exhausted." She arose from her chair and gave each of the girls a peck on the cheek. "Can I carry this in for you Kate?" she offered, motioning toward the tray of empty coffee cups.

Kate, Annie and Nance quipped simultaneously, "I GOT IT!"

"Ha, ha," said Jordan dryly.

"Let me know if there is anything you need," said Kate.

"I will. 'Night"

"Good night. Night."

"I'm going to bed, too," said Kate, stretching sleepily. She rose from her chair and picked up the tray. "Do you girls need anything else?"

"No. We're fine," Annie and Nance answered.

Annie hopped up and opened the screen door for Kate. "It was a good day today, don't you think?" she asked.

"Yes, Annie," Kate smiled. "It was a good day."

"Don't forget, we're fishing in the morning," said Annie.

"Wouldn't miss it for the world."

Annie plopped back onto her chair, pulling the quilt up around her.

Who-who-whoo, who-who-whoo. The owls were chattering again.

"You know, Nance," Annie began, "I used to wonder if anybody would ever want me after what I went through with cancer. I remember one day looking in the mirror and I didn't even recognize myself. I didn't feel well, I was bald and skinny and my color wasn't good. I figured at that point, the only way I could improve my looks was to smile. So that's exactly what I started to do, I started to smile. I started to smile a lot. Then I noticed people were smiling back at me and before long I started to feel happy."

Nance nodded, contemplating her words.

"If you think about it," Annie added, "most people don't need a facelift, they just need to smile."

"Ain't that the truth," Nance chuckled.

"Did you know," Annie revealed, "more men hit on me during my illness than any other time in my life?"

"Really?" Nance asked.

"Really. One guy even followed me home from the grocery store," Annie continued. "At first I wondered if these guys sensed I was ill and maybe some sort of primordial 'man must take care of woman' thing existed. But in the end, I honestly believe it was the fact that I was smiling a lot and all my walls were down. Let's face it, I had nowhere to hide. But I still had concerns about my cancer history and being desirable," she went on. "Then one day, I was sitting in this little woodland chapel in the middle of Wyoming and I was feeling a bit down and homesick. I remember thinking exactly as you, 'What if no one ever wants me?' I had some of my drawings in my hand and as I sat there, I started to flip through them. I thought about what people say about my work. They always say, 'Don't change a thing because it is their imperfectness that gives them their charm and makes them beautiful,' and I thought, 'Gosh, you could say the same about me. My body may not be perfect anymore but that doesn't mean I am not beautiful.'"

Nance smiled and nodded.

"What I'm really trying to say Nance, we do not need to have perfect bodies to be beautiful people. And let's face it, it's all gonna head south sooner or later."

"*Great*," Nance responded, none too cheerfully.

"Judy likes to say at her age all you have is your posture and your jewelry. I'm workin' on my posture," Annie grinned.

Nance laughed and it quickly turned into a yawn; exhaustion was taking a firm grip on her. "I've got to get some sleep," she said, rising from her chair. "Thanks for cheering me up Annie—for the most part."

"Anytime," Annie smiled.

FIVE
Lost and Found

There is nothing like returning to a place that remains unchanged to find the ways in which you yourself have altered.
Nelson Mandela

In the morning, Annie, wearing her lucky fishing vest, headed down to the boathouse with their fishing gear. As she approached the dock, Colby, loading life preservers onto their rental, a fourteen-foot open skiff, turned to greet her. "Morning, Annie, she's gassed up and ready to go."

"Great," Annie said, handing him her small bucket. "I just need a bag of ice and some bait."

"Trout strips?" Colby asked. "The stinky ones work the best."

"Yep, the stinkier the better," grinned Annie.

"No problem." Colby took her bucket and headed off toward the boathouse.

Annie sat down on the edge of the dock to wait. Kate and Jordan were on their way. Nance, too tired to get up so early, had decided to sleep in.

This was Annie's favorite time of the day. The lake was so quiet and still. Today, a fine mist was lingering, resisting the morning light as it began to peek over the ridge. She reached down and dipped her hand into the clear water. It felt cool as it washed across her palm and flowed gently between her fingers. Her thoughts again drifted back to her parents. She thought about the early years here at the lake when her mother and father were happy. The three of them used to fish together. She knew without a doubt there *had* been love between her parents. It was important for Annie to remember that, it somehow softened the more painful memories.

When Colby came back with a bag of ice and the bait, Kate and Jordan were following not far behind. Kate had on her official fishing vest, while Jordan seemed to be seeking seclusion beneath a black baseball cap. Concerned, Annie offered Jordan some coffee from her thermos and was glad when she accepted.

After giving Colby their basic itinerary, Annie started the small motor on the back of the boat and they puttered out onto the lake. The mist curled gently around them as they slowly made their way across the silvery water. Soon, golden sunlight beamed over the ridge and the mist began to dissipate. By the time they reached the western shore of the lake, the sky had almost completely cleared. As they turned south, Annie quietly pointed to a black bear sow and her year-old cub. They were fervently foraging for blueberries, fattening up for the long impending winter months.

Annie turned the motor off just prior to reaching her favorite fishing spot near a fallen old tree. They drifted to the exact spot she had hoped for and she quietly motioned for Kate to drop the anchor. Obviously hoping to catch the first fish, she and Kate quickly baited their hooks and plopped them into the water.

Jordan, sitting on the center seat of the boat, appeared only slightly more awake after the coffee. Annie watched her fumble with her bait then carelessly drop it over the edge of the boat.

Within minutes, Annie had her first strike and excitedly landed a nice trout. Before disengaging the hook, she reached into one of the many pockets on her vest and pulled out her new fishing gadget: a small red-and-white counter. It was identical to the one her mother had used at the grocery store to keep track of her spending. She clicked it once then dropped the gadget back in her pocket.

"What was that?" asked Jordan, her tone gloomy.

"My fish counter," responded Annie, "so I can keep track of how many fish I catch." She carefully took the fish off the hook and placed it in the cooler, turning her head so Jordan and Kate wouldn't see her suppressed giggle.

"Oookay," Jordan responded.

Within minutes, Annie jubilantly landed another fish. She pulled out her counter and clicked again. *This is working perfectly,* she chuckled to herself.

Jordan looked at Kate and frowned. Kate shrugged.

Annie caught another, *Click.*

And another, *Click.*

At first, Kate, too, found it amusing, but after fish number four even she was getting annoyed. It didn't help that Annie was the only one catching fish.

Click.

"Okay!" Jordan said loudly, the boat rocking precariously as she lunged at Annie. "Give me that thing."

"Hey!" Annie protested as Jordan wrestled the counter from her hand and tossed it toward Kate.

Unaware of the incoming projectile, Kate could only watch as the counter flew past her into the water. She watched regretfully as it slowly sank to the bottom of the lake. Cringing, she looked back at Annie. "Oops—sorry."

"That wasn't very nice," Annie frowned. "It took me forever to find one of those things."

"Annie, it was an accident," Kate responded. "Really, I'm sorry."

Annie's brow furrowed angrily and she went back to fishing in cold silence.

Kate gave Jordan the stink-eye.

Jordan winced in remorse. She sank down in her seat and pulled her cap down over her eyes.

Before long, Kate, needing bait, politely asked Annie to hand her a piece from the bucket.

"Sure," said Annie, a deceptive smile on her face.

Kate squinted at her. She noticed the tone of her voice was just a little too sweet.

Annie reached into the bucket and pulled out a rather gnarly looking piece of bait. But instead of handing it to Kate, she flung it at her and watched with glee as it stuck to her arm.

"Ewwww, gross," Kate squealed.

Annie began to laugh, claiming it was an accident.

Kate, not amused, retaliated; she peeled the nasty piece of bait off her arm and flung it back. Annie screamed as the gooey glob stuck to the front of her vest. She quickly grabbed more bait from the bucket and began fast-balling it at Kate. Kate, now *in it,* just as quickly flung them back. Their laughter and shrieks filled the air as an all-out bait war commenced.

"STOP—DAMMIT—STOP!" Jordan yelled.

Suddenly aware of Jordan's angry cries, Kate and Annie abruptly stopped. An uncomfortable silence fell across the boat as they realized Jordan was plastered with at least a dozen pieces of bait clinging to various parts of her clothing, sunglasses and hat. Her face was flushed red with anger as she assessed the gooey bits not only on herself but on Kate and

Annie, too. Simultaneously they all burst out laughing.

Whoosh. A huge fish hit Annie's bait. She grabbed the rod just before it slipped over the edge of the boat. Her line whirred off the reel as the fish ran toward the shoreline for cover. *"This is a big one!"* she exclaimed, holding on tight.

"You got it, Annie," Kate encouraged as the big fish fought back, jumping twice in an attempt to release the hook.

"Jordan, get the net ready!" Annie shouted as she worked the fish closer to the boat.

"Easy . . . easy," Jordan coached. The fish made another short run toward the old fallen tree before Jordan finally was able to scoop it on board.

"All right, Annie!" Kate congratulated, admiring the catch.

"Nice," said Jordan.

"Yesss," Annie celebrated, "I'd give myself *two* clicks for that one."

* * * * *

Back at the cabin, Nance awoke shortly after the girls left. She felt rested and refreshed. She really needed a good night's sleep and after the previous long day of traveling she was glad to have the morning free. Besides, fishing was not her forte', especially after the summer Annie accidentally hooked her in the side of the head.

Nance stretched languidly and for a moment resisted the temptation to rise from bed. But she was back at the Buckskin and she did not want to waste a moment of the day. Still in her red plaid flannel pajamas, she made a fresh cup of coffee and carried it and a blueberry muffin to the porch, settling into one of the big chairs. The morning mist was just beginning to rise over the lake. *So quiet here*, she thought, taking a sip from her cup, *no wonder I slept so well.*

As far as Nance could discern, nothing much had changed here and she felt the urge to explore. She decided it would be nice to take a walk along the lake trail. Later she could have lunch in the Old Tyme Diner up at the lodge. The gift shop looked pretty interesting, too.

In her bedroom, she pulled on her standard black stretch jogging pants, perfectly suitable for the day. The air had felt a little cool so she zipped her grey hoodie up over her tee shirt then tucked her cell phone in her pocket, just in case *someone* tried to call.

By the time Nance walked past the lodge, the mist had completely cleared, replaced by bright morning sunlight. Looking out at the lake, she delighted in the way its perfect stillness mirrored the forest. Near the boathouse, a pair of mergansers, the fishing ducks known for their colorful plumage, flitted excitedly along the shore.

"Good morning," Colby waved as she passed by.

"Morning," she waved back.

Once past the lodge, Nance crossed an old wooden bridge that marked the beginning of the lake trail. The bridge spanned a small stream and she stopped for a moment to admire the colorful river rocks in the clear shallow water, just as she had often done as a young girl. The memory made her smile and she continued her walk along the shady sun-dappled trail. It curved invitingly around the edge of expansive Buckskin Lake. To her left, a tree-filled foothill steepened and eventually gave way to sparse rocky outcrops and the summit of Great Spirit Mountain.

Great Spirit Mountain had been named for the magnificent carving of a full-size Indian Chief that had been discovered carved into its granite side. A challenging footpath led from the lake trail up to the wide natural rock ledge where one would find the Indian Chief sitting cross-legged, looking stoically out over the valley. Though time was taking its toll on the carving, it was still rich in detail. His magnificent headdress of feathers cascaded past his broad shoulders and an elaborate breastplate identified him as someone very important to his tribe. His right hand was raised and on its open palm was carved an oval shield with a dove at its center. The wings and tail feathers were spread wide as it flew upwards. On the breast of the dove, a heart was carved. As legend had it, the shield stood for protection, the dovc stood for peace, and the heart stood for bravery.

Most everyone that encountered the carving of the Indian Chief came off the mountain and spoke of how spiritual it felt there. Feeling sentimental, Nance thought about the numerous times she and the girls had gone up there as children and sat with the Great Spirit overlooking the valley. It was always the highlight of their vacation and the view there was magnificent. But as she stood looking up the steep ascent of the footpath, a voice in her head said, *Well, that ain't gonna happen.*

Nance continued her walk along the edge of the lake. The air was beginning to warm so she stopped briefly to remove her hoodie and tied it around her waist. Her thoughts went back to one very memorable day. It was the day the girls had raced up the side of the mountain to where the Great Spirit sat. One might say it was the beginning of a legend. Annie, being the youngest, was only about ten at the time. Kate had just turned twelve, which would have made Jordan and her eleven. From the day Annie had arrived that particular year, the girls had all noticed something was not right. Annie's already small frame had lost weight and she was noticeably pale. There were dark circles under her eyes and her disheveled hair hung limply around her thin face. Normally, Annie looked forward to her summer days at the cabin and would have been bubbly, inquisitive and full of energy. Nature would have exploded around her and she would have loved every moment immersed in its beauty. She had an incredible knack for spotting wildlife, but it was the smaller details of nature that delighted Annie the most. She could find a universe in a dewdrop or spot a tiny colorful bird in a field full of wildflowers. However, the most troublesome part about Annie that year was how distant she had become. When one would ask her a question most times she would answer, if only briefly, but she would not look up, she would just keep looking down at the ground.

It was during that time, before their divorce, Annie's parents had owned the cabin on the property next to Kate's. They were a good distance apart, as were all the cabins but still visible. At night, Kate and Annie had devised a flashlight signal system so they could communicate with each other. It wasn't a very complicated system, just consisting of two signals. Two flashes had meant "Hello. I'm here," then, when sleepiness began to settle in, three quick flashes had meant "Goodnight." But this summer, Kate's signals had gone unanswered. When she had asked Annie about it, all Annie did was shrug.

Something else was different, too. At night, one could hear Annie's parents, Ken and Mary, yelling at each other.

"I'm sick of you being drunk all the time!" Annie's mother had yelled. "No wonder you can't keep a job!"

"Well maybe you should get a job!" Annie's father had yelled back. "You don't do anything around here anyway. When's the last time you cooked a decent meal?"

"Look who's talking!" Annie's mother had hollered. "All you do is lay on the couch all day."

"Go to hell!" her father had retaliated. The cabin's screen door could be heard slamming behind him.

"I'm dumping this booze down the sink!" Mary had threatened.

"You better not!" the door slamming again. "Give me that bottle!"

Every night, arguing and loud noises could be heard emanating from Annie's cabin and she had continued not to answer Kate's signals. Kate had become very worried about her friend. One night, as she lay in her bed, she had overheard her own parents talking about the situation. They had been trying to be discreet so Kate had silently snuck up to her door to hear their conversation.

"We should do something," Kate's mother, Clair, had said in a worried tone.

"What?" Bill, Kate's father had asked, looking up from his book. He was a strong supporter of minding his own business.

"I don't know," Clair had said, "but this can't continue. You've seen Annie; she looks terrible."

Bill had grumbled but finally agreed, "Okay, you're right. We can talk to some of the other parents about it."

Kate had snuck back to her bed and pulled the quilt up around her. From where she lay she could see the full moon rising over the lake. It was beautiful and she hoped that her friend, Annie, was looking at it, too.

The next day the four girls had met at the boathouse, their usual meeting spot. Each of them was dressed in shorts, tee shirts and not-so-white sneakers. The boat master, Mr. Lewis, a tall slender man with a clipboard in hand, had greeted them. All of the parents appreciated the fact that Mr. Lewis had made it a point to keep track of any children that ventured off on their own.

"Good morning, girls. Where you off to today?" Mr. Lewis had asked.

"We're going up Great Spirit Mountain," Kate had informed him. Being the oldest she naturally took the role of spokesperson.

"Okay," Mr. Lewis had said, writing down their destination on the clipboard. "What time will you be back?" he inquired, peering over his glasses.

"Three o'clock," Kate had told him. She watched Mr. Lewis jot down the information then proudly showed him her new watch.

"Uh-huh," Mr. Lewis had approved, "very nice. You got plenty of water along?" he asked, looking at the girls' small backpacks.

"Yes, sir, and our moms packed our lunches," Kate had answered.

"And where is your backpack young lady?" Mr. Lewis had asked Annie.

Kate had spun around. She was surprised to see Annie did not have one. "Annie, where's your backpack?" she asked.

"I forgot it," Annie had replied, kicking a small rock near her foot.

Kate had quickly turned to Mr. Lewis and said, "I'll take one of those waters please." She had reached in her pocket, handed him fifty cents then shoved the extra bottle of water into her backpack.

"Be careful, girls," Mr. Lewis had called out as they headed along the shore toward the lake trail. "Remember, three sharp. Don't make me come looking for you," he had warned. He hung the clipboard on its hook by the door and picked up the house phone. "Jackie, send me down a fresh box of Band-Aids please."

Conversation had flown between Kate, Nance and Jordan as they walked along the trail towards the base of Great Spirit Mountain. They had so much to catch up on since last year and this would have been their first trip up to see the Indian carving this summer. For them, it would be an easy traverse up the steep path to the rock outcropping where the Great Spirit sat. Annie however, had lagged quietly behind, her eyes still looking down at the ground. Kate, hoping to pull Annie out of her shell, had asked, "Look Annie, did you see that bird?"

"No . . . missed it," Annie had responded in a small voice.

Catching on to what Kate was trying to do, Nance had asked, "Annie, aren't you excited about seeing the Great Spirit?"

"Sure," Annie had answered, barely audible.

Nance had looked at Kate and shrugged.

Then, Kate had had an idea. It began with a story. A story so vivid that years later Nance had questioned Kate about its origin. She told Nance she had no idea where it came from; it was almost as if someone was placing the very words in her head as she spoke them.

"The other night I was sittin' up at the lodge minding my own business," Kate had begun, "when this old Indian came out of nowhere and took a seat in the rocker next to me. I looked at him out of the corner of my eye—so as not to be too obvious. Clear across his face ran a jagged scar and he wore a patch over his right eye, like he'd been attacked by a bear—or a mountain lion or somethin'."

"Really?" Nance had asked, quickening her pace to walk closer to Kate.

"Yep. He must have been a hundred-years-old," Kate had expressed. "He wore an eagle feather and had long black braids all the way down to his waist."

"Well, did he say anything to you?" Jordan had asked. She, too, had quickly become caught up in Kate's story.

"He sure did," Kate had answered. "He leaned forward in his chair and drew his face *real* close to mine."

"Well, what did he say?" Nance had asked, her voice rising.

"Yes, what did he say?" Jordan had pleaded.

"He asked," Kate had responded, taking a quick glance behind her to see if Annie had been listening then continued her answer in a voice deep and dramatic, "'do you know the Legend of the Shield?'"

"The Legend of the Shield?" Jordan had repeated.

"I never heard of the Legend of the Shield," Nance had said. "Well, what did you say?"

"I said to the old Indian—matter-of-factly of course, 'I know the Legend of the Shield. That is if you're talking about the one on the hand of the Great Spirit,'" Kate had answered. "Then the old Indian snapped back at me, '*Well, what do you know?'* she elaborated with a scowl.

"Oh! Oh, my!" Jordan and Nance had both jumped back in alarm.

Kate, again had glanced back at Annie. She could see her pace had picked up, if only just a little. She went on with her story, "Well, I told him I know that the shield stands for protection, the dove stands for peace and the heart stands for courage."

"Really?" Jordan had asked, hearing this story for the first time. "Then what happened?"

"The old Indian slapped his knee real hard and set back in his rocker—glaring with his one beady eye," Kate had said, mimicking the look.

Nance remembered how she and Jordan had again pulled back in alarm.

"Then he leaned forward real close again," Kate had continued. "He looked around to make sure no one else was listening. I leaned in, too, 'cause I felt like he was about to tell me somethin' important. Then he said, 'There's magic in that shield.'"

"Magic," Nance and Jordan had murmured to each other, both with eyes as wide as silver dollars.

"'What kind of magic?' I asked—skeptical of course," Kate had said. "'Why there's enough magic in that shield to carry you safely to the end of your days,' he said. He told me legend has it that the first person to lay a hand on the shield after a full moon will receive the Great Spirit and all its power into their very own body. The shield will protect them from evil, the dove will bring them peace and the heart will bring them courage."

"Wow!" Nance had exclaimed. "I never heard that

before, have you Jordan?"

"No," Jordan had responded. "What did you say then, Kate?"

"Well, when I turned to look at the Indian, he was gone," Kate had then spun around quickly, stopping the girls in their tracks, "*into thin air I tell you!*"

Jordan and Nance had gasped. The air was thick with their child-like imagination and they momentarily chattered back and forth with excitement.

"It was a full moon last night," Annie's small voice had come from behind.

"What did you say?" Kate had asked as she stopped and waited for Annie to catch up.

"It was a full moon last night," Annie had repeated.

"Yes, I know, Annie," Kate had responded then turned back around and continued to walk, hoping for something more.

Annie remained quiet and the silence had hung heavy in the air but only until they reached the trailhead of the mountain path that led up to the carving of the Great Spirit. There, Annie had turned to Kate and through expressive eyes had asked, "Do you think anyone's been up there yet, since the full moon?"

"I doubt it," Kate had answered. "Mr. Lewis didn't mention anybody else heading this way yet today. I reckon it's likely one of us is a good candidate."

Without warning, Nance and Jordan had let out "*Whoops*" and simultaneously started up the path to the Great Spirit. Their missions alike: to be the first to touch the shield. Annie flung herself onto the steep trail right behind them, scrambling up the trail with everything she had. Kate had followed with panicked thoughts running through her mind. She couldn't let Nance or Jordan get there before Annie.

It had not been long before Annie realized she could never catch up with Jordan and Nance so she split off and headed up a more difficult but shorter route.

"Annie!" Kate had hollered. "Don't go that way, it's too dangerous!" But Annie had seemed completely oblivious to Kate's concerns or the danger she was exposing herself to. Kate told Nance years later, she had glimpsed a determination in Annie's face that she had never seen before.

For a moment, Kate had hesitated and wondered if she should follow Annie but instead thought, *I've got to stop Jordan and Nance, Annie has to be the one to touch the shield first.* She had willed herself to climb even harder up the path. Jordan and Nance, a good fifteen feet ahead of her, were squealing loudly as they easily navigated the rocky slope.

From where Kate was, she could see Annie was struggling. She cringed several times when she saw her lose her footing and backslide on the rocks. *This was so stupid,* she had said to herself, *what if Annie gets hurt?* The scary thought fueled her ascent even more and she easily passed Nance then grabbed Jordan's ankle just as she had reached the edge of the outcropping where the Great Spirit sat.

"Hey!" Jordan had yelled angrily as Kate pulled her down from the ledge.

Nance had come up quickly from behind and Kate had reached out and grabbed her shirt to stop her. *"No!"* Kate had yelled. *"Let Annie!"*

Jordan and Nance had looked at each other confused at first, then the three of them looked over at Annie. They had gasped at what they saw. Annie was precariously perched on the edge of the overhang with her legs dangling. She was kicking furtively in the air as small rocks careened to the valley floor hundreds of feet below her.

"Annie, be careful!" Kate had shouted but Annie had not heard her. Her small hands were clawing at the thin dirt, desperate for something to cling to, but she found nothing but hard rock, shallow tufts of grass and loose stones. It was clear to Kate, Jordan and Nance that Annie was losing the battle as she slowly slipped ever closer to what would be a devastating drop.

This can't be happening! Kate had thought, panicking as Annie, blinded by dirt, her determination now tempered by fear, desperately groped the ground for any possible handhold. Her legs and feet flailed as she searched unsuccessfully for anything that would prevent her fall. The girls, completely out of reach, could only watch helplessly as Annie's frantic attempts failed.

Then, there had been a moment of hope; Annie with one hand had grabbed hold of a small branch and was clutching it with every ounce of her being. "Hang on Annie!" Kate had called out, only to watch in horror as the branch snapped. Kate, Jordan and Nance had wailed, burying their faces as a scream pierced the air. A confusing flutter of black and white had followed—then dead silence.

Kate, her eyes blurring with tears, had been the first to lift her head. She was unable to breathe, her heart pounding with fear. But, *something* had registered in her mind. *That sound,* she thought, *that wasn't Annie screaming.* Confused, she commanded her eyes to focus and looked around. An eagle alighting on a nearby tree soon caught her eye, but *where,* was Annie?

Jordan and Nance had slowly raised their heads, dread and anguish resonating on their faces. A small moan came from above. Kate had motioned toward the ledge and the three of them had hesitantly peeked over the edge. There, slowly rising to her feet, was Annie. Somehow, she had survived.

Kate had pressed her finger to her lips so Nance and Jordan would remain quiet, to see what Annie would do next. Perceiving that she was the only one there, Annie had taken a deep breath and pushed her matted bangs away from her face. The girls could see that she was completely covered with dirt. There were scratches on her arms and legs and there was blood dripping from a small cut under her left eye. Mustering what strength she had left, Annie had limped over to the carving of the Great Spirit and raised her trembling right hand. She closed her eyes and gently placed her open palm upon the shield.

Kate, Jordan and Nance had watched in silence, their mouths agape. After a moment, when Annie had lowered her hand, they hopped up onto the ledge and hurried over to where she still stood in front of the Great Spirit.

"Nice job, Annie!" Kate had expressed.

"Yeah, Annie," Jordan had nervously added, "you really knocked it out of the park!"

"Ye-ah, Annie," Nance's voice had trembled. She was clearly shaken.

What they saw next they were never to forget. When Annie had turned toward them, her face appeared to be glowing. She looked serene, like peacefulness had washed across her. Unresponsive, she stepped past them and walked back toward the edge of the outcropping with its perilous drop-off. Nance and Jordan had both grabbed Kate's arms and the three had frozen in fear. They all sighed in relief when Annie sat down and they rushed over to join her.

"A-Annie . . . ," Kate had stammered, "are you okay?"

Annie, still silent, had turned to look at her, a distant look in her eyes. At first, she had not seemed to recognize Kate, but then, the fog lifted and her eyes began to sparkle. "Kate," Annie had smiled, "I'm hungry."

Kate had quickly pulled her backpack off and dug inside for the sandwich her mother had made. She un-wrapped it and handed half to Annie along with the extra bottle of water. "Here," Kate had said as she happily fought back tears, "it's your favorite—peanut butter."

That day had quickly returned to normal as the girls chatted and laughed, enjoying their lunches and the view. The deep blue sky had been so clear that one could see for miles. Below them, the river ribboned its way through the lush green foliage of the valley. The air was fresh and it cooled as the day grew on.

"We'd better go," Kate had said after a while, looking at her watch, "or Mr. Lewis will be out looking for us." Reluctantly, they got up and gathered their backpacks. For good measure, one by one as they passed the Great Spirit carving they tapped the shield on his raised hand. They were just beginning their descent when they had been startled by yet another loud primitive scream. They spun around just in time to see the bald eagle fly by. As he soared past, they were sure he had acknowledged them with a playful tip of its wing.

"Goodbye, Mr. Eagle," Annie had called out to the magnificent bird. "Thank you for sharing your beautiful view."

Kate had put her arm around Annie and together they

headed back down the path. Though she could not describe it, Kate knew something magical had happened that day. And thus the beginning of the Legend of the Shield.

When the girls had arrived back at the boathouse, they found Annie's mother anxiously waiting for her. She was flanked by a very nervous Mr. Lewis. "Annie, where in the hell have you been?" her mother had asked angrily.

"Momma . . . ," Annie had tried to explain; she *had* told her where she was going that morning.

"Look at you!" her mother had yelled, roughly brushing twigs and grass from Annie's clothing. "Wait till your father sees what you've done to your clothes."

Annie's face had paled and Kate saddened as she saw the sparkle once again fade from her eyes.

"Now calm down . . . ," Mr. Lewis had begun.

"It's none of your business, Mr. Lewis," Mary had responded curtly then yanked Annie by the arm and started up the path to their cabin.

"Well it *is* my business," Mr. Lewis had called out after her, "I look out for these girls." He shook his head and approached Nance, Jordan and Kate, clearly concerned. "You girls all right?"

"Yes, Mr. Lewis," Kate had responded. Jordan and Nance had nodded, but none of them could mask the anguish on their faces.

Mr. Lewis had kindly told them they could find their folks waiting for them at Kate's. They scurried on their way in silence. As they approached the cabin, they had known something was wrong. Half a dozen golf carts were parked out front. When they had entered the door, all of the adults there quickly rose and said their goodbyes. Jordan and Nance were shuffled out by their parents. When Kate had asked what was going on she was told everything was fine, but she had had a gut feeling that it wasn't.

That night, Kate had again heard Annie's parents fighting as they had done every night since arriving at the lake. Where Kate lay in her bed, she could see the light was out in Annie's room. *I'll signal Annie and let her know I am up*, she had thought, *surely she will answer tonight*. She pulled her flashlight out of the drawer of the night stand and aiming straight at Annie's window, she pushed the button twice. No response had come back. After a minute, Kate had sent two more flashes. Again—nothing.

Disappointed, Kate had laid her head down on the pillow, her eyes still scanning the darkness with hope. Sadness once again began to flood her thoughts. Then—*it happened!* Two flashes of light came from Annie's bedroom window. Kate had quickly sat up and fumbled for her flashlight. She pushed the button two times and waved excitedly, even though she knew Annie could not see her hand in the darkness. Two quick flashes beamed back at her. Kate had felt elated and as if an enormous weight had been lifted off of her. With a relieved smile, she had laid her head back down on the pillow and before long, she had fallen asleep. That night, neither girl had ever signaled "Goodnight."

Early the next day, the girls had had plans to meet at Kate's to go swimming. Jordan and Nance had shown up at nine o'clock, as was the plan. Kate had looked peculiarly at Nance as she already had her swim cap on and was wearing a purple sea serpent life preserver around her waist. Nance had answered Kate's curious look with an embarrassed, "My mother." The real truth was she had loved her purple sea serpent life preserver. Jordan, already an excellent swimmer, had her swim goggles perched on her head.

"Where's Annie?" Kate had asked.

Jordan and Nance had looked at each other and shrugged. Thinking nothing of it, the girls, chatting excitedly, had flip-flopped their way up the path to Annie's cabin. But they soon found trouble had beaten them there. Apparently, Annie's parents had found out about the 'town meeting' and amidst a slurry of vocal objections they were leaving. Already too close for comfort, the girls had quickly hidden behind the corner of the cabin. Kate had glanced back home and saw her father had stepped out onto the deck of their cabin and was keeping close tabs on what was happening. Kate's mother was peeking nervously over the café curtains in the kitchen window.

In front of Annie's cabin, several pieces of luggage had been strewn on the ground and her father was cursing as he picked them up and threw them onto a golf cart. Annie's outraged mother had practically dragged Annie down the steps of the cabin over to the cart and shoved her on the back. Annie sat unblinking and motionless. As the golf cart jolted away, Kate, Jordan and Nance had quickly stepped out from behind the cabin and sadly raised their hands to wave goodbye. To their surprise, Annie had smiled broadly, happy to see her friends. She, too, had raised her hand. On her open palm the girls could see a rough drawing; it was of a shield with a dove and a heart.

* * * * *

Back in the present, Nance smiled as she recalled this

story and other happier memories from her childhood here at the lake, there were so many. She, Jordan, Kate and Annie were inseparable in those early days and their innocent adventures strengthened their bond. She walked a little further along the shore and settled onto a rustic wood bench that graced the edge of the lake. She took a deep breath. The air smelled crisp and fresh. She watched quietly as a pair of loons cavorted under the low sweeping branch of a willow tree. Their summer plumage beginning to fade, they snorkeled and dived for small fish. Nance had always loved the way the willows swayed in the slightest of breezes. She closed her eyes and listened to the quiet murmurings of nature.

SNAP—CRACK—SNAP.

Nance was jolted out of the stillness by the sound of twigs breaking and small rocks dislodging on the side of the steep incline behind her.

CRACK—SNAP—SNAP.

She hopped up off the bench. Someone or *something* was coming down the side of the mountain and whatever it was it was big and coming her way fast! Fearful thoughts began to race through her mind as she searched upward. *Landslide* was her first inclination but the sounds were isolated, not wide-spread. *What if it's a bear—or a moose? What was I told—run if it's a bear, freeze if it's a moose? No, no,* she thought, beginning to panic, *it's the other way around! Run if it's a moose, freeze if it's a bear.* As the sounds came closer, instinctively Nance backed as close as she could to the edge of the water. She would dive in if she had to. *Then what?* Her heart was pounding so hard she couldn't think clearly.

SNAP—CRACK—CRACK.

Suddenly, a mountain bike burst through an opening in

the brush. Nance let out a fearful yelp as it skidded to an abrupt halt just a few feet in front of her.

An intimidating rider dressed in all black, face concealed by a helmet, hopped off the bike. The rider undid the buckle and whipped the helmet off. To Nance's surprise, it revealed a small elderly woman.

"Wow, that was intense," said the rider as she set her bike and helmet down. She checked her watch and grinned. "I just beat my best time down the mountain."

Nance blinked in disbelief. She was unable to move, her mouth agape.

"I'm sorry," said the woman, stepping forward. "Did I frighten you?"

"*That—was amazing!*" Nance blurted.

"Thanks," said the woman, fluffing her short curly hair with a black gloved hand, "I'm gearing up for the Senior Citizen Mountain Bike Expo. No eighty-five-year-old from the flatlands is going to whoop my butt *next* year." she said defiantly. Stepping forward she extended her hand. "The name's Betty, Betty Carter."

"Nance Morgan," Nance reciprocated, "nice to meet you."

Betty briefly stretched her back. "Mind if I set for a moment?" she asked, motioning toward the bench.

"No, not at all," said Nance, sitting back down.

Betty pulled a water bottle from the frame of her mountain bike and joined Nance on the bench. "Water?" she offered.

"No, thanks," answered Nance. She looked curiously at Betty. "That looked pretty dangerous, aren't you afraid of getting hurt?" she asked. *Betty looked reasonably fit,* she thought, *but, c'mon!*

"No," Betty shrugged, "not when I compare it to the free dive I did with bull sharks last year. Now *that* was dangerous!"

"Geez," said Nance, visibly alarmed.

Betty smiled and looked out at the lake. "This is one of my favorite spots."

"Mine, too," Nance agreed, her eyes scanning the view, "always has been."

Betty looked over at her. "I don't believe I've ever seen you here before."

"It's been a while," Nance responded. "I used to come here as a little girl."

"Oh," Betty said with a smile, "then you have buried treasures here."

Nance tilted her head, "Buried treasures?"

"Oh, yes," Betty grinned, "there are always buried treasures in our childhood. We just have to find them."

Nance smiled back at Betty, she was not quite sure what to make of the statement or this feisty older woman. She looked out at the lake again and her mind began to drift.

After a few minutes, Betty could see Nance was deep in thought. "Well . . . I'll let you be," she said and began to rise from the bench.

"No. Please stay," said Nance. "I was just thinking about how this place hasn't changed much." Then her eyes lowered towards the ground, "And about how I used to climb this mountain."

Betty nodded, encouraging her to go on.

"But, I'm pretty out of shape now," Nance continued, "and I'm not sure I have what it takes anymore." Looking up at Betty, she asked, "I don't mean to be rude, but would you mind if I ask how old you are?"

"I'm eighty-three," Betty said proudly.

"Wow, I would have guessed much younger," Nance responded.

"Thank you," said Betty. "And as far as this mountain goes, if I can do it, you can do it."

"I don't know," said Nance, shaking her head.

"Listen, I've got to go right now, but why don't you come by my cabin sometime and we can chat." Betty arose from the bench and pulled on her helmet. Riding off down the lake trail, she called back, "Cabin fifty-three."

You go girl, thought Nance. She watched until Betty was out of sight. Instinctively her next thought was, *Ooo—lunchtime.*

* * * * *

Back at the lodge, Nance sat on one of the red vinyl-covered swivel stools at the counter of the Old Tyme Diner. In true diner style, its floor was large black and white tiles and the red color of the stools was repeated in a long, curvy, M-shaped countertop. Framed pictures on the walls were interesting old black-and-white photos taken of the area when the lodge first came into existence.

Nance ordered the deluxe cheeseburger with pickles, coleslaw and fries. Afterward, even though she was quite full, she indulged in an ice cream sundae. *I worked out today,* she reasoned with herself. Next, she stopped in the lodge's small gift shop and picked up a beige tee shirt bearing the Buckskin logo to add to her growing collection of drab-colored clothing—plus four candy bars.

Contented, Nance left the lodge and strolled down toward the lake. She checked her watch, *Almost two*, she noted. *The girls will be back from fishing soon.* She settled onto a bench under a large old oak not far from the boat landing. From there, she had a good overview of the lake.

Before long, Nance noticed the five Swedes, well, she could hear them, long before she could see them coming around the bend of the lake in kayaks. They were loudly hooting and hollering, obviously in a race to the shore. Karl, the largest of the five Swedes was clearly in the forefront. He beached his kayak first and hopped out to triumphantly claim his victory. The others landed shortly behind him. Disembarking, they scoffed sportingly at their loss. After securing their boats and gear, all, except for Karl and Olaf, headed off towards the lodge.

Nance, still on the bench, was discreetly enjoying the show. She especially liked watching Karl, a fine specimen of a man, having so much fun. He was doing a recap of his victory dance when he turned around and was surprised to see Nance looking his way. He swiftly composed himself, smiled and waved.

Embarrassed to be caught, Nance waved back then looked quickly away; she did not want to appear overly interested or like she was gawking or anything. She was pretending to peruse some brochures she had picked up at the lodge when Karl approached and asked if he could join her.

"Sure," said Nance, politely moving over. She felt a bit flustered at first, but thankfully her good manners kicked in. "My name's Nance," she said, offering her hand.

"Karl," he responded in his Swedish accent, his large

hand gently taking hers.

"Nice to meet you," Nance smiled.

"Nice to meet you," Karl smiled.

"Beautiful day," said Nance.

"Ya, beautiful," Karl nodded.

An awkward silence followed as they both gazed out at the lake.

Finally, Nance asked, "First time here?"

"Ya, first time," Karl answered.

Another awkward silence followed.

"You seem to be having a good time," Nance noted, hoping to spur more conversation.

"Oh, ya, wonderful," Karl responded, again without elaboration.

Oh, my, thought Nance, *I thought I was shy.*

Karl seemed to know what she was thinking. "I'm sorry," he said, "it's just . . . ," he hesitated, "you are *so* pretty."

"Oh," Nance responded with surprise. "Thank you." She blushed and brushed her bangs out of her face. Then, for just a moment, she hesitated. *He was talking to me, right?*

"*Hel-lo!*" came another man's voice. Olaf approached them with a big grin on his face. Nance remembered him from the day before on The Swan. Without asking, he boldly settled onto the bench on the other side of Nance, making for rather tight quarters.

Déjà vu, thought Nance, recalling the boat ride.

"My brother, Olaf," said Karl.

"*Hel-lo*!" said Olaf again. He took her hand and shook it enthusiastically.

"Na-a-nce," she replied, her voice shaking along with the exuberant handshake.

The words *awkward silence* suddenly had more meaning as Nance once again became part of a Swedish sandwich. Although today, Nance could not help but notice, a *very muscular* Swedish sandwich as both men were sporting tank tops and shorts.

Karl was obviously annoyed by Olaf's intrusion and Nance could feel him glaring over her head at him. Olaf on the other hand, continued to grin straight at her. Unsure of what to do with herself she began to peruse her brochures, but to be honest, she was unable to focus. Her rescue came in the form of a small, overly friendly chipmunk. He scampered their way, stopped in front of Olaf and sat up on his hind legs. His head bobbed back and forth, obviously in search of a treat.

"Awww . . . isn't that cute?" Nance commented.

"Ya, cute," Karl agreed.

"I don't have anything for you little buddy," Olaf told the curious chipmunk.

The chipmunk responded by moving in closer, his little feet shifting left to right with excitement.

"Maybe I have something for him," said Nance, reaching into her gift shop bag.

The chipmunk, still at Olaf's feet, tilted his head in an adorable manner, his large dark eyes bright with expectancy. Suddenly, to everyone's surprise, the chipmunk opened his mouth—far wider than anyone would ever expect possible and promptly chomped down on Olaf's big toe.

Olaf flew off the bench yelping in pain and fervently shaking his foot. The chipmunk however managed to hang on. When it finally released his toe it ran up a nearby tree, barking in protest.

"*Oh, my, God! Are you okay?*" asked Nance, leaping

up from the bench in alarm. She wanted to help Olaf who was now hopping around on one foot in agony.

Karl wasn't any help; he was bent over laughing so hard tears were streaming down his face. "You scream like a girl, Olaf," he teased through his laughter.

Nance, taking the incentive, quickly ran over to the boathouse and grabbed a handful of ice from the freezer. When she came back, Karl did his best to regain his composure, wanting to be a gentleman and not seem cruel. He watched as Nance gently inspected Olaf's toe. It was beginning to turn purple.

"The skin is not broken," said Nance, "that's good." Olaf cringed when she tried to put ice on it. "Oh, I'm sorry," she apologized, taking much greater care as she re-applied the ice.

Olaf, quickly sensing an opportunity began making a *much* bigger issue out of the bite than was necessary. He was obviously enjoying the attention and he was also aware this *greatly* annoyed Karl.

"Should I get the lodge doctor to look at it?" Nance asked.

"No," Olaf answered weakly, "but I might need help getting back to my cabin."

Karl squinted suspiciously at him.

Olaf moaned then discreetly gave Karl a big wink.

Karl stood up. "Don't worry, Olaf," he said, "I'll help you." He firmly took hold of his brother's arm and pulled him up off the bench.

Olaf winced and shot back an angry look, "How nice of you, Karl."

Karl grinned and squeezed his arm even tighter.

"Keep ice on it," Nance called out as she watched Karl and Olaf head up the path toward their cabin. A few minutes later when the girls had docked the boat, she could still hear Olaf yelping in the distance as Karl roughly pushed him along on his now throbbing big toe.

"Hey, Nance, what's going on?" asked Kate, Annie and Jordan in tow.

"I'm not really sure," answered Nance, her eyes still following the men. "Whoa!" she stepped back, suddenly alarmed by the girls' appearance—not to mention the smell. "What happened to you guys?" she asked.

"Bait fight," said Kate.

"Oh," Nance raised an eyebrow, "*right.* Sorry I missed that."

SIX
Maiden Voyage

The definition of insanity is doing the same thing over and over and expecting different results.
Albert Einstein

As the daylight came to a close, the air cooled. Kate built a fire in the stone hearth and it soon crackled invitingly. She poured four glasses of wine and set out a plate of assorted cheeses for everyone to nibble on then set about preparing the main course. Today's catch of fresh fish would be combined with leeks, carrots, potatoes, garlic, spinach, tomatoes and assorted seasonings for a spicy stew. The savory broth simmered slowly; the fish would be added after the vegetables were tender and infused with flavor. In the meantime, Jordan washed organic field greens and sliced tomatoes and cucumbers for a salad while Nance whipped up a simple dressing of fresh herbs, olive oil, and red wine vinegar.

"Need any help, Kate?" Annie asked, looking around at all the busy hands.

"No, I'm good," Kate answered, she had moved on to baking the biscuits she had prepared earlier in the day.

"Jordan, need me to chop anything?" Annie asked.

"No, thanks, Annie, I'm almost done," Jordan replied.

"Nance?"

"No."

"Okay, I'll set the table," said Annie, picking up the soup bowls and the silverware Kate had placed on the counter.

"Thanks, Annie," said Kate, sharing a smile with Jordan and Nance. Annie, having racked up a considerable record of botched recipes was almost always relegated to setting the table. It had been determined years ago that wild innovation and lack of attention were Annie's downfalls in the kitchen. However, she had learned many valuable lessons from her mistakes. Among them—just because it comes in a yellow box doesn't mean it's cornstarch; baking soda also comes in a yellow box and tastes really bad when used in place of cornstarch. Don't cook chicken and dumplings for a new husband in the same non-stick coated pot used to dye a sexy nightgown navy blue. This will cause distress when the hungry husband comes home and lifts the lid to see blue bubbles gurgling up through his dinner. Another memorable dish was "Dial-a-Pie," so named by Kate for the key lime pie Annie brought to the table sloshing in a pool of uncooked egg yolk. And not to forget, "Butt Plugs," appropriately named by her ex-husband for her rock hard cornbread—no further explanation required. This exclusion from cooking was no secret to Annie and she happily chatted as she performed her table setting duties.

"Aargh, these bangs are driving me crazy," Nance complained, pushing them out of her eyes for the hundredth time.

"I can trim them for you," offered Annie.

"Uh, are you forgetting you accidentally cut off your eyelashes while trimming your own bangs?" reminded Kate.

"Well . . . yes," Annie shrugged, "but I only cut off the left one."

"Oh, *that* makes it okay," said Kate with a chuckle. "There's a scissors in the kitchen drawer if you need it Nance."

"Thanks," said Nance, "but what I really need is a visit to the hairdresser."

"How long has it been?" asked Kate.

"Months," Nance responded. "Since Randall stopped calling, I just don't seem to care about *anything* anymore."

"It's normal to feel down after a relationship ends, Nance," said Kate. "You'll know when it's time to move on."

"I hope that will be soon."

After a more than satisfying dinner, the girls quickly changed into their pajamas. After all, jammie hangin' was still the general rule. They refilled their glasses of wine and settled in front of the fireplace. The flame had died down and the room had become quite chilly. Jordan, Nance and Annie piled under their quilts while Kate added fresh wood to the fire. Within minutes it was once again burning with gusto. Simultaneously they all threw off their quilts.

Kate, still perched next to the fire asked Nance how she had spent her day. She did not want her to slip back into the Randall pit again.

"I went for a walk along the lake trail, I had lunch at the lodge," Nance recounted, "*oh*—and I met a woman named Betty."

"Do you mean Betty Carter?" asked Kate.

"Uh-huh," Nance responded. "It was crazy. I was sitting on a bench—the one near the path up to the Great Spirit, when she came flying down the side of the mountain on a bike. Scared the *be-jeebies* out of me."

Kate laughed, "That sounds like Betty. She's quite amazing."

"She is," Nance agreed. "She invited me to visit her at her cabin sometime. I'd like to do that."

"Well, her cabin is easy to find, it's up on the hill just past the lodge. It's the one with all the sporting equipment outside; she's quite active—to say the least. Nothing seems to slow her down," added Kate. "I hope I have both her energy *and* her tenacity at that age."

"Speaking of tenacity," said Nance, "Annie, tell us about your trip to Alaska." She was eager to hear about this recent trip.

Annie's face lit up. She was very excited to share her story and got very animated as she spoke. "I did everything," she began. "First of all, it feels very different there; you know you're not in Kansas anymore. It feels very . . . well . . . *wild.* I flew into Anchorage, rented a car and drove the Seward Highway to the coast. Just offshore were white Beluga whales—right where I'd read they would be. They're the only whales that can turn their heads," she demonstrated. "When I got to Seward I hiked up the side of a mountain and stood next to a massive glacier. It's named Exit Glacier, because it's retreating."

"What do you mean?" asked Nance.

"It's melting," answered Annie.

"Oh," responded Nance. "Global warming?"

"It's likely," Annie nodded. "It was this beautiful iridescent blue color. From afar, the glacier looked like a perfectly smooth sheet of ice, but up close it was very jagged and full of deep crevasses. And it sounded like it was alive—moaning, creaking and cracking. It was incredible!"

"Oh, wow," said Nance.

"That evening I went to a restaurant and dined on a delicious meal of Alaskan King Crab," Annie reminisced, savoring the memory with great pleasure.

"All by yourself?" Nance asked.

"Of course—I was in Alaska by myself," Annie

answered, baffled by the question. "The next morning, I took a ship out on the Gulf of Alaska where *huge* waves crashed over the bow," she motioned with her arms. "After an hour of rough going we entered a cove and parked next to a mile-wide glacier where you would wait for a loud *CRACK—like a shotgun going off*—and everyone would scramble to see a big chunk of ice break off and crash into the sea. The crew even fished a piece of the ice out of the water so we could see it up close."

"Cool," said Jordan. "Was there any wildlife?"

"Oh, plenty," Annie responded. There were sea otters floating on their backs cracking open crabs and seals clustered together on the rocks. There were mountain goats, puffins and eagles perched on the cliffs. And waterfalls cascading everywhere. Before heading back to shore we stopped on Fox Island and had a wild Alaskan salmon barbeque. It was wonderful. The following day I took *another* ship back out to Fox Island and kayaked in six-hundred-feet deep water. It was pouring rain. By the way, it rains all the time there. Did you know Seward is a temporal rainforest?"

"Really?" asked Nance. "A rainforest . . . in Alaska?"

"Yes, there were ferns growing everywhere."

"Huh," said Jordan, "Who'd a thought."

"Before leaving Seward," Annie continued, "I took a raft trip down a glacier-fed river—in the rain, observed a salmon run—in the rain, and toured a fascinating Alaskan Sea Life Exhibit."

"How did you arrange all this," Nance asked.

"Travel agent," Annie answered then continued her story. "From Seward I made my way up to Denali National Park, a *big* dream of mine. I rode the bus ninety-two miles deep into the park two days in a row. The whole area was carpeted with blueberries and cranberries and I saw *fifteen grizzlies* the first day!" she beamed. "I also saw lynx, caribou, moose, ptarmigan and big horn sheep. I really hoped to see wolves and I was not disappointed. I got some *great* pictures."

"Did you bring them?" asked Nance.

"No, forgot them," Annie frowned. She glanced over at Kate, "I guess I should have made a list. Anyways, after Denali, I took an eight hour train ride back to Anchorage and I had a fabulous dinner in the dining car," she said, a wistful, dreamy look on her face."

"Oh, I love trains," said Nance. "I'd love to take a long trip on one someday."

"Me, too," Jordan agreed.

"And that was my trip," Annie concluded. "I do want to go back someday because I did not get to see orcas. Maybe next year."

"Sounds great," said Jordan.

Nance, having listened to Annie's story with great interest, asked, "Weren't you afraid to travel so far by yourself?"

"Well, all of you were busy at the time; I didn't have any options."

"What about Ben?" asked Nance.

"He wasn't fully in my life yet. Oh," Annie suddenly understood the *real* question, "you mean . . . without a man."

"Well . . . yes," admitted Nance.

"Of course it would have been nice to have Ben along," Annie agreed. "And I was terrified. I remember my first trip to Jackson Hole, Wyoming. It was right after completing my treatments. I'd never even rented a car by myself. Suddenly, there I was at the base of the Teton Mountains in a car I had never driven before. I remember thinking, '*Oh, my, God, I am so far from home.*' But within twenty minutes I saw my first elk and my fear just melted away. It felt exhilarating. I had always wanted to go to Grand Teton because I had heard it was one of the best wildlife viewing areas in the nation. It's also right down the road from Yellowstone National Park. Prior to my cancer, I might have put it off forever," Annie added thoughtfully, "but without a guarantee that my cancer would not come back, I didn't know what the future would hold. And like I said, I didn't have a man in my life at the time or anybody else willing to go, so there was no other option but to make the trip by myself. Plus, I didn't want to wait until I was too old to get around." She looked at Nance, "I know you've always wanted to travel. You can't just wait for a man to make your dreams come true; you have to do it now—for yourself. You just have to take that first step. I promise if you do, you won't regret it."

Nance bit her lip; just the thought of this was both scary and exciting.

Annie admitted she did take precautions when she traveled. She did not go out at night or venture into remote areas alone. On occasion she traveled with groups but mostly found she liked the luxury of her own pace. "Another thing I've learned," she added, "When you travel alone you have a tendency to talk to and meet more people. I've always found them to be incredibly helpful and more than generous with their time, especially if they knew I was traveling alone."

"That's good," Nance responded, taking in the information.

"More wine?" asked Kate. Everyone reached out with

their glasses.

"What are we doing tomorrow?" asked Jordan. She set her glass down and stretched her feet towards the warmth of the fire.

"Fishing?" Annie hoped, raising her hand to vote.

"You're kidding, right?" Jordan reacted strongly. "I'll probably have to throw out the shirt I wore today."

"Sorry."

"How about sleeping in?" Nance's eyebrows danced.

Kate and Jordan quickly raised their hands in unison.

* * * * *

The next day, one by one, the girls stumbled into the kitchen for coffee. Kate had prepared a tray of buttery croissants, honey and fresh fruit. She carried it out onto the porch where they could enjoy what was left of the morning. It was an oddly balmy day; the weather felt unseasonably warm. With no pre-set plans, the girls decided on a hike along the lake trail where Nance had walked the day before. If they looped back at the old swimming hole it would get them back just before lunchtime.

"Make sure you take enough water," Kate reminded, always thinking ahead. "We won't need much else; we'll only be gone a couple of hours."

"I'm taking my camera," said Annie, heading down to her room.

"Of course," said Kate.

"Do you think shorts will be warm enough?" Jordan asked.

"Definitely, that's what I'm wearing," Kate answered.

"Did you pack shorts, Nance?"

"I've got some jean crops along," she answered.

Fifteen minutes later they were ready to head out. Kate and Annie slipped on small backpacks. Kate carried the water bottles in hers while Annie's carried her camera equipment.

The lake trail at Buckskin had a long history. It was well-known to be an original Native American passageway. For fun, Kate, Jordan and Nance kept an eye out for arrowheads and pottery shards, just as they had done as children. Annie, as usual, found endless opportunities for photographs. She kept stopping to take a picture and then had to jog to catch up. Wildlife was usually abundant along the trail even at this time of day. The area hosted a healthy population of moose, white-tailed deer, fishers, martens, beavers, foxes and otters. There were black bears in the area, too, but a sighting on the trail was unlikely. For their own safety, a conscious effort was made by all to keep the bears adverse to human contact.

By the time the girls reached their halfway point, the old swimming hole, the sun, much stronger than expected for this time of year, began to take its toll. Nance, her face flushed from the heat, stopped to rest on the small rustic bench there. Kate handed her a bottle of water and Nance took a long cool sip. "I am so hot," she groaned. "Is it me or is everyone feeling the same way?"

"No, it's definitely not just you," said Annie, sitting down. She pulled her hair back in a ponytail and fanned her neck.

"Look," Jordan said excitedly, "the rope—it's still here!" The rope swing hung where it always had from the heavy limb of an old oak tree at the shoreline. "And the lake float!" she added, pointing to the small floating wood dock a short swim from the shore.

"I told you," said Nance, "this place never changes."

"Oh, I used to *love* swinging out and dropping into the water," Jordan reminisced, taking hold of the rope. She turned to the girls, "Hey, do you want to go in?"

"What? Swimming?" protested Nance. "Are you mad? It's too cold."

Jordan knelt down and dipped her hand into the water. "It's not that bad," she said. "It's always ten degrees warmer here. Remember? This is where the hot spring comes out."

Kate dipped her hand in the water and agreed, "It really isn't that cold, Nance. Feel it."

Nance got up from the bench and skeptically knelt at the water's edge. "It's not that warm either," she frowned.

"Come on, Nance. It'll be like old times," Jordan pleaded. "You just won't be wearing your purple sea serpent life preserver. What's the matter? Can't swim without it?"

"Maybe—maybe not," Nance smirked.

"I'll go," said Annie.

"C'mon, Nance," Kate urged, "we'll just do a quick swim out to the lake float and back—cool ourselves off. Work up an appetite for lunch."

"I already have an appetite for lunch," Nance responded. "And need I remind you we are not wearing swimsuits?"

"We can just go in our clothes," Jordan shrugged.

"These jean crops would take *forever* to dry," Nance baulked, "if they don't drag me to the bottom of the lake first." Not to mention, she did not want the girls to see the candy bars she had stuffed in her pockets. She had promised them she would start making healthier choices.

Annie, not wasting any time, set her camera and backpack on the bench and quickly stripped down to her underwear. “I’m ready,” she announced. Jordan and Kate promptly followed suit, stowing their clothes on the bench. They looked expectantly at Nance.

Nance sighed.

“Nobody’s around, Nance,” said Jordan, “and besides, we’re not naked, we have underwear on. Have you been to the beach lately? Bikinis are made of *far* less material.”

“Okay,” Nance reluctantly agreed, “but you better look the other way; I wouldn’t want to cause any sudden blindness.” She squinted at Jordan, “And don’t give me any of that granny-panty stuff.” She began to undress and noticed Annie’s hand slowly reaching for her camera. “Hey! Don’t you dare, Annie.” Annie looked away like she had no idea what Nance was talking about.

Jordan let out a “*Whoop*” as she swung out on the rope and plopped into the water. Kate swung out behind her and after a brief discussion a race to the lake float began. They figured they were due for a rematch, but in reality, neither one could remember the details of their last race. Five minutes later, Kate reached the float first, barely ahead of Jordan and they both climbed aboard. Nance, in the meantime, was creeping into the water very slowly. The water still had a bite to it and she was trying to avoid an all-out icy introduction. But Annie, squealing with delight, swung out on the rope and plopped into the water next to her, soaking her completely.

“Thanks, Annie,” said Nance, sarcasm exuding in her voice.

Annie grinned and began a leisurely back paddle

toward the float. When she climbed on board she found Kate and Jordan discussing the finer points of their competition, just like the old days. There was always some sort of twist to their races such as: you can only kick with one foot or backstroke only. By the time Nance climbed up on the float they had already worked out the rules for their next rematch.

The warmth of the sun felt good and they all lay back on the gently rocking float to soak it in. "What a beautiful day," Jordan commented, watching tall cottony cloud puffs drift slowly across the azure blue sky.

"Doesn't get much better than this," Kate agreed, her eyes closed against the bright sunlight.

"Mmm-mmm," Nance mumbled with detachment. She could get used to this.

Suddenly—Annie sat up straight.

"What's the matter, Annie?" Kate asked, opening one eye. She had felt the raft slightly shift.

"I heard voices," said Annie.

"Uh-huh, and what are they telling you to do?" Kate asked.

"No, really," said Annie, her eyes scanning the shoreline. *"Look! It's the Swedes!"*

Nance sat up straight, squealed and dropped into the water. Kate, Jordan and Annie slid off the raft right behind her and they all quickly began swimming towards the shore.

"Don't panic," Kate called out, "we have plenty of time. It's only a five minute swim."

"Is that a challenge?" Jordan asked.

"Always," Kate countered with a wry smile then dug in.

Four minutes later Jordan and Kate simultaneously

reached the shore. Nance and Annie arrived thirty seconds later, record time for both of them. Soaking wet and without towels, they hurriedly began to pull on their clothing.

"Where's my crops?" asked Nance, looking around in alarm.

"Where did you leave them?" asked Jordan.

"They were right here, on the bench next to yours," answered Nance, her voice rising.

Jordan started to leaf through whatever articles of clothing were left on the bench. She shook her head.

"Are these bear prints?" asked Annie, looking down at the ground.

Kate, hopping over on one leg as she pulled up her shorts, looked at the prints. She began to worry when she spotted the remainder of several candy bar wrappers nearby. "Nance, did you have candy bars in your pockets?" she asked.

"Maybe one . . . or two," Nance stammered as full blown panic began to set in. *"What am I going to wear back to the cabin?"*

"You better find something quick," said Jordan, scanning the area, "or hide, the Swedes sound pretty close."

"Give me your tee shirt!" Nance demanded, lunging toward her.

"Are you crazy?" Jordan yelped, hopping backwards to avoid Nance's frantic grip.

"Wait—I've got it!" Annie cried out. She was peering inside the metal refuse container maintained by the lodge.

"I'm not wearing anything out of a garbage can," Nance vehemently stated.

Annie held something up.

Nance frowned, "Crap! Let's do it and get the hell out

of here!"

Finally, with the problem somewhat solved, the girls headed up the trail toward the lodge. Two minutes later, the path narrowed where they met up with the Swedes, causing everyone to pass in single file. Led by Grant, the men were all shirtless and carrying towels draped across one body part or another, obviously on their way for a swim.

"Be careful, girls," Grant warned, "we just passed some bear prints on the trail. They looked fresh."

Kate, passing him first, responded, "Thanks, Grant. We saw some evidence, too, by the swimming hole."

"Remember," he cautioned, "do not run from a bear."

Annie passed him next followed by Jordan. "Oh, hello," Grant said to Jordan as she passed. He gave her as wide a clearance as he could but they were still close—too close, for Jordan. His hands were raised in surrender. She was obviously not amused by this gesture.

Nance, pulling up the rear, hoped to pass by the men unnoticed, but her silence only drew *more* attention from Karl. She deliberately looked down as she walked by and she could sense his eyes were upon her. He turned around with one last hope of engaging her but instead was taken aback by what he saw. Bouncing stiffly along on Nance's rear end was a skirt made of cardboard. It had been fashioned out of a familiar looking red-and-white beer carton. Karl, baffled yet intrigued, stopped and watched as she continued on her way.

Olaf, who had been walking in front of Karl, stopped to watch, too. He placed his hand on his big brother's shoulder and said, "What a woman."

* * * * *

Back at the cabin, the girls giggled through lunch. The morning had given them plenty to laugh about. "Do we have any plans?" asked Jordan, helping to clear the dishes from the table. "I wouldn't mind taking a nap."

"No, of course," Kate replied, "take a nap, you're on vacation. I'm going to check out the fire pit; it should be a nice night to build a fire outside."

"I'll help," said Annie, hopping up. She loved building camp fires.

Nance decided it would be a good time to pay Betty a visit. Betty's cabin was a pleasant fifteen minute walk from Kate's on Buckskin's back loop trail. She knew the cabin number but really did not need it because like Kate had said, there was sporting paraphernalia everywhere. Against one wall leaned a red kayak along with a canoe, a paddle board and a selection of fishing rods. Near the door, more outdoor gear: snowshoes, life preservers and a net hung on hooks. Her familiar black mountain bike leaned against the porch railing.

Nance approached the screen door and was surprised to hear Latin music playing loudly. Horns blared while a deep gritty voice sang, *"Let's do the Mambo! Shimmy, shimmy Mambo!"* When she peeked in, there was Betty wearing a dark-colored leotard and leggings. She was energetically wiggling and shaking her hips to the music. A dance video projected on her small TV.

"Come on in," Betty motioned to Nance. She nodded toward the TV. "Try it," she shouted above the music, "it's a blast!"

Nance shook her head. She hadn't danced in years.

"Come on," Betty insisted. She tapped a button on the controller and the music changed to a lively twist, her hips already in full swing.

Oh, what the heck, Nance thought to herself. She was going to feel awkward if she danced or not and it did look kind of fun. She stiffly began to move.

"Put your hips into it. Like this," Betty demonstrated.

Following Betty's lead, Nance started to put some effort into it. They twisted backwards and they twisted forward, moving their shoulders with the beat. They twisted to the left and they twisted to the right. They even twisted high and low. Nance was just getting into the rhythm when the music ended and Betty decided to take a break.

"Whooo," puffed Betty as she plopped onto a chair. "Great workout. How about a cup of tea?" she asked, popping back up just as Nance began to sit down.

"Uh, sure," Nance responded, following Betty into the kitchen. "Woooo, I'm a bit out of breath," she said, sitting down at the small table.

As Betty prepared a pot of tea, Nance looked about. "The layout of this cabin is just like Kate's—Kate Harrison's," she noted. "I'm staying with her and a couple of other girls."

"Oh, yes, Kate . . . nice girl," said Betty. "Are you hungry? I've got some awesome power bars."

"No, thank you," Nance responded politely.

"How about a banana?" Betty asked, motioning toward the fruit bowl on the table.

"No, thanks. I'm fine," said Nance. She looked around the cheerfully decorated kitchen. Red and white resonated everywhere, from the gingham curtains and plaid dishtowels to the Bing cherry design on her dishes, cups and teapot. On the wall near the table were several framed pictures of Betty with very recognizable landmarks in the distance. In one photo, she wore khaki safari clothes and sat on a camel in front of the pyramids. In another photo, she was riding a donkey along the edge of a steep cliff overlooking the Grand Canyon. A third photo of Betty, sporting a stylish black beret, had the Eiffel Tower looming behind her.

Betty set the teapot on the table along with cups, spoons, sugar and cream. She handed Nance a red-checkered cloth napkin then settled into the other spindle-back chair. She began to pour their tea. “Sugar?” she asked.

“Yes, please.”

Betty spooned a small amount of sugar into Nance’s cup. “Cream?” she asked.

“Yes, please. Just a bit.”

Betty passed the steaming cup to Nance.

“Thank you,” said Nance. She stirred her cup to help it cool. “Do you live here all alone?” she asked. She had not noticed a companion with Betty in any of the photos on the wall.

“For now,” Betty responded, “but I’ve got my eyes open,” she winked.

Nance chuckled. She couldn’t help but be charmed by Betty’s upbeat attitude. “Were you ever married?” she asked. “I don’t mean to pry; it’s just that I’m intrigued by how adventuresome you are.” She nodded toward the photos on the wall.

“Sure, I was married,” Betty answered with a big smile, “for fifty-four wonderful years. Until my husband, Ted, died,” she added, her smile turning to a frown.

“I’m sorry,” said Nance.

“Oh, don’t be sorry,” said Betty. “After dating a few frogs I met another wonderful man, Jed. So I married him.”

Nance's face brightened, "Oh, that's nice."

"Then he died," said Betty.

"Gosh, I'm *sooo* sorry, Betty."

"Oh," Betty waved off the comment. "I had a *great* life with each of them—full of adventure."

Nance sipped her tea and thought for a moment. She had to ask, "Betty, you were fortunate to have had two wonderful relationships in your life. What was it about Ted and Jed . . . I mean . . . how did you know when a man was right for you?"

"Oh, I only marry a man if his name rhymes with wed," Betty responded.

Nance looked at her blankly.

"I'm just kidding," laughed Betty. "Knowing if it was right was the easy part. When it came to the nitty-gritty of it, if I didn't feel it was 100 percent right for me then the answer was 100 percent 'No.' Let's face it, sometimes when you kiss a frog—it's just a frog."

Nance laughed. She loved Betty's candidness.

"So tell me about you, Nance, what do you do?" Betty asked, leaning forward with great interest.

Nance hesitated. "Well . . . I guess that's a good question; I'm trying to figure that out myself. I was married for twenty-two years, but sadly it ended in divorce about three years ago. I have two beautiful kids in college," she said, her face brightening. "I also do a lot of volunteer work."

"That's wonderful," said Betty.

"Honestly though," Nance added, "lately I've been pretty lonely—not too successful with the dating thing."

Betty nodded for her to go on.

"About a year and a half ago, I met a man that I fell

head over heels for, an airline pilot. His name is Randall. I really thought we were perfect for each other, but a few months ago he stopped calling. I've tried many times to reach him, but he doesn't return any of my phone calls or e-mails."

"Oh," said Betty, looking sympathetic.

"I don't know what happened," Nance continued, looking down into her cup of tea. "Of course he traveled a lot as a pilot, and his job was *very* stressful," she emphasized, "so when he was in town I did everything I could to make his life easier. I would help him out by picking up groceries and his dry cleaning. I would cook him nice dinners and set a pretty table. Often when he was away, I sent him cute little cards or left messages on his answering machine to let him know how much I was thinking about him. I even cleaned his apartment and did his laundry."

Nance looked up sadly from her teacup and found Betty with an appalled look on her face. "Oh, honey," Betty said, "do for a man like that and he'll plop down on the couch and kick his feet up."

"Uh, that's pretty much what happened," Nance admitted.

"Save that stuff for your girlfriends," Betty stressed, "they'll appreciate it."

"But, I just don't know how else to be," Nance shrugged. "I'm used to being a homemaker and taking care of people."

"Well what do you like to do?" asked Betty, patting Nance on the hand.

"I haven't given it much thought."

"Think back—to when you were a little girl. What made you happy, what were your dreams back then?" asked

Betty.

Nance thought about it for a minute. "Well, I always liked playing with makeup and fixing my friends hair. Oh!" her face lit up like a light bulb, "I've always wanted to travel. Especially after hearing my friend, Annie, tell her stories. And now," she looked up, "seeing these pictures of you—very inspiring."

"*You* can do that," Betty assured.

"What? Go to a foreign country?"

"Yes."

"No," Nance quickly disputed, "I'm not that brave. And besides, today's travel is so exhausting; I would never have the stamina for it."

"Hogwash! I travel all the time," said Betty. "You just gotta prepare—tweak your energy a bit. Heck, I probably wouldn't even know my own age if I could get people to quit reminding me," she added, looking somewhat irritated by the thought. "What kind of exercise do you do?"

"Uh, exercise?"

"Yes. What do you do to stay strong?" asked Betty.

Nance shook her head. "I don't really exercise."

"Why?" Betty asked. "I do and I'm almost twice your age. What's your problem?"

"I've got bad knees," Nance answered.

"So do I," said Betty.

"My joints get really achy when I exert too much," said Nance.

"I've had a hip replacement," Betty countered.

"Astigmatism," Nance motioned toward one eye. "Vision gets blurry at times."

"Blind in one eye," Betty fired back.

"I got Vertigo once, it was awful," said Nance.

"They make pills for that."

Nance's brow furrowed; she was not getting the sympathy she was expecting from this feisty old lady. She sat back in her chair and eyed Betty for a second, then dug back in with a vengeance. Her excuses, now barely holding weight.

"Leg cramps."

"Bananas," said Betty as she shoved the fruit bowl across the table at her.

"Weak bladder," said Nance firmly.

"Diapers," Betty retorted.

"I might be losing my hearing."

Betty, still unyielding, unclipped a hearing aid from her ear and threw it on the table.

Frustrated and devoid of excuses, Nance blurted her most honest response, "I'm afraid to travel by myself!"

Betty nodded, "Now we're gettin' somewhere." She rose from the table.

"Where are you going?" asked Nance.

"How do you feel about boxing?" asked Betty. She picked up a pair of red boxing gloves from a chair and without warning tossed them to Nance.

Nance clumsily caught them. "Well, I've never really done it," she answered.

"Come with me," said Betty, "we need to toughen you up."

Nance, perplexed, followed Betty outside to the back of the cabin where a makeshift boxing ring complete with starting bell, helmets and training weights had been constructed. A large red punching bag hung from a nearby tree. Betty helped Nance put on the gloves and led her over to the suspended bag.

"Hit it," said Betty.

"O-kay," Nance said and gingerly tapped the big bag. It moved ever so slightly.

"You call that a punch?" Betty frowned. "Hit it again."

Nance gave the bag a slightly harder hit. Again, it barely moved.

"Harder," Betty said loudly. "Pretend it's your last boyfriend. What was his name, Crandall?"

"Randall," Nance corrected, "but I'm not mad at him."

"Oh, so you like the way he treated you?" Betty stated more than asked.

"Well . . . no, not really," Nance responded, making an effort to push her bangs out of her eyes with one of the large gloves.

"Then show him what you think about the way he treated you," said Betty. "Pretend he's the bag."

"Okay," said Nance. She planted her feet firmly then punched the bag with more conviction. In a very civil voice she said, "The way you treated me was not very nice."

"Louder and harder," said Betty.

Nance punched the bag again, "The way you treated me was not very nice."

Betty pushed the bag back and yelled, "Louder!"

Nance again punched the bag, this time raising her voice considerably, "The way you treated me was not nice!"

Betty pushed the bag back again and it bumped hard against Nance. She did not lose her footing and this time Nance needed no encouragement to express her feelings. "THE WAY YOU TREATED ME WAS NOT NICE! THE WAY YOU TREATED ME WAS NOT NICE!" she yelled, fiercely punching the bag.

"*That's* what I'm talking about," Betty grinned, bringing the swinging bag to a stop.

After a few more rounds, Nance was puffing hard as Betty untied and removed the gloves. "Ow," Nance said, manipulating her wrist, "that hurts." She looked up at Betty with a satisfied smile, "But at the same time feels *really* good."

Betty nodded her head and winked.

Later, energized by what had become a rousing afternoon at Betty's, Nance shadowboxed on the path back to Kate's cabin. Jabbing the air and kicking her feet, she realized an elderly couple walking her way was hesitating on the path ahead. She politely composed herself and passed them. "Lovely day isn't it?" she said, smiling back at their startled faces. In the clear, she resumed boxing and mused to herself, *That's right—I'm crazy!*

* * * * *

Lured by the amber glow of the late afternoon, Kate stepped out onto the porch of the cabin. *Tonight the weather is perfect for a fire*, she thought. The air was crisp and cool with barely a whisper of a breeze. Many years ago when she was a child, on one lovely autumn day, she and her father hand-collected rocks from the creek bed and assembled a small fire pit. That same afternoon, they picked up twigs and small pieces of wood and her father taught her the *right* way to assemble them. It had been a very special day to Kate and the many marshmallow roasts and cookouts under the stars that followed were just a few of the simple pleasures that gave her memories that would last her lifetime.

Annie stepped outside to join her and together they carefully selected several nicely-seasoned logs from the wood stack beside the cabin. She watched attentively as Kate crisscrossed them in the fire pit then intertwined plenty of small twigs and pieces of dry brush. As the evening approached, the air did indeed cool significantly and it only took one perfectly placed match to ignite a strong flame. Before long it turned into a truly mesmerizing fire of brilliant orange, gold and blue flames. It flicked and curled vigorously, inviting with its welcome warmth.

The girls changed into comfortable warm clothes and carried out blankets, glasses and the sacrificial bottle of wine. When Kate showed up with a tray of marshmallows, chocolate bars and graham crackers, Nance rubbed her hands together, "Oooo, we're making s'mores," she said with delight.

Annie reached over and snapped off a piece of dark chocolate, her favorite. However when it came to marshmallows, she wanted nothing more than to enjoy it solo, toasted to the perfect golden brown.

Soon, everyone had a skewered marshmallow and was searching for the perfect spot to toast it. There was a lot of heavy concentration going on when out of nowhere, Jordan announced, "Hey, did I tell you I'm opening a restaurant?"

"*Really?*" the other girls looked her way. This came as a complete surprise.

"Uh-huh," Jordan continued in a serious tone, "I'm calling it 'Peckers.' All of the servers will be men wearing Speedos."

The others, albeit in shock, nodded in approval.

"We're going to have foot-long hotdogs on the menu,"

Jordan went on, "but when it arrives at the table it will really only be six inches."

Annie coughed out a sip of her wine.

"Where do you come up with this stuff?" Kate asked, also wiping wine from her chin.

Jordan laughed, skewered another marshmallow and perched it over the fire; her first one hadn't faired so well. Nance, Annie and Kate did the same and again jockeyed for a spot. Before long, everyone had perfectly toasted marshmallows prompting Jordan to start up again, "Kate, hand me two graham crackers please. I'm going to pretend this marshmallow is Rodney's head when I smush it between them."

"*Someone's* feeling feisty," Kate chuckled, keeping her eye on her own marshmallow as she passed Jordan the crackers.

Nance, having assembled her first s'more of the evening, took a gooey bite. "Oh, this is *so* good," she said catching chocolate as it dripped. "I thought you didn't want me eating this stuff."

"Moderation, my dear, moderation," Kate answered.

Annie was heavily concentrating on marshmallow number six, three of which had plummeted off her skewer into the fire. She was determined not to lose this one.

Jordan held up her skewer with two badly burnt marshmallows dangling from it. "Annie, what does this remind you of?" she asked.

"Ewww, that's gross," said Annie, leaning away.

Jordan laughed as the marshmallows dropped into the fire and began to sizzle.

Kate laughed, too, adding, "Man-bashing is not a

sport, Jordan."

"Speak for yourself," Jordan shrugged.

"Not every man is like Rodney," Kate added on a serious note.

"Yeah, you're blaming every guy you meet for his actions," said Nance.

"Look who's talking," said Jordan.

"Rodney was a jerk," said Annie.

"All men are jerks," Jordan responded.

"Ed's not a jerk," said Kate in defense.

"No, Ed is not a jerk. Ed is great," admitted Jordan.

"Ben's not a jerk," said Annie.

"I haven't met Ben," said Jordan.

"Karl's not a jerk," said Nance.

The others looked at her then at each other with surprise.

"You barely know Karl," Jordan countered, "give it time."

"You just haven't met the right guy, Jordan," Kate commented.

"I don't want to meet the *right* guy," Jordan responded, a hint of despair in her voice. "Honestly, it's like I've been thrown off the football field and I'm pissed about it. I don't want to play the game anymore."

"Well, good luck with that," said Kate. "I've always believed you can't make love happen and I certainly don't believe you can stop it from happening either."

Everyone was quiet for a moment, all eyes gazing upon the crackling fire. Perhaps reviewing the reality of this comment personally—or the consequences. Finally, Jordan looked up and quipped, "Hey, did I mention how great it is to have you guys spelunking through my brain?"

Kate laughed, "Talk about the dark side of the moon."

"Walk toward the light, Kate, walk toward the light," teased Nance.

"Yeah, I've fallen and I can't get up," laughed Annie. Everyone looked at her strangely then laughed with her.

Kate turned her focus back to Jordan. "Look where you are now, Jordan. You have a successful business, your health is excellent and you've got your whole life ahead of you," said Kate. "We should be celebrating!"

Jordan smiled appreciatively but she still could not resist the irony. She lifted her wine glass and said, "Well, then here's to me—great at business but crappy at love."

Annie added with a grin, "And here's to me—great at love but crappy at business."

"True," Kate laughed, "I can attest to that." She raised her glass. "To great friends and to good health."

"Yes. Great friends and good health."

Clink, clink—clink.

* * * * *

"Are you sure this will hold me?" asked Nance as she nervously inspected the rock-climbing harness she held in her hands. Kate gave her a reassuring look as she helped her step into it.

"Gosh, I haven't climbed in so long," Nance said. She looked anxiously up at the lodge's indoor climbing wall. With her eyes she traced the route Jordan had climbed with ease only minutes earlier.

"This is very much like the outdoor route we'll be

climbing today," said Kate. "You can do it."

"Okay," Nance responded, her eyes continuing to study the wall. "Should I go that way?" she asked, pointing to her possible first move.

"That's good," Kate replied.

"Okay, where next?" Nance asked.

"Well," Kate considered, "you've got two choices, far left or straight up."

"Okay," said Nance, clipping her bangs back, "but if I die let it be known, I'm willing you my cat. His name is Trouble and trust me, he lives up to his name."

"Here, Jordan, you belay her," said Kate, pushing the rope toward her.

"Hell no, I know that cat very well," said Jordan, stepping back. "I've got the scars to prove it."

Nance tapped Kate on the shoulder then discreetly nodded towards the entrance door. Kate turned to see Karl heading their way and she quickly surmised an opportunity.

"Hello," Karl greeted.

"Hey, Karl," Kate responded. "You've done a lot of climbing from what I've heard."

"Ya. Since so big," he motioned with his hand.

"Great! Would you mind belaying Nance?" Kate asked.

"Ya, good," Karl responded, taking the rope from her.

Kate smiled at Nance then she and Jordan retreated to a nearby bench to watch.

Nance momentarily squinted back at Kate then greeted Karl. Realizing there was no way out of the situation, she turned a serious focus to the wall. This was no time for distractions; she used to be pretty good at climbing and she certainly was not going to embarrass herself now. *The hardest step is the first step*, she reminded herself and reached for a handhold.

Kate was happy to see Nance climbing slowly, putting a lot of thought into her moves. "I knew she could do it," she quietly commented to Jordan.

"Huh-uh," Jordan agreed.

They continued to watch as Karl patiently belayed Nance. He only offered advice when she seemed to be stuck; she needed to be able to make these decisions on her own, especially on the side of a real mountain.

"He's a good teacher," Kate noted, "very patient."

"Not hard on the eyes either," mused Jordan.

"Mm-mm," Kate agreed.

"I think they have a crush on each other," said Jordan.

"Guys!" Nance called down. "We're not deaf you know."

Fifteen minutes later, Nance reached the top of the wall and Karl slowly released the rope, lowering her back down. She was beaming when she reached the floor.

Karl, grinning, gave her a high five. Excusing himself he left to join his brothers who were tackling a more difficult route at the other end of the room.

Flushed, Nance approached Kate and Jordan. "That was fun," she grinned.

"Which part," Kate asked, "the climbing or Karl?"

Nance smiled coyly.

"Yea," nodded Jordan, "somehow we got the sense Karl could handle Trouble.

"Mmm-mm, me, too," Nance agreed, looking his way.

"Want to go again?" Jordan asked, hopping up from

her seat.

"Sure," said Nance, "I need *a lot* more practice."

Kate leaned back and relaxed. *Things were going well,* she thought, watching Jordan and Nance work together. She noticed Annie approaching. "Where have you been?" she asked. "We've been here almost an hour."

Annie grumbled something and plopped down on the bench next to Kate. Never to be one that could hide her emotions, Annie's forehead was furrowed and a look of worry was on her face.

"What's the matter?" Kate asked, concerned.

"Oh, just a restless night," Annie responded, her downcast eyes revealing more.

"I kind of thought that," said Kate, "that's why we let you sleep in. Nightmares?" she asked.

"No, not so much. More worrisome thoughts."

"About what?"

"Different things."

"Like what?" Kate pressed, knowing her friend's capacity to tumbleweed.

"Just silly stuff . . . and I have a bad headache, too."

"I've got some aspirin back at the cabin," Kate offered.

"It's probably a brain tumor," Annie blurted, "knowing my luck." She immediately felt silly.

"Ah, brain tumor, brain shroomer. After what you've survived—*bring it on,*" said Kate.

Annie laughed, "How do you do that? You can change my outlook in an instant."

Kate laughed, "It's a gift."

"It's just that ever since I got cancer . . . ," Annie began.

"I know, Annie," Kate placed her hand on Annie's forearm. "The aspirin is in the kitchen cabinet by the fridge."

"Okay," said Annie, already feeling relief as she got up from the bench. "Thanks."

"Wait there for us," added Kate. "As soon as Nance completes this climb we'll head back and have a quick bite to eat before we catch the van to the climbing area."

"Okay," answered Annie. "Do you want me to make some sandwiches?"

Kate hesitated.

"I think I can manage sandwiches," Annie responded. "Trust me," she grinned and headed out.

* * * * *

After lunch, the girls showed up at the lodge for their scheduled ride to the climbing area. Their destination: Fortress Ridge, a popular mile-long granite wall. A natural formation, Fortress Ridge had hundreds of different climbing routes with various degrees of difficulty. Today the girls would tackle the route known as 'Maiden Voyage' for obvious reasons. It was an easy bolted route specifically designed for beginners. For the safety of the climbers, the lodge maintained the integrity of the bolts and anchors. There were two pitches and each pitch would take about thirty minutes. Kate felt it would be a good starting point for Nance to get her feet wet.

The forty-minute drive in the lodge's transport van was slow and bumpy at times but the views more than made up for the ride. Plus, their driver, Colby, was always entertaining. He had a lot of knowledge about the area including recent wildlife sightings. In the lower elevations, a wide meadow still covered with thick mars of grass and lingering wildflowers hosted a small herd of white-tailed deer. Startled, the does bounded away while one antlered buck, a ten-point, stood his ground. His soft velvet-covered antlers backlit by the sun.

When they reached the top of the first ridge, the mountains rose quickly and the road began to switchback up the steeper incline. Soon there were mountains looming on both sides and it was good to know that among the precipitous cliffs and exposed rock ledges, nesting Peregrine falcons were finally making a comeback.

The road leveled out and turned west, hugging the shore of a river that eventually dropped into Buckskin Lake. Ten minutes later, the van clacked across a narrow bridge then parked next to several other transport vehicles. Here at the base of the mountain, a popular camping area was abuzz with adventurers of all ages. Not everyone was here to climb; there were several people fly-fishing where the quickly moving river swept past a shallow sandbar. From the camping area, a short trail led to the base of Fortress Ridge.

Kate exited the van first. She quickly pulled her long dark hair back into a tight braid then retrieved her climbing gear from the back. She threw the bulk of it over her shoulder and waited for the other girls. Jordan grabbed the balance of the gear while Nance retrieved the small backpack of water and snacks. Annie toted a lighter version of her camera equipment.

In the past, Kate had carried tons of gear on extensive climbing trips around the world. She would train for months before a major climb, hiking with a backpack weighing fifty pounds or more. Those years of mountain climbing and hiking had given her a strong body confidence. This climb, requiring minimal gear, would be a breeze for her. As she walked the short distance to the climbing wall, she inhaled deeply and noticed how especially clean and pure the air smelled. It was always this way close to the mountains; it was as if the air wafted straight down from heaven. To her, climbing was the essence of beauty and adventure and she knew well the gratifying spiritual and physical challenge of it. She could not even begin to imagine her life without it.

When they reached the base of the Maiden Voyage route the girls could see the Swedes, their brawny shoulders and tank tops giving them away. Led by Grant, they were tackling a more difficult climb further down the ridge. Many other climbers were in various degrees of accomplishing their goals.

After a short discussion, it was decided that Kate would belay and Annie would climb first so that once she finished the first pitch she could take pictures of the other girls as they ascended. Annie, though not as experienced as Kate, was also an avid climber. She climbed easily, clipping the rope into a carabineer at each bolt along the route until she reached the ledge. She safely anchored herself then signaled to Kate all was secure.

"Okay, Nance. You're up," said Kate.

Nance, already in her climbing harness, looked up nervously. "This is *much* different from climbing in the gym," she said.

"You can do this Nance, you did great this morning," Kate reassured as she helped clip her to the rope. "I promise it will all come back to you."

"Okay," Nance responded, unconvincingly.

"What did you say?" Kate leaned forward and cupped her ear.

"Okay!" said Nance with more conviction and began her ascent.

Several minutes into the climb, Nance could feel her heart start to pound from the exertion. Although she knew climbing was not totally about strength, physically she felt completely out of her element. Apart from this morning, the last time she had climbed she was in her twenties, before her life became one adjustment after another to accommodate her husband and growing family. In this moment of apprehension, she wished she had stayed more active through the years, and not only for the health benefits; she regretted that she had never really shared this part of herself with her children.

As Nance slowly climbed the wall, Kate and Jordan called out suggestions for foot and handholds. Fortunately, the bolts were placed within easy reach, but that was not enough to keep Nance from visibly shaking. She was still struggling when she saw Betty climbing a nearby route with the ease of a mountain goat. Betty waved and gave her a thumbs up. It fueled Nance's determination. *Not only is Betty doing a more difficult climb,* she thought, *she's eighty-three for God's sake. I can do this!*

"You're doing great, Nance," Kate called out from below.

"Hey, Kate," came a man's voice on the trail.

"Hey, Adrian," Kate smiled, recognizing the voice. She quickly glanced at the young man as he passed, still keeping her focus on Nance.

"Kate," came another man's voice.

"Jeffrey."

"*Hey, Kate*," came a woman's voice.

"*Drew,*" Kate grinned, "I heard you were here." She motioned with her elbow, "This is Jordan. Jordan—Drew."

"Nice to meet you," said Jordan, extending her hand. Drew, a small woman in a ski cap and braids, smiled up at her. She was strappy—not an ounce of fat on her.

"You, too," Drew replied, shifting the climbing gear on her shoulder and firmly taking Jordan's hand. She tilted her head upward and looked curiously at Nance. "First climb?" she asked.

"No," responded Kate, "it's just been a while."

"Cool. Hey, we're climbing Chimney tomorrow if you guys want to join us," Drew offered, referring to a challenging route in the same area.

"Thanks. We just might do that," Kate replied.

"Cool. See ya."

"See ya," Kate answered.

"Who was that?" asked Jordan as she watched the spunky gear-laden woman continue down the trail.

"That's Drew. I've been climbing with her for years," responded Kate. "Oh, and don't let her size fool you, she's climbed El Cap."

"*Really.*" Jordan was impressed.

"Really."

When Nance finally succeeded in leveraging herself up onto the first ledge, Annie was there to greet her. She locked herself into the anchor provided and took a deep breath. Annie signaled to Kate all was good.

Kate called out, "Great job, Nance!"

Nance, still a little breathless, stuck her arm out and gave a thumbs up.

Jordan was the next to climb. Kate noticing slight hesitation, asked, “When’s the last time you climbed?”

“Well over a year ago. I belonged to a climbing gym for a while, used to go two or three times a week,” Jordan answered.

“Why did you stop going?”

“Rodney didn’t like climbing,” Jordan replied. She immediately realized how stupid that sounded, considering how much she loved the sport.

Jordan began her climb and completed the first pitch in twenty-five minutes, surprising herself how easy it was for her. She pulled herself up onto the ledge where Annie and Nance were waiting and clipped into an anchor. Kate quickly followed with Jordan belaying her from above.

“Good job, guys,” said Kate, sharing a high five.

“I’ve got some great photos,” said Annie, reviewing them. “Let me get one of you guys together.” Jordan, Kate and Nance leaned together and grinned back. Jordan took a selfie of the four of them on her phone.

After a brief rest, Kate asked, “Everybody ready?”

The consensus was, “Yes.”

Nance again looked intimidated as she checked out the next leg of the climb. This second pitch on the route was more difficult than the first. The route zigzagged between several splits in the rock and around a large overhanging boulder. Annie and Kate eyed the route carefully, knowing even beginners’ routes can have their challenges.

“Nance,” Kate asked, “are you up for this? We can go back down now if you want.”

Nance looked back up and said, “No, I want to try.”

“Good,” Kate answered. “Same protocol—first Annie,

then you, Jordan, then me."

Annie attached her camera to her harness with a carabineer and began cautiously making her way up the second route. "Be careful," Annie warned as she encountered difficulties, "the foothold is tricky here . . . this handhold is a nail-biter . . . don't go this way." After around thirty minutes, she reached the top and signaled, "All good."

Next it was Nance's turn. She had been watching Annie's movements intently. Shortly after she began the climb, she could feel the strong afternoon sun beating against her neck and small beads of sweat began to form on her upper lip. This was definitely a more complicated route than the first. Her heart once again began to pound, this time as much from fear as exertion. When she reached a particularly difficult spot she called out, "I don't know what to do here," her fingers beginning to tremble as she clung to the rock.

"There's a good foothold below your left knee, Nance," Kate called out, sensing Nance's apprehension. "You're not going to fall, I have you," she reassured.

Nance shakily dragged her left foot up, pressing against the wall until she found the hold. She then found a shallow handhold and pulled her body up a dozen inches.

"There's another foothold out to the right," Kate called out.

Nance slowly slid her right leg up and found the new foothold. This allowed her to reach a more secure handhold. She breathed deeply and rested for a moment.

"You're halfway to the top," Annie called out from above. "You're doing amazing."

I can do this, Nance thought again with even more determination than before. She looked up and carefully plotted her next move. She accomplished it and looked for the next. One by one, slowly but surely, she achieved each new goal. As she continued the balance of the climb, Nance's confidence and stamina began to kick in. Her mind automatically began to focus and decipher each new challenge that came her way. *It's like a dance*, she thought, as every part of her body began to adapt and stretch to each new song. She actually started to enjoy herself. Even the protruding boulder was less of a hindrance than she originally feared. When she reached the top of the pitch, she felt relieved, energized and exhilarated all at once. There was this great moment of pride and accomplishment captured forever in a picture that Annie snapped as she came over the edge.

Jordan began the second leg of the climb. Invigorated by the ease of the first pitch she started up with complete confidence, certain it would be a breeze. She even started showing off a bit as her natural competitiveness began to kick in. She made a few risky moves that frankly made Kate cringe. Unfortunately, overconfidence can backfire—and it did. Minutes from reaching the top, Jordan miscalculated a hold and lost her grip. She cried out and dropped several feet before the belay rope tightened, preventing her from falling further.

"I've got you, Jordan!" Kate called out from below.

Annie and Nance were peaking over the ledge from above and gasped when they saw her drop. Though it was just a short fall, they could see she had banged her knee hard against the rock. Jordan, momentarily dazed, looked down to see her knee bleeding profusely.

"Do you need help?" Annie asked, calling down to her.

Shaken, Jordan called back, "No . . . I-I'm okay."

Anne signaled a thumbs up to ease Kate's concerns.

Jordan took a deep breath, regained her composure then continued the climb. When she reached the top, she was embarrassed to find several other climbers, including Grant, gathered around. They had heard Jordan's scream and were there to help if needed. Still shaky, she sat down and rolled up the leg of her climbing capris. Her knee was banged up and bleeding but no deep wounds.

Grant, seeing there were no serious concerns, disappeared momentarily then came back with a bottle of water and a roll of climber's tape. Nance handed him a couple of tissues out of her backpack and he proceeded to inspect Jordan's injury. She winced when he touched her bloody knee and he stopped momentarily to discern her reaction. "Nothing is broken," he assured her, "but it's definitely badly scraped. I'm going to rinse it with some water and put some tape on it to keep the dirt out."

Jordan stiffened and looked away; she was an admitted wimp when it came to pain. Grant rinsed the area and carefully dabbed it dry. He folded a clean tissue into a square to cover the scrape then gently began to apply the tape.

"Ow!" Jordan yelped.

"I barely touched you," Grant responded, one eyebrow raised.

Jordan shot him an angry look and fidgeted defensively.

Grant shook his head and continued to apply the tape.

Jordan, beginning to feel foolish for making such a rookie mistake, began to babble. "I can't believe that happened—I've been climbing for years—do you know Steve Ellis? Yeah, I've climbed with him—major stuff."

Grant did not respond with anything more than an

unimpressed look which made Jordan talk even more. He finished taping her knee and looked at her sternly. "That's what we need, another cocky climber around here," he said, then got up and walked away.

Surprised and embarrassed by his reaction, Jordan turned and called out a sincere, "Thank you," but Grant did not acknowledge her. *Well I guess I deserved that*, she thought, feeling even more like a fool.

Click-click.

"Annie! Get that camera out of my face!" she yelled, batting at the camera.

That afternoon the girls walked and Jordan limped back to the cabin. She had refused Colby's offer of a ride on one of the lodge's golf carts.

"Does it hurt?" asked Kate.

"Not nearly as much as my ego," Jordan grumbled.

"We'll get some ice on it right away," said Kate. "Annie and I will probably climb with Drew tomorrow; I was hoping you would join us. Do you think you'll be up for it?"

"Are you kidding?" Jordan responded. "I've got to redeem myself—I'm there!" Suddenly, something dark and fuzzy whizzed past her feet causing her to spin painfully around. "Ow-ow. What was that?"

Dr. Judy Conrad approached them from behind. One of her two miniature poodles, Tom-Tom, had gotten off his leash. She was having quite a bit of trouble catching him as she was holding the other in her arms.

"Awww . . . is this the blind one?" Annie asked, patting the cradled grey poodle on the head.

"Blind one? That's the blind one," Judy pointed at the little black dog fervently zig-zagging the path. He did not seem to have a care in the world as he *yipped* excitedly, delighted by the freedom and the smells.

"We'll help you catch him," Kate offered, setting down the climbing gear.

Nance and Annie dropped their packs, each of them having premonitions this would be harder than it looked. Jordan was thankful to be disqualified from the task.

"He bites," Judy reminded.

Annie and Nance gave Kate a *thanks-a-lot* smile then spread out and took a position on the path. Kate, holding the leash, would have to hook it onto his harness using the element of surprise. One thinks that would be easy with a poodle who was blind but that was definitely not the case. Tom-Tom was a stout little bundle of energy and had a knack for slipping through fingers. In his unpredictable fervor, he trotted towards Annie then changed course at the last minute. Nance lunged for him, grazing his short fluffy tail as he went by. Tom-Tom retaliated with a growl and a quick nip to the air. He shifted his gears towards Jordan but somehow sensed a roadblock and banked to the right passing Kate before she had a chance to react. Now back in Annie's realm, he avoided her outstretched arms with a U-turn. He headed Kate's way again and this time she was ready for him. She quickly hooked the leash onto his harness. She stood up, holding the angry nipping dog at a distance with an outstretched arm.

"He's like one of those wind-up, chattering teeth toys," said Kate, happy to relinquish the controls to Judy.

"Thank you," said Judy.

"No problem," said Kate, picking up the climbing gear. "Oh, Judy, we're cooking hotdogs over my fire pit tonight. Will you join us?" she asked.

"Love to."

"Sans the poodle," said Kate with a wink.

"Ditto."

* * * * *

By the time Judy joined the girls at Kate's fire pit, the fire was already settling in with glowing embers. It was another perfectly clear night under a star-studded sky though cooler than the night before. Kate and Annie had carried two trays heaped with food and condiments down from the cabin. They also brought Jordan a small bag of ice for her knee. Nance wore her most comfortable jogging pants and a perfectly suitable oversized sweatshirt. The others wore jeans and long-sleeved shirts layered with various forms of fleece and flannel.

"How is your knee, Jordan?" asked Annie as she hung a small cast iron pot of beans on a shepherds hook over the coals.

"It's fine," Jordan responded, "just bruised."

"It was fun though, yes?" Annie asked.

"Yeah," Jordan chuckled, "it was."

Kate used several flat rocks as makeshift condiment tables and stuck hotdogs on long forks to be grilled over the fire until their skins blistered and crisped. She carefully toasted buns on a small grate fashioned years ago for just that purpose. When enough hotdogs were ready and the beans bubbled hot, they indulged. They even had potato chips, a food normally exiled from their perspective nutritional pyramids.

Laughter and conversation flew as the girls filled Judy

in about the last couple of days. Everyone stuck another dog on their stick to roast. Suddenly, the evening took an unexpected turn when Nance blurted out the words, "*I knew it was wrong from the beginning!*"

"What?" everyone questioned, turning toward Nance.

"My relationship with Randall," Nance confessed, "I knew it was wrong from day one."

"Okay," said Kate calmly.

Nance continued, "I remember driving over to his house and thinking, '*No, no, no, this does not feel right,*' but when I arrived and he answered the door looking so sexy and so handsome my thoughts changed to, '*Oh, yes.*' The truth is I lied to all of you *and* to myself," she admitted. "He was never all that nice to me. He was always telling me to lose weight or pointing out things that made me feel insecure about who I was. Even so, night after night, I sat by the phone—waiting for him to call."

The girls looked at her sympathetically.

"He even stood me up several times," Nance added sadly. "In my head, I created this wonderful man that never truly existed. In reality, he was nothing like the man I envisioned him to be. It's just . . . when I was in his arms and when we made love it made me feel so safe, so desirable." Tears were welling up in her eyes. "Why do I still miss him so much even though I realize now he never loved me? *What is wrong with me?*"

"Oh, Nance," Kate reached out. Jordan and Annie leaned in, too, wanting to give their friend solace.

"It's the 'Penis God Syndrome.'"

All of the girls spun around to look at Judy. "Huh? What did you say?" Had they heard what they thought they'd heard?

"The Penis God Syndrome," Judy repeated in her dry tone of voice. "Very common."

"What do you mean, Judy?" asked Kate.

"It's when a woman puts a man on a pedestal, believing he is the source of all happiness, security and self-worth. It can be very enticing to think of a man in this way but very unrealistic. In what has become her idealized world, everything begins to revolve around this man," Judy explained further, "waiting for him to call—waiting for him to get home—anticipating his every need."

This caught Nance's attention; she knew exactly what Judy was talking about.

"Even if he mistreats her," Judy continued, "she ignores the warning signs, allowing her emotions and the desire to be loved to rule her decision-making process. As the relationship progresses, the woman's personal growth all but comes to a complete standstill. She begins to abandon the things that made her who she is as the man becomes the center of her universe. They may be incompatible, or the man may be unworthy of her devotion or even incapable of deep love, but that is never taken into consideration."

"That doesn't sound like much of a foundation," commented Kate.

"It isn't," said Judy, shaking her head. "When the relationship begins to dissolve, the woman wonders what she can do differently to please him. Her personal life takes a back seat and she no longer benefits from those funny stories told by her friends or the excitement of learning something new. In essence, she has given the man complete control over her life, her happiness and her self-worth. Leaving him is never given a second thought. Because of low self-esteem, she doubts that anyone else will ever want her."

The girls were quiet. They knew what Judy was saying was true. They had personally witnessed it in various degrees many times with women they knew. Women that fell in love quickly and abandoned their dreams, choosing instead to follow a man. Some of the women ended up happy, but many, did not. When they changed who they were to please another, everyone had suffered in the end. Consequently they ended up bitter or depressed.

"So you've seen this a lot, Judy?" asked Nance, drying her tears with her sleeve.

"I've seen it a million times in my practice," Judy responded. "Anytime you depend on any person outside of yourself for happiness, you are setting yourself up for a big disappointment. Happiness must come from within. But think about it, this is not just a one-sided problem," Judy continued, "it is also unfair to the man. Imagine having to live up to that kind of responsibility. He's only human. He's not a God."

"What about affection?" Nance asked. "Sorry to be so blunt, but . . . ," she hesitated, "what about sex? I miss that closeness."

"Yeah, what about sex?" Jordan asked. She, too, was taking notes.

"Then the Penis God rises to his full glory," said Judy, lifting her skewered hotdog into the air. "We become blind to the truth. The man now becomes perfect in our eyes and he can do no wrong. We begin to ignore *all* the red flags and the only thing that matters is the next encounter. The only way to be true to ourselves . . . ," Judy continued, raising her hotdog higher, "the only way to break the spell . . . ," she paused, "the

Penis God must die." She lowered her hotdog and shrugged. "Once the Penis God is dead, the sugar-coating may be gone but you can begin to look at the man realistically and make intelligent decisions."

The girls, somewhat stunned, looked at each other. Then, Annie, out-of-the-blue, stuck her skewered hotdog high in the air and announced, *"The Penis God must die."*

"Yes! The Penis God must die," Nance concurred, raising *her* hotdog.

Jordan and Kate quickly followed suit and raised their hotdogs in a dramatic gesture of solidarity.

Suddenly, Annie's hotdog flopped off its skewer into the fire, hissing loudly as it blackened and shriveled in the flames. "*Oooo*," the girls echoed—cringing at the sight.

The following hour, enjoying the meal and the fire, was undoubtedly more upbeat. People say food enjoyed in the outdoors tastes better. It is especially so when it is seasoned with laughter and the company of good friends. It was still early when Judy arose and bid the girls goodnight. She groaned as she stretched a kink out of her back. She liked to joke about how old age had slowed her down, but the fact was she had one of the fullest and most accomplished lives of anyone they knew.

"Do you want me to walk you to your cabin, Judy?" Kate asked.

"No, I'll be fine," Judy answered. "You girls come by anytime, I'm here till the lodge closes for the season."

"Thanks, Judy."

"Goodnight."

"Goodnight."

As the evening came to a close, Kate and Jordan

lingered by what was left of the fire while Nance went ahead up to the cabin. Annie caught up to her, a blanket clutched around her shoulders. "You know, Nance," she said, "I was thinking."

"What?" asked Nance.

"If who Randall was you made up in your head," Annie reasoned, "then that man never truly existed."

"Okay," Nance responded, unsure of where this was going, "and?"

"Well," Annie continued, "if the man you loved never truly existed then technically he would not be able to break your heart."

Nance chuckled and put her arm around Annie as they walked. "Yeah, technically, I guess you're right."

* * * * *

The next morning the girls were all up early. It was a designated free day for everyone to do as they pleased. Kate, Jordan and Annie headed out for another climbing trip with Drew and her friends. Nance had other plans; she was looking forward to going to Betty's for another round of boxing and dancing. She truly had enjoyed her first visit and Betty was a hoot to hang with. She dug through her luggage for something she actually *wanted* to wear. She chose a light-blue zip-front jogging set and pulled it on. *It's a bit snug,* she thought, *but not uncomfortable, and besides, I like it.*

As she walked along in the early morning light, she thought about the conversation of the night before. *Darn . . . that's kind of a bummer to be responsible for my own happiness—goodbye white picket fence,* she thought in jest.

But on the other hand, she surmised, *it's quite invigorating to realize I can take the reins. However, none of this is going to matter if I don't start taking care of myself, I'll never have the life I want.* She decided to up her pace and powerwalk to Betty's. She put her elbows into it, swinging them back and forth as she went. Five minutes in, her face was flushed and she was huffing and puffing but she persisted nonetheless.

Nance's thoughts went back to the conversation with Judy the night before. The words made her giggle as she repeated them in her head. *The Penis God.* "Oh!" she yelped aloud. Out of nowhere, Karl had trotted up beside her. *Oh, my,* Nance's mind raced, *did I say that out loud?*

"Hello!" Karl said cheerfully, adapting to her pace. "May I join you?"

"Uh . . . sure," she hesitantly agreed, "though I'm not sure if I can keep up with you."

"No worries," Karl grinned.

"O-Okay," she responded, still a bit startled.

As they continued along the path, side by side, Nance was sure they looked quite comical; she with her elbows swinging to and fro walking at full speed and big Karl doing no more than a slow jog. Regardless, his company felt good and she was tired of trying to please others. With Randall, that had become a full-time job with no pay and no benefits.

When they came upon a bench, Nance, tuckered and out of breath, plopped down. Karl, showing no sign of fatigue sat down next to her and politely waited for her to recover.

"Water?" Karl offered, unclipping a bottle from a loop on his jogging pants.

"Yes, thank you," she answered. She took a big sip of the cool water then handed the bottle back to him. He took a long drink then re-clipped the bottle.

Nance's breathing soon returned to normal and her awareness of Karl sitting next to her heightened. *Wow, this is a big man,* she thought to herself. *Intimidating at first, that is until you experience the kindness in his eyes and his easy smile.* Her curiosity began to surface. "Are you on some sort of group tour?" she asked, referring to the other Swedes he was traveling with.

"No, they are all my brothers," Karl answered.

"Really? How many siblings do you have?" Nance asked.

"Four brothers, two sisters."

"Wow, that's great," Nance said. "You seem to be having a wonderful time together."

"Ya," Karl nodded in retrospect.

"I must say," mused Nance, "Olaf is quite a character."

"Ya," Karl laughed in agreement. "Olaf . . . he thinks he is looking out for me, but it is *me* that is really looking out for him. He is always getting into trouble."

"How so?" asked Nance.

"Well, last year in Australia, we rented a car and for many days were driving the outback. It was very hot and one day we stopped by a watering hole to eat lunch—too dangerous to swim. In the shallows was this little croc," he continued, "and Olaf, always trying to outdo the brothers, decided to catch it."

"Oh, geez," said Nance.

"Ya," Karl agreed, nodding his head.

"So we stand there, watching Olaf as he chases this poor little guy around in the water when suddenly, a huge crocodile appeared out of nowhere and lunged at Olaf, missing his leg by inches."

"Oh, my," Nance responded with alarm.

"Ya, we never saw him move so fast," Karl said, beginning to chuckle.

Nance began to chuckle, too.

"We all laughed real hard till we realized Olaf no longer had the car keys in his pocket."

"Oh, no! In the water?" asked Nance.

"Ya," said Karl. "We sat there six hours in brutal heat till an old Aussie finally came along and hotwired the car for us."

"No!" said Nance, now laughing hard.

"Ya, is true," said Karl. "Though not so funny then. I tell you another story. One time we were all hiking quietly through an open meadow, hoping to see wildlife," Karl began. "Suddenly, Olaf started screaming and ran by us like a 747 with . . . ," he began laughing.

Nance started to giggle, "With what?"

". . . with . . . with a swarm of bees on his ass!" Karl burst out laughing.

Nance did, too.

"Oh, I'm sorry," Karl apologized, catching that he had just used profanity. "Hanging with the brothers too much."

Nance shrugged it off then ventured to ask, "No lady in your life?"

"No," Karl looked down at the ground. "She passed away. Three years ago . . . cancer."

"Oh . . . I'm terribly sorry," said Nance, regretting her question.

"No, no . . . we had a good life," Karl responded, managing a smile.

Nance smiled back. They continued to sit there quietly for a moment, taking in the surrounding beauty. It was a comfortable moment, natural—not awkward in the least. Karl felt it, too.

I wonder? Nance thought. She turned to Karl and asked, "Do you like to dance?"

"Love to but not too good," he shrugged.

"Come with me," she said, hopping up from the bench and extending her hand.

Five minutes later when Betty came to the door of her cabin, Nance was standing there with Karl. "Betty, would you teach Karl some dance moves?" she asked, a hopeful look on her face.

"Sure," Betty grinned, eagerly taking hold of Karl's big arm. She escorted him inside oblivious to the screen door as it almost closed on Nance.

Nance rolled her eyes and followed them inside.

SEVEN
Passing Storms

In three words I can sum up everything I've learned about life, it goes on.
Robert Frost

The day had been a physically strenuous one for all of the girls. After dinner, Kate, Jordan and Nance retired early to their bedrooms leaving Annie on the cabin porch alone. She sipped from a cup of tea and watched in fascination as lightening flashed in the distance, silhouetting the mountains. *Storm brewing*, she thought, noticing the way the trees were beginning to sway in the wind. Her thoughts went to a distant memory. It had been a stormy night like tonight. Rain was coming down in buckets as a man ran toward a hospital emergency room. In his arms, he carried a small limp child. His frantic wife followed closely behind him. When they entered the hospital, a gurney was waiting. He carefully laid the child down then watched helplessly as the nurses rushed her away.

The attending doctor walked quickly toward them, "Ken—Mary, we're going to take good care of Annie," he reassured.

"Dr. Richards, thank you for coming," said Ken, catching his breath, his face distraught with worry.

Tears were flowing down Mary's cheeks, "Yes, thank you, Dr. Richards."

"I don't know what happened," said Ken, searching for answers. "We were having dinner . . . Mary and I were arguing about something. All of a sudden, Annie got up from her chair and collapsed on the floor in pain."

"Has Annie been complaining about anything?" Dr. Richards asked.

"The last couple of days she's had a stomachache," said Mary, "but honestly, I did not think it was anything serious."

"It may not be. I'll have to run some tests. Get dried off and get yourselves some coffee; this is going to take some time. I'll look for you in the waiting room as soon as I know something," said Dr. Richards then he hurried off down the hall.

Ken slumped onto a nearby bench and buried his face in his hands. Mary placed her hand on his shoulder. "Is this our fault?" he asked.

"I don't know, Kenny," she said, shaking her head as she looked around at the bleak environment. "Come on, let's get some coffee; it's going to be a long night."

Hours later, when Dr. Richards finally appeared in the waiting room, Ken and Mary sprang to their feet. "Annie is a very sick girl," he informed them. "I'm afraid she has a bleeding ulcer."

"*A bleeding ulcer,*" Ken responded with alarm. *"She's only eleven."*

Mary's knees weakened and she sat back down in a chair.

"It is unusual," Dr. Richards agreed. "Has she been under a lot of stress lately?"

Ken and Mary looked at each other, then Ken's eyes lowered to the floor.

"We argue quite a bit," Mary answered, feeling ashamed. "Do you think that could be the cause of Annie's illness?"

"Most definitely," answered Dr. Richards. He paused for a moment, acknowledging their grief-filled faces. He had known both of them since they were children. "Listen," he said, "if there is anything I do know for sure, it's that you both love your daughter very much. Right now you need to do what is best for her health."

"Of course," Mary and Ken agreed.

"You can see her now," said Dr. Richards. "She's sleeping peacefully. I'm going to keep her under observation for a couple of days. We'll talk more after she's stabilized."

"Thank you, Dr. Richards. Thank you very much," said Ken, taking Mary by the hand.

They walked into the room where Annie lay sleeping. Nervously they looked around at the IV and the monitors that were hooked up to the child they loved so much. She looked so pale and fragile. They quietly slipped into chairs and stayed by her bedside throughout the night. When Annie awoke the next morning, both of them were there to greet her. She was confused at first but happy to see her parents and reached out for their embrace.

"Are you in any pain?" Mary asked, stroking her hair.

"No, Mommy," Annie responded, her voice a bit hoarse. "Can I have some water?"

"Only ice chips," Ken answered, reaching for the cup on the nightstand.

The nurse came in shortly carrying a tray of assorted liquids and gelatin. She suggested to Annie's parents that they take a break and get some coffee while she tended to Annie.

Out in the hallway, disheartened, Ken leaned against the wall. "We can't do this anymore Mary . . . we can't do this to Annie," he said.

"I know," Mary quietly agreed, "but a divorce isn't going to be easy on her either."

"No," said Ken, "but it can't be any worse than what we're putting her through now."

"What about Dr. Conrad?" suggested Mary. "Maybe she could help. Dr. Richards said she is an excellent psychologist."

"No! Not Judy Conrad," Ken responded angrily. "You know she was part of that posse out at the lake."

"Yes," Mary motioned for him to calm down, "I know, but we've known her for years and we know she's a good person. She only did what she did out of concern for Annie."

His voice calm again, Ken conceded, "Let's get through this first then we'll figure it out."

Mary nodded in agreement.

Several days later when Annie was feeling better, Dr. Conrad met Ken and Mary in the hallway outside her room. They spoke briefly then Mary went in and retrieved Annie. Still looking pale, her white nightgown hung loosely on her small frame. She clung to a teddy bear with a large pink bow Ken had bought for her in the hospital gift shop.

"Hello, Annie," said Dr. Conrad, reaching out her hand.

"Hello," Annie responded shyly. She reached for her mother's arm.

"My name is Judy. Would you like to take a walk with me?"

Annie looked up and searched her mother's face for reassurance.

"It's okay," Mary nodded and smiled. Ken nodded, too.

"Okay," Annie agreed and stretched her hand out to Judy's.

"I heard you like to draw," said Judy, noticing a faded drawing on Annie's palm.

"Yes," Annie responded. "I like pictures."

"There's a playroom at the end of the hall with lots of colored pencils and paper, let's go there and we can chat," said Judy.

Ken and Mary watched them slowly walk down the hallway hand-in-hand. Their hearts were breaking for their little girl and for themselves as well. They never expected their marriage to follow the path it had. Now, their daughter's wellbeing was their priority.

Mary looked over at Ken, his strong masculine frame looking so tired and vulnerable. Even though they would be separating, without a doubt she still loved him. Sensing his pain, a tear fell on her cheek; she knew the marriage had been difficult on both of them. They had definitely brought out the worst in each other—nothing had come naturally. From the beginning, their differences were obvious. If one had seen family photos from their childhood days they would have been easy to sort. Mary, having come from society, had pictures of smiling women in fancy dresses and men in crisp dapper suits. They attended dance recitals, took piano lessons and played tennis and croquet. They belonged to country clubs and vacationed in all the fashionable places. Ken's family worked the earth. The few family pictures he had were of humble farmhouses, horses and plows. Aged early by hard work, stern expressions dominated the weathered faces of both the men and the women in his photos. Children wearing tattered overalls and second-hand dresses stood stoically nearby.

In her early twenties, Mary, bright and spirited, held a lucrative job at the State Department in Washington, D.C. She loved her work and like her mother was active in many local charities. When a friend asked her to deliver a car to Miami during her two-week vacation, she jumped at a chance for adventure. There, she met Ken, fresh out of the Navy, and quickly fell in love. Though she'd had many suitors through the years, she found Ken's magnetic charm and spontaneous nature to be irresistible. She left D.C. behind and happily moved to Miami where they were soon married.

As the years went by and Ken struggled to provide, Mary became more and more disappointed in her new lifestyle. Extremely intelligent, she would lash out verbally with angry words that could cut like a knife. Annie could remember innumerable times begging her mother to stop but she wouldn't, instead she'd push and push until Ken would lose his temper. Ken, realizing he could never please Mary, began to drink heavily. Physical violence often reared its ugly head. In an innocent attempt to keep the peace, Annie became 'Daddy's little helper,' but her mother jealously misunderstood her actions. Soon she began to take her unhappiness out on Annie, too.

Through the years, Annie noticed her mother's moods would cycle. There were periods of extreme elation followed by a period of rage, then of depression. Each cycle would take about a year to complete then it would start all over again. Whether the psychosis triggered her unhappiness or the unhappiness triggered her psychosis, Annie never really knew. She wished she had known her mother before illness and unhappiness staked its claim. She longed for the camaraderie that she saw between other mothers and daughters. In the end, she never blamed either parent. She knew it took two and both had equally contributed to the demise of the marriage. After they divorced, her parents both seemed happier in their new lives, however, neither ever remarried.

Because Annie's illness had preceded her parent's decision to divorce, there was a period of time she felt guilty for perhaps being the cause. But with age came acceptance. As an adult, she no longer blamed herself for her parent's problems, just as they were not responsible for any of *hers*. She thought about them often, but she hated when the bad memories crept in, prompted by some minute trigger buried somewhere in her subconscious. She was working on that.

Her parent's marriage had been difficult to say the least, but their relationship changed in their final years when her mother had a succession of strokes and her father descended rapidly into the quicksand of Alzheimer's disease. Suddenly, Annie found herself taking care of both of them. Oddly, they seemed to forget their anger toward each other and in some innocent way, love bloomed again. They spent many days sitting and holding each other's hand or taking long walks as Ken pushed Mary in her wheelchair. Gone were the expectations, the prejudices and the anger. The liquor was gone, too. Once Annie became her father's caretaker she would not buy it for him and he never did ask. On occasion, Annie would buy him an apple beer and watch in amusement as he relished it, never knowing the difference. He barely spoke anymore, however, upon seeing the word "liquor" on a storefront he would spell it out as they drove by. "L-I-Q-U-O-R."

* * * * *

Annie finished her tea and retired to her bedroom. Finding comfort in the sound of a wind chime tinkling in the distance she quickly fell asleep.

However it wasn't the same for Jordan. She, too, heard the wind chime. Like men, it both delighted and annoyed her. Throughout the night, the lightning continued to illuminate the sky as thunder rumbled threateningly in the distance. Though it did not rain, there was uneasiness in the air. As the dark hours crept slowly along, Jordan tossed and turned in her bed, unable to sleep. Instead, her mind flooded with thoughts about her past relationships. She had given each one-hundred percent and now felt betrayed and angry toward not only the men who had hurt her, but all men. Staying mad made her feel strong and in control. At times her thoughts softened and she found herself fighting back tears. She had not cried since her breakup with Rodney. She knew that if she cried she would lose the edge—the anger edge that was protecting her from being hurt again. But deep in her heart, she knew that letting go of it was the only way to have a chance at finding real love. She would have to become vulnerable again and someday take the leap of faith that true love requires.

Frustrated, Jordan sat up in her bed and drew her knees to her chest. She stared out the window at the ominous weather. She knew it would be hard to once again lay her life out like a deck of cards. She thought about Karen, a friend of hers who had dated a man named Harry. A pretty redhead, Karen would hide things about herself that she felt would scare Harry off. With the passing of a dear friend, she had reluctantly come to own a family of seven cats. She grew to love them and was committed to their care but knew Harry did not like cats, so on their first date she wanted to make sure they were completely out of sight. Before Harry's arrival, she put them on the back porch assuming they would retreat into the yard, but instead they all sat expectantly looking in through the sliding glass door. Karen hurriedly prepared a bowl of food for them and was happy when they followed her into the yard, out of view from the house. She gave them each a quick pat then rushed back into the house to finish dressing. This was her first date in a long time and she was both nervous and excited. Minutes before Harry's expected arrival, she once again found the cats gathered at the door, looking in. Her nerves beginning to unravel, she quickly, but gently, chased the cats off the back porch then turned the sprinklers on, hoping to keep them further out in the yard. Back in the house, she took a deep breath, smoothed her dress and tried to calm herself. She was still primping in the bathroom mirror when the doorbell rang. As she approached the front door, out of the corner of her eye, something caught her attention. She turned toward the sliding glass door to find seven confused soaking-wet cats staring back at her. She panicked and quickly pulled the drapes closed, hiding them from view. She took another deep breath, centered herself and proceeded to answer the door.

This was just one of the many innocent untruths Karen had brought to the table while dating Harry. If Harry did something that did not sit well with Karen she never complained or voiced her opinion—always choosing to not rock the boat. Their relationship went on for almost a year, but she would tell Jordan many times over, she never really felt loved. *How could she,* Jordan wondered, *if she never revealed who she was, how could she ever truly feel loved?*

When Karen eventually ended her relationship with

Harry, she yelled at him with pent-up frustration, "I'm breaking up with you Harry—*AND I HAVE SEVEN CATS!"*

As the night went on, Jordan continued to toss and turn. Eventually she fell asleep but awoke the next day feeling tired and confused. As she lingered in bed, all of the thoughts of the previous night began to creep back in. She pulled her pillow over her eyes and wondered if she would ever calm the war that was going on in her head. After a few minutes, she knew lying in bed was futile. She arose and looked out the window. It was an unusually gray morning, but she could see sunlight trying to peak over the ridge. *I need a good run*, she thought, *running always clears my mind.* It was drizzly but not too wet for a quick spin along the lake trail. And there were plenty of tall trees there to shelter her from the rain. She slipped into a navy blue jogging set, hoping the long sleeves would lock out any chills the dampness might incur. She quickly combed and pulled her hair back, securing it in a ponytail.

Annie and Kate were still in their pajamas on the porch enjoying coffee when Jordan greeted and quickly passed them. Her mind was too occupied to hear Kate call out about the incoming storm.

As Jordan jogged, her mind began racing back and forth with opposing arguments. Instead of fighting these thoughts, she allowed herself to free associate. There was no way she wanted to experience the pain she felt when her relationship with Rodney ended, but if she was honest with herself, she knew with the *right* person she would prefer to be in a relationship.

Jordan waved to Colby as she passed the boathouse. He appeared to be securing the boats, but she thought nothing of it. By the time she crossed the small wooden bridge, she once again found herself fighting back tears. She was beginning to realize anger was like having another relationship unto itself. It required maintenance and devotion. It needed to be fed. She also realized that by staying angry she was giving Rodney control over her future. She *wanted* to love again. All men were not jerks; Grant was testimony to the fact that there were nice men out there. *Dammit*, she thought as the first tear splashed upon her cheek.

On cue, what had been a drizzle of rain suddenly began to come down in freezing cold buckets. When lightening cracked loudly nearby followed by a huge boom of thunder, Jordan screamed; she did not mind rain, but she was terrified of lightening. Frozen in her tracks, she looked desperately around for cover, but there were no options nearby. Her only choice was to run up a service road in hopes of finding refuge there. As she ran past the "Employees Only" sign she thought, *Surely there is some shelter there.* Her eyes blurred by the rain, she ducked into the first building she saw and pulled the door closed with both hands. Feeling safe, she sighed audibly in relief.

"Hello, Peaches," a familiar voice said from behind. "Good to see you."

Jordan spun around—completely caught off guard. It was Grant, and he wasn't exactly smiling. Before she could respond he pulled a towel from a shelf and tossed it to her. Somehow she managed to catch it. She dried her face and looked around, trying to get her bearings. The room was full of pottery pieces in various stages of completion. "What is this?" she asked as her eyes began to focus. "You're a p-potter?"

"Yes," Grant responded. "You got a problem with that?"

"No," said Jordan.

"Well you seem to have a problem with everything else I do," said Grant.

"Uh . . . about that," said Jordan, "I owe you an apology."

Grant, although hesitant at first to trust these unexpected and amicable words, nodded. His face softened. "Okay," he said, "I can appreciate that." He could see the honesty in her eyes . . . *her beautiful brown eyes*.

Outside the wind howled as the storm intensified. Jordan's jogging suit was soaking wet and she was beginning to shiver. "Come on," Grant motioned for her to follow, "we need to get you into some dry clothes. I'll make some fresh coffee."

They walked up a short stairwell to a mudroom where Jordan slipped off her wet sneakers then followed Grant through a door. She was completely surprised when she suddenly found herself standing in his living room. Before she got a chance to take it all in, Grant handed her some dry clothing and pointed down the hallway to the bathroom.

Jordan found the bathroom bright and immaculate with slate-colored towels and granite countertops. She quickly slipped into the powder-blue hoodie and black pants Grant had given her to wear. *Huh . . . women's clothing*, she noted. She wrung out her jogging suit over the sink and caught a glimpse of herself in the mirror. She cringed; her friend's strung-out wet cats came to mind.

When she came out of the bathroom, Grant took her wet clothing to the mudroom and she heard the dryer start to hum. He came back and began to make coffee in the open kitchen. It was separated from the living area by a butcher-block island with tall swivel stools.

Jordan took the opportunity to look around Grant's living room. With its wood-beamed ceilings, stone fireplace and colorful art, it was stunning. Even though it was dark and stormy out, tall windows filled the room with light and commanded a sweeping view of the lake.

Grant eyed her cautiously from the kitchen as she walked about. Yes, she was as beautiful as he remembered. Even soaking wet he was captivated by her, but he was nobody's fool—you didn't have to bite him twice.

"I never knew this house was here," said Jordan as she looked out the window, trying to determine its exact location in the landscape.

"That was the plan when I built it," said Grant. "I like my privacy."

Out on the lake, Jordan could see the rain falling in sheets, angled by the wind. It looked cold and scary, making the crackle and snap of a fire beginning in the hearth all the more welcome. Its warmth pulled her in briefly, but her eyes were attracted more to the paintings and pottery that accented the room. She lingered in front of one particularly gorgeous ceramic vase. The colors of autumn—red, gold and amber with lingering swirls of green, seemed to come alive. *There's something very familiar about this piece*, she thought.

"What do you take in your coffee?" Grant asked.

"A little cream and very little sugar," she answered, still searching her mind for clues.

He walked over and handed her a steaming cup of coffee then turned to the vase she was admiring. He, too, lingered, looking at it thoughtfully. "I made that piece for my parents," he said.

"It's beautiful," said Jordan.

"Mm-mm. Thanks."

She took a sip of her coffee when suddenly—it hit her. *Grant—Grant Kingsley.* How is it she had not put two-and-two together? "Are you *the* Grant Kingsley?" she asked in astonishment.

"Yep," said Grant. "At least I was the last time I checked my driver's license."

"Grant Kingsley—the Master Potter?"

"Mm-mm."

"Your work is all over galleries in New York. *I love your pottery,"* Jordan gushed.

"Well . . . thank you," Grant grinned.

Jordan bent down and admired the details of the pottery piece. "How did you come up with this color combination? It's so unique."

"I don't know . . . it just comes naturally," Grant answered. "Studying nature helps, that's where I get a lot of my inspiration."

"I took a pottery class once, let's just say *my* mother never had any of *my* pieces on display," said Jordan.

"Maybe you just need a little guidance," said Grant, motioning her over to the fire.

"Maybe," she responded.

Grant settled into one of the over-size armchairs near the hearth.

"I can't believe it," mused Jordan, settling into another. "Grant Kingsley," she smiled, shaking her head.

Grant smiled back.

Jordan took a sip of her coffee, it was perfect and soothing. She leaned forward toward the warmth of the fire, cupping the stoneware mug with both hands. She wanted to know more about this man full of surprises. She looked over at Grant and asked, “So do you live here year-round?”

“Yes. I keep an apartment in the city, for business purposes, but mostly I call this home,” he answered.

“Nice,” said Jordan, nodding approval.

“I lived away for a while,” Grant elaborated, “went to college and art school, traveled to Europe, but no matter where I lived, I felt like I was always chasing a dream. Then one day I realized in doing so I was sacrificing the things that meant the most to me. I missed my life here and I missed spending time with my folks, so when they needed my help running the lodge, I didn’t hesitate. I’m just glad I figured it out before it was too late.”

“I heard your parents had passed away. I’m sorry for your loss,” said Jordan.

“Thank you.”

“What do you do during the winter?” Jordan asked, drawing another delicious sip of her coffee.

“Well, I snowshoe, I cross-country ski, I ice fish, make pottery. I also have a lot of maintenance and repairs to do to the lodge before we reopen in the spring,” Grant answered.

“My gosh it must get cold up here,” Jordan surmised.

“*Major cold*,” said Grant. “It may sound strange but winter is one of my favorite seasons here. It’s incredibly surreal to experience—magnificent and humbling at the same time.”

Jordan took a moment to imagine what he described then asked, “Doesn’t it get lonely up here?”

"Umm . . . ," Grant began, "I miss the folks, but you'd be surprised how many people come and go here in the winter. I also like to check in on the few private owners that live here year-round."

Jordan nodded and looked out at the lake. "This view . . . it's incredible. I'm sure that's why you picked this as your home site."

"Yes . . . that and the fact this hill was a secret getaway for me as a kid. I used to have a tree fort in that big tree over there," Grant said, pointing toward a tall oak.

"That was *your* tree fort?" Jordan asked. "So *you're* the one that used to bomb us with water balloons."

"Me? Never," Grant chuckled.

Jordan laughed. Their eyes lingered for a moment until a crack of thunder caused her to jump. Luckily her coffee was almost finished because it would have gone everywhere.

"So how do you like living in the city?" Grant asked.

"How do you know I live in the city?" asked Jordan.

"I can tell a citified girl when I meet one," he asserted with a grin.

"Well . . . I don't hate it," Jordan answered honestly, "but like you, at times I just feel like something is missing. It's *great* being back here surrounded by so much nature."

"*That's what I'm talking about*," said Grant, sitting forward in his chair. "This place . . . it gets in your blood."

Jordan saw his face light up with the passion of a man that knows what he likes. Their eyes again locked for a moment and she had to look away.

Outside, the rain had once again become just a drizzle. The sun peaked out from behind the clouds, revealing a double rainbow over the lake. "Wow, look at that," Jordan pointed,

"I've never seen a double rainbow before."

"Quick—make a wish," Grant urged.

"O-okay," said Jordan, squeezing her eyes shut. She had no problem formulating her wish. When she reopened her eyes, Grant was grinning at her.

"You made that up didn't you?" she accused.

"Uh-uh."

"Very funny," Jordan laughed. "Well," she said rising from the chair, "the rain has stopped. Thank you for the coffee, it was delicious." She walked her empty cup over to the kitchen counter and set it down.

Grant retrieved her items from the dryer and she proceeded to the bathroom to change. She neatly folded the clothing Grant had lent her and placed them on the counter. Secretly, she hoped the wish she had made would come true; she hoped the clothing Grant had lent her did not belong to someone special in his life.

As she walked home the clouds began dissipating, revealing patches of deep azure blue. The air smelled fresh and drops of rain were dripping from the lush greenery along the trail. Pinecones glistened like gold in the emerging sunlight as birds chirped like heralds. The world was new again.

* * * * *

Clearing storms often make for beautiful sunsets. Knowing this, Kate had suggested to the girls that they go to the lodge to enjoy it and the spectacular view of the lake. Even better, tonight there would be a bonfire in the large stone fire pit below the deck. Upon arrival at the lodge, they were happy to find dry, cooler air had replaced the rain and a nice-sized group of people already assembled around a large, blazing fire.

"I love this," said Annie, looking around. "There are so many interesting people here. Look, there's Mountain Bum," she said, pointing him out to Nance and Jordan. "He drives up here every year in time for the spring wildflower bloom and stays in the area till the first snow."

"That's cool," said Jordan, observing the neatly dressed silver-haired man. "What does he do here?" she asked.

"He's an incredible photographer," Annie answered. "He sells his photography all over the world. We became friends a couple of years ago. He lost his daughter last year to breast cancer," Annie shook her head sadly. "She was only in her forties, left behind three small children."

"Oh, that's too bad," Jordan sympathized, looking his way.

"I know," Annie agreed. "I hate hearing that stuff, but it also reminds me to live every day to the fullest."

Everyone nodded in agreement.

"I'm going to say hello," said Annie, heading off in his direction.

Kate spotted Drew and waved to her. She was chatting with her rock climbing friends and the three younger Swedes, Viktor, Mikael and Niels.

Nance, noticing the fine-looking men surrounding Drew, commented, "She really attracts the guys. It must be because she is so outgoing."

"It's true," Kate said, looking Drew's way, "she does attract a lot of guys, and she *is* quite outgoing. But I don't think *that's* what appeals to them."

"What do you think it is?" asked Jordan, curious, too.

"Well, we've been on a lot of climbs together and she has this great spirit about her," Kate answered. "You really get the sense that she loves her life and lives it on her terms. It's quite captivating."

"Huh," Jordan and Nance pondered, continuing to look Drew's way.

"I'm going over," said Kate. "Anybody want to join me?"

"I'll go," Nance piped, noticing Karl heading toward the same group.

"I'm good," said Jordan. "This chair's got my name on it," she said, settling into one of the Adirondacks near the fire. She sat forward, stretching out her hands to warm them. The vigorous swirl of the flames captivated as they reached upward and unfurled into the evening sky.

The sunset, as promised, competed for Jordan's attention with pink, orange and lavender splashed clouds. She sat back and felt her body relax into the chair. Briefly she closed her eyes, taking in the intoxicating sounds and smells of the night: the crackle of the fire, the crisp mountain air, and the sweet woodsy smell of pine. When she re-opened her eyes, she glanced about at the happy, diverse group of people sharing the evening. *There is symmetry here*, she thought. *Everyone is different yet they have one common ground, they love being here in this awe-inspiring, wonderful place*. It felt good, balanced, especially when compared to her life in the city where she often felt disconnected.

She again sat forward in her chair and extended her hands toward the warmth of the fire. Not far away she noticed Grant stacking on more wood. Taking advantage of her obscurity, she took a moment to check him out. *That is one fine-looking man*, she admitted to herself. He was tall and very nicely proportioned. He was lean and muscular, but not too muscular. She liked the way his strong forearms bulged out from under the rolled up sleeves of his blue plaid shirt. When he pushed his sun-streaked hair back from his face, she saw he had left a smudge of soot on his cheek.

Jordan rose from her chair and approached him. “Nice,” she complimented.

He turned and smiled at her, cocking his head inquisitively.

“I . . . I mean the fire,” she stammered. “That’s a *seriously* nice fire.”

“Well,” he responded. “I don’t play around; I quit school ‘cause of recess.”

Jordan looked at him, unsure if he was being serious, then laughed. “Is that why you have soot on your face?” she asked.

“Where?” he asked, wiping his chin with his shirt.

“Your cheek.”

Grant wiped his cheek on his sleeve and looked over for approval.

“You got it,” said Jordan.

“Enjoying the evening?” he asked.

“Yes,” she assured. “Very much.”

“Good. I don’t mean to rush off, but I’m apparently the go-to guy around here,” said Grant.

“Aren’t you?” asked Jordan.

“Shhh,” he motioned, looking around as he backed away. “I’ll see you tomorrow on the float trip.”

“What float trip?” she asked.

"The one Kate just signed you up for," he said, pointing across the deck to where she was talking to Colby. He was jotting something down on a clipboard.

"See you then," said Grant, smiling as he went.

See you then, she thought, watching him go.

* * * * *

The girls were all looking forward to the nice change of pace the river float offered. Early the next morning, all in good spirits, they headed down to the boathouse where they were to meet Grant.

"Another perfect day," commented Nance.

Kate, Annie and Jordan agreed. Except for the brief downpour yesterday, weather had definitely been their friend this week. Today looked just as promising.

Suddenly, Jordan froze in her tracks. Everyone stopped with her.

"What's the matter, Jordan?" Kate asked.

"Nothing," Jordan replied as she resumed walking.

The girls looked toward the boathouse where Jordan had been focused and saw the possible cause. Leaning flirtatiously over the counter talking to Grant was a tall blonde. As the girls approached from behind, all they could see was long shapely legs and layer upon layer of golden-blonde hair cascading down her back. She wore short shorts and a white tank top that complimented her perfect tan. Grant, standing behind the counter, was grinning from ear-to-ear, his muscular arms extended above his head as he gripped a low rafter. A sexy masculine stance few women can resist. Any hopes by Jordan that this girl was not pretty were dashed when she turned around, still laughing from something Grant had said. She was *absolutely* gorgeous.

Noticing their approach, Grant stepped from behind the counter to greet them, "Good morning," he said cheerfully.

"Good morning," all but Jordan responded.

"Follow me, girls, your chariot awaits," he said, bowing with his arm outstretched toward the lodge.

The girls filed past him. Jordan happened to notice the pretty blonde pick up a hoodie from the counter, the same powder-blue hoodie *she* had worn at Grant's the previous day. *Okay*, she thought, *Grant's a nice guy. Of course he has a girlfriend.*

At the lodge, four vans towing rafts awaited them along with the other guests taking the trip. Nance was happy to see Karl and his brothers were among them. They acknowledged each other with a nod and a smile.

"Good morning, everybody," said Grant. "We are your raft operators. Most of you know Colby and Tim, and this pretty lady is Krista."

Krista grinned and gave a little wave. Jordan noticed the lightweight plaid shirt she had donned over her tank top made her no less attractive. Even from her woman's view, Krista still looked as alluring as ever.

"You girls are with me," he motioned to Kate, Annie, Nance and Jordan. "Everyone else please line up in front of one of the other raft operators."

Olaf, Mikael, Viktor and Niels quickly lined up in front of Krista. Karl hesitated. He looked at Nance and shrugged then reluctantly joined his brothers. A young family and an elderly couple lined up in front of Tim while two young women lined up in front of Colby.

Krista gave Grant a pleading look.

"Okay guys—break it up," said Grant. "Olaf and Karl, you're on Colby's raft."

Olaf, always ready to seize an opportunity, puffed out his chest and grinned as he walked over to Colby's lineup. The two young women began to giggle and blush. Karl joined them, again glancing over at Nance with a smile.

Nance smiled back.

Once the vans were fully loaded, they were off to the raft landing, a thirty minute ride from the lodge. Although the river would have plenty of whitewater action, the float trip was just a relaxing scenic boat ride with a shore picnic midway. Kate and Annie always took at least one float trip every time they came up to the cabin. It was a nice break from their active pursuits.

When they reached the landing, the operators loaded coolers, blankets and an assortment of necessary gear onto the rafts. Grant had everyone put their personals in waterproof bags. Not only to keep their items safe but also due to the exuberant splashing wars that tended to break out when other rafts got too close. After a mandatory safety briefing and everyone had their life jackets on, one by one the rafts set off down the river.

Annie was excited because the protected river corridor with its natural beauty and undeveloped character offered endless photographic opportunities. And there was always plenty of wildlife to be seen. This time of year, white-tailed deer could be found feasting on the white cedar that lined the river. Plentiful berries in the area lured a diversity of large and small animals, while dams and hardwoods bore evidence to an active beaver population. Though the fast-moving water might at times make it difficult to get a good picture, the light was perfect. Annie did not mind one way or the other, she was happy just to be there, and of course—she was digital.

An hour into the float as the rafts neared a bend in the river, Grant motioned for the raft Tim was operating to go on ahead for the safety of the elderly couple as well as the family with two small children. Annie, recognizing the drill, quickly packed her camera away in her waterproof bag and picked up an oar. Kate, Nance and Jordan followed suit.

"Okay, girls," instructed Grant, "when we come around this bend, look straight ahead; you're going to see a big swirl in the water. That's where we're going to take our stand. We're going to catch them by surprise; they'll never know what hit 'em."

"Aye, Captain!" the girls chimed.

When they flew around the bend, Grant dug in with his oar and expertly spun the raft, monopolizing a small eddy. This gave them the reprieve they needed from the fast-moving water to launch their attack.

"Get ready," Grant forewarned, keeping his voice low. "I want you to give 'em all you've got. We only have a minute to soak them. Keep in mind, that is exactly what they intend to do to you. No mercy!"

"No mercy!" the girls echoed. They tapped their oars together and poised themselves for battle.

Colby's raft flew around the bend first, the fast-moving current forcing them within easy reach of Grant's raft and splashing oars. Catching them by surprise as hoped, the girls soaked Colby, Karl, Olaf and the two girls amid loud squeals and screams. Unable to catch the eddy, the water quickly pushed Colby's raft down the river with trailing shouts of revenge. Kate, Jordan, Nance and Annie, giddy with victory, celebrated with high fives.

Grant, craning to look upstream, motioned with his hand, "Okay, quiet girls."

Restraining their revelry, the girls repositioned themselves—awaiting their next victims. Krista's raft flew around the corner and again they used the element of surprise to soak her and the occupants of her boat: Viktor, Niels and Mikael. They waved their fists in the air as the current dragged them quickly away.

Grant and the girls celebrated this second victory with gleeful shouts and more high fives. All things considered, they were about as dry as they could be.

Suddenly, out of nowhere, a kayak pulled up next to them. Grant and the girls were perplexed to see old Mr. Lewis steadying it with expertise. Betty, sitting in the front of the kayak, asked in a calm even voice, "Excuse me . . . do you have any Grey Poupon?" Before anyone could register what was happening, she yelled, "Suckers!" and gleefully began blasting the raft with a water cannon.

The girls screamed as they attempted to dodge the icy water, but it was useless—everyone was saturated. Then, just as suddenly as they had appeared, Mr. Lewis caught the river flow and they disappeared down the river. Grant dug his oar in, catapulting the raft back out onto the fast-moving water, but the raft was no match for Mr. Lewis' kayak.

Ten minutes later, Grant beached the raft next to the others at the picnic site. The girls were cold and wet but still laughing. As they exited the raft, Colby greeted them and they happily accepted the towels he offered. He pointed them toward a steaming pot of coffee perking invitingly on a grate over a small fire. Nearby, propped up on sticks, was an assortment of clothes and socks in various stages of drying. As they and other guests approached the fire, Krista handed each of them a gourmet box lunch and a drink. Blankets were spread out on sunny patches of grass and everyone claimed a cozy spot to eat.

After enjoying the food, Kate, Jordan and Annie found a familiar rock perch above the shoreline where they could soak in a little sun. Kate and Jordan proceeded to have a lively debate about the term "gourmet box lunch." Jordan thought the term was an oxymoron. In her view, the words "box lunch" completely negated the word "gourmet." However, Kate thought there was no reason for this to devalue the contents. For instance, take a diamond, no matter how it is packaged—it is still a diamond.

In the meantime, Annie reached for her camera. Using her long lens she panned the area for photographs. Below she spotted Grant interacting with the young family. He had a small fishing pole and was teaching the little girl how to fish. The girl, who appeared to be about five, was squealing with delight as small fish nibbled at her line, causing the bobber to dance and dart across the shallows.

"Look, isn't Grant sweet," said Annie. "He's teaching the little girl how to fish. He really is the whole package," she mused and looked purposefully at Jordan.

Jordan, purposefully unmoved, laid back, propping her head up with her jacket. "Ahh . . . men,'" she mused, "one of life's great mysteries."

"Why do you say that?" asked Kate.

"Because that's what they are to me," she answered, "a *big* mystery, and frankly, who wants to dig."

"This is going nowhere good," said Kate, recognizing Jordan's sarcasm. She went back to reading her book.

"Personally," Annie stated, "I've contemplated a few."

"A few what?" asked Jordan.

"A few of life's mysteries."

"*Oh, really*," Jordan asked, "like what?"

Kate looked up over her book. *And here we go.*

"Well, for instance," Annie answered, "I've always wondered if flies burn their feet when they land on hot food. Like, 'Ow—Ooo,'" she demonstrated.

Kate and Jordan looked at her strangely, then, for just a moment, pondered the answer themselves.

"Or . . . ," Annie went on, shifting uncomfortably, "what kind of underwear won't ride up the crack of my a--?"

"Look at Nance," Kate conveniently interrupted. Down at the water's edge, Nance was playfully dipping her toes in the water and laughing at something Karl was saying.

Annie picked up her camera and focused. "She looks happy," she said and snapped a couple of pictures. She then scanned the busy scene below for another picture-worthy subject. "*Whoa,*" finding it, she froze her camera. "Look at Grant."

"What?" asked Kate. She picked up her binoculars to see what Annie was looking at. *"Ohhhh."*

Down below, Grant had removed his shirt and was taking a long drink of water from his canteen. Muscular and rippled in all the right places, he was a sight to behold.

"Let me see," said Jordan, pulling at the binocs.

"Poor thing," Kate joked, reluctantly handing over the glasses, "so pitiful to look at."

Jordan scanned until she found Grant standing

knee-deep in the water next to one of the rafts. She focused in just in time for him to catch her looking his way. He was chuckling as he turned his back to her and pulled on a fresh shirt.

Jordan, embarrassed for having been caught, quickly put the binoculars down. She grabbed her book and nervously began to flip through it.

"You're holding the book upside down," said Kate.

Jordan, her face pinking up, flipped the book over and continued to feign reading.

"That's my book," said Annie.

"*Whatever,*" said Jordan, tossing the book aside. She rose and headed toward an alternative route down from the perch that would not put her in Grant's immediate vicinity. "I'm going down by the water."

"Don't go that way, Jordan. It's too steep," said Kate.

"I can manage," Jordan replied then she proceeded to half skid down the hill. She settled onto a small patch of grass near the river's edge. Shaking off her thoughts, Jordan took a deep breath and released it. Nature always had a way of keeping her out of her head. She ran her fingers through the thick grass, feeling its coolness. She looked around and skyward. Soothed by the slow sway of the trees and the occasional drifts of clouds, her mind soon quieted. She leaned back and closed her eyes, tilting her head to feel the warmth of the sun on her face.

"My, my . . . little Jordy Taylor."

Recognizing the voice, Jordan quickly sat up.

"May I join you?" asked Grant.

"Sure," said Jordan, brushing the grass from her hands. "And technically, it's Stewart now."

"Oh . . . sorry," said Grant, taking a seat. "I did not ask the other day. Are you married?"

"Divorced."

"Oh, sorry . . . me, too," he responded.

"Sorry."

"How long were you married?" Grant asked.

"About fifteen years," said Jordan, flicking a leaf off her shorts. The breeze caught it and carried it to the water's edge. "Then one day he left me for greener pastures," she said, solemnly watching as the current swept the leaf away.

"Well, you know what they say about that," said Grant.

"What?" asked Jordan, her eyes still following the leaf.

"The grass is always greener till you have to mow it."

Jordan thought about it then turned toward Grant, "*Thank you.*"

"No problem," said Grant with a smile.

A brief moment of silence followed before they both began to speak in unison. They both laughed and became quiet again.

Grant ventured first, "How long has it been since you've been here?"

"Oh, gosh . . . probably close to thirty years," she surmised.

"I remember Mr. Lewis used to call you girls the Scraped Knee Gang," said Grant. "Looks like you still belong to the same club," he teased and lightly thumped her knee.

"Ow," Jordan winced, swatting at his hand.

Grant laughed. "So, are you having fun today?"

"Yes," Jordan answered.

"You're pretty good with that oar," Grant chuckled.

"Thank you," Jordan chuckled, too. After a brief quiet moment, she looked over at him and smiled, "I heard you were teaching the little girl to fish."

"Yeah, little kids are such a blast."

"That was very sweet," said Jordan.

"That's just the kind of guy I am," Grant grinned. "Besides, teach a girl to fish and she'll bring home dinner."

Jordan laughed.

"But, on a serious note," Grant added, "I love that saying: 'If you plant nature in the heart of a child, it seeds the forests of our future.'"

Jordan nodded in agreement.

Suddenly distracted, Grant glanced back toward the landing. "I've got to go," he said, rising.

Jordan glanced around to see what he was looking at. She quickly keyed in on Krista who was walking in the opposite direction. She discreetly disappeared behind a group of trees.

"Okay," Jordan said, feeling somewhat confused. She watched for a moment as he walked away. *Krista*, she thought, annoyed. *Whatever. I am not going to let it ruin this beautiful day*. She laid back in the grass, clasping her hands behind her head for support. This time she took several deep breaths, consciously clearing her mind and releasing her tension. She closed her eyes and listened to the ever-so-slight breeze that whispered through the trees. Before long, in tune with every bird chirp and every water gurgle, Jordan fell asleep.

* * * * *

Of course, Krista knew that he was following her. He

had been sending suggestive looks her way ever since they had seen each other at the boathouse that morning. She had not been completely innocent either; at the landing when he had helped to secure her raft, she made sure she was perfectly positioned when she leaned forward, allowing her breasts to peek out and entice from her tank top.

As she walked along the secret path to their private secluded meadow, the sun was coming down hard but felt good against her skin. She stopped and peeled off her flannel shirt, dropping it on a nearby rock then seductively stretched her lithe body in all directions. She could feel his eyes hungering for her from behind and her heart pounded in anticipation. When she reached the familiar grassy meadow, she was delighted to find it covered with tiny pink flowers. Consciously continuing the seduction, she loosened her hair and long golden curls cascaded down her back. She knelt down and plucked a flower, lingering for a moment as she inhaled its sweet aroma.

When she stood back up, he was suddenly upon her, gripping her shoulders from behind. He whispered in her ear, "Those are poisonous you know."

Krista quickly threw the flower down and spun around only to be caught in his arms. "Not really, if they were poisonous do you think I would do this?" he asked and playfully pushed her down into the lush grass.

She laughed and started to get up, but he quickly straddled and restrained her. She playfully squirmed beneath him only to have him hold her tighter. Soon, her futile resistance turned to ecstasy in the arms of the man she loved.

Back on their rocky perch, Kate and Annie were still enjoying the sun. Annie lazily picked up her camera and once again began to scan the area for photos. “Well . . . ,” she said, slowly setting her camera back down, “I don’t think Jordan has to worry about Krista.”

“Why?” asked Kate, looking up over her book.

“She and Colby are kind of busy over there beyond the trees,” Annie answered, nodding their way.

“You mean . . .?” asked Kate, raising her eyebrows.

“Yep,” said Annie.

* * * * *

Grant returned with two bottles of cold water only to find Jordan asleep where he’d left her twenty minutes earlier. He paused for a moment, debating whether or not he should wake her; she looked so peaceful. To him, she was every bit the beauty he remembered from their teenage years. He had a wild crush on her back then and felt a lot of those same feelings beginning to stir now. Although he found her unpredictable nature both a draw and a hindrance.

Jordan, suddenly aware of a presence, jolted awake with a loud snort.

“Now *there’s* the Jordy Taylor I remember,” Grant chuckled as he handed her a bottle of water. “Sorry to wake you, but we’re boarding in about ten minutes.”

“Okay,” Jordan said stiffly as she rose and brushed her hair away from her face. She ignored his offering of water and marched off toward the raft landing.

“Ooo-kay,” said Grant, baffled once again. He grimaced as he watched her go, the seat of her shorts plastered with mud, leaves and grass.

EIGHT

Red sky at morning . . .

It is easy to fly into a passion—anybody can do that—but to be angry with the right person and to the right extent and at the right time and with the right object and in the right way— that is not easy, and it is not everyone who can do it.

Aristotle

Annie opened her eyes to a room basked in pink light. Peaking sleepily out her bedroom window, she was awed by the sight of the sun rising below ribbons of bright red clouds. She lingered there only long enough to remember it was Jeep day.

Still in her pink flowered nightgown, she crept quietly down the hall to the kitchen and plugged in the coffeemaker. Her norm would be to wake slowly, preferably on the porch enjoying every last drop of her coffee, but today was different. Always eager for opportunities to explore new areas, she had been greatly anticipating this Jeep rental day. Although driving would be confined only to designated trails, they would be able to go much further than a day's hike would allow and offered views of the forest she had not yet seen.

Like most outings, today would include a picnic lunch so Annie set about making potato salad. Everyone seemed to love her potato salad and it was the one dish she had actually mastered. She quickly peeled some potatoes and set them on the stove to boil. From the refrigerator she retrieved the requisite vegetables, mayonnaise and a couple of hard-boiled eggs. She set them on the counter and shifted her attention to the sight and sound of fresh-brewing coffee. Aware of her tendency to become distracted, she made note of the time when the potatoes began to boil.

Annie poured a cup of much-needed coffee and sat down at the table to enjoy it. *Oh, this is sooo good*, she thought, closing her eyes. *I wonder if we have any cookies left.* Rising from the table, she spotted one lone oatmeal raisin cookie in the jar by the kitchen window. She retrieved it and enjoyed a quick bite, noticing the changing light in the yard. The sunlight was slowly awakening all the little critters and birds. She continued sipping her coffee and nibbling at her cookie, intrigued by the activity coming to life outside the window. A squirrel hopped past carrying shredded bark for a nest. A jay upturned leaves, hunting for some morning treats. House finches were playfully flitting from branch to branch. To her, house finches had one of the prettiest avian voices. She stepped out onto the porch to better hear them. She did not have the best hearing anymore and at times she found an old adage to be true: When you lose your eyesight—it pisses *you* off. When you lose your hearing—it pisses everyone else off.

Suddenly, something caught Annie's eye. It was a Zebra Longwing butterfly. In hopes of getting a closer look, she set her coffee cup down and stepped down into the yard. She stood perfectly still, her eyes following the butterfly as it swirled and looped from bush to bush. When it finally landed, Annie approached it ever so slowly. Having come surprisingly close, she watched in wonder as the butterfly sipped from a glistening dewdrop—just wishing she had her camera in hand. Within seconds the butterfly again was airborne. Annie watched with joy as the tiny acrobat circled her then quickly disappeared.

What a beautiful morning, Annie thought, feeling the rising sun caress her shoulders. As she looked about, she fantasized she could walk like a friend among the birds and the wildlife she saw. When she stretched out her arms, birds would land upon her and sing to her. Friendly butterflies would tickle her face with their soft fluttering wings and make her laugh. Deer would nudge her for affection and she would kiss their noses and tend to them like a loving mother. In the summer she would cavort with the otters in the river and follow the swans through the tall reeds, revealing their secret places. She would win the trust of and play tag with the timid fox that followed their kayaks along the shore. And in the fall, she would tussle with the bears then lay exhausted, belly-up in the thick cool grass.

"Annie," Kate called out from the cabin door.

Annie, her eyes closed and her arms extended, did not respond; she was still deep in her fantasy.

"Annie," Kate repeated louder.

"Oh!" Annie jumped, suddenly remembering the boiling pot on the stove. She ran inside the cabin, relieved to find Kate had already rescued the potatoes.

"Their okay, Annie," said Kate. "You've got to stay in the room when you're cooking," she reminded—*again*.

"I know. I'm sorry."

"What's all the commotion?" asked a groggy Jordan, Nance in tow.

"Annie's cooking," responded Kate.

"Oh," Jordan acknowledged, not giving it another thought. "Any coffee?"

"Yes," said Kate. "We should eat a little something before we go, too."

"What time do you want to leave?" asked Jordan, shuffling toward the coffeemaker.

"Well the entire loop takes four hours," answered Kate, "and if we allow a couple hours for down time," she surmised, "ten o'clock should be okay."

"Sounds good," said Jordan.

About 9:30, after completing their picnic preparations, Annie and Kate headed up to the lodge to pick up the Jeep; there was no reason to haul the cooler and stuff all that way. As they approached the vehicles, Kate asked Annie, "Which one do you want?" Although different in color, each Jeep was painted with some variation of camouflage. Kate did not have a color preference but she knew Annie would.

"The blue one," Annie immediately answered.

They entered the lodge where Colby approached them carrying the rental papers and a set of keys. Kate greeted him, but Annie did not. Instead, she grabbed a newspaper off a table and quickly buried her face in it.

Colby had Kate sign the papers and gave her a map of the designated trails. "This is the four-hour loop," he showed her on the map. "The trail is clearly marked so I know you won't have any trouble following it, Kate." He glanced over at Annie, who immediately looked up at the ceiling. "You are driving—right?" he asked uneasily.

"Yes," Kate responded, also noticing Annie's weird behavior.

"Mirror Lake is a perfect spot to picnic. It's about midway through your drive. There's a beautiful view from here," he pointed to a pull off, "and here. You *must* be back by four because we are expecting storms again later this evening. Oh," he added, handing her the keys, "cell phone coverage is sketchy; if you need to call us you may have to drive a ways before you get a signal."

"Thanks, Colby," said Kate, eyeing Annie as she bee-lined it for the door. Joining her outside, she asked, "*What is wrong with you, Annie.*"

"I saw him naked you know."

"Oh," chuckled Kate, "that's right."

Back at the cabin, provisions and gear were quickly loaded and the canvas top of the Jeep was lowered and secured. "This is going to be fun!" said Annie as she hopped up into the front passenger seat (luck of the draw). Jordan and Nance climbed in the back.

Once they found the trailhead, Jordan took over as navigator, though they found the rugged road clearly marked with signs at pivotal turns. Soon they were driving in new territory and they pulled over frequently to savor the views and allow Annie to take pictures. Wildlife was scarce while driving, likely due to the sound of the Jeep, but came alive when they stopped. Before long, steep inclines transitioned them from a landscape dominated by hardwoods into the balsam firs and red spruce of the higher elevations.

At Mirror Lake, perfectly named for its reflection of the tall trees that surrounded it, they found a sun-filtered spot and spread blankets. The picnic basket was unpacked and they enjoyed their sandwiches of roast turkey with cranberry mayonnaise and fresh sprouts on crusty rolls. Nance had made a green bean salad and tossed it with vinaigrette. Annie's potato salad and assorted crudité rounded out the meal.

After lunch, Jordan headed down to the shore of the lake. Annie grabbed a blanket and followed after her. There, Jordan, adept at skipping stones, tried to teach Annie the skill, but after twenty or so failed attempts, Annie gave up. She found a small clearing, spread her blanket and engrossed herself in cloud watching, one of her favorite pastimes. Above, plump white clouds floated by like huge parade balloons. Higher up, others resembling torn cotton were moving more quickly, abstracted by unseen winds. It was always comforting for her to watch clouds, losing herself in the moment, immersed in something so peaceful. When she was ill from chemotherapy she would watch clouds while lying on the grass in her backyard, bundled up in a blanket. On her toughest days she would close her eyes and imagine herself sleeping at God's feet, her hand touching the edge of his robe.

"I wish I could knock that chip off Jordan's shoulder," Nance commented to Kate, watching Jordan expertly skip stones on the lake. "You know, we've always been so close, like you and Annie . . . up until her relationship with Rodney began to fall apart."

"It just takes time, Nance," Kate responded. Jordan likes to think she's tough but we know the softer, loving side of her."

"She's been happier here than I've seen her in a long time," said Nance, "but then some thought comes into her mind and she's distant again—or angry. I know not to take it personally, but it's hard."

"That's all you can do," said Kate.

"Annie stays in good spirits," noted Nance, looking her way.

"Umm . . . she has to work at it," responded Kate. "She can get bogged down with troubling thoughts and worry. It's tough after having such a serious illness. But she's made a commitment to try to focus on what's important to her and to do more of the things that make her happy. Things like watching the sunset, traveling, taking pictures and spending time with friends. No matter what happens she wants to live her life to the fullest and to face the future with courage."

"That's great," said Nance.

Packing out their trash, the girls loaded into the Jeep for the next leg of the trip. An hour later, while enjoying the outstanding view from Heartbreak Ridge, Kate surprised them with slices of her excellent apple pie and a thermos full of hot coffee. To their delight, often with Kate, a trip had a culinary map as well.

Taking in the panoramic view, Annie pointed out several lakes sparkling below. Sporadic dots of orange, yellow and red trees revealed the quickly approaching change of season. Far in the distance they could see the darkening clouds of the storm Colby had warned them about, no threat at the moment. At three o'clock, with an hour left to get back to the lodge, they loaded back in the Jeep for the final segment of their trip. If they only knew how ironic their visit to Heartbreak Ridge would be, considering what was about to happen next.

The day had been good one. During the drive down they were enjoying that quiet, content, sleepy feeling that comes with the end of a perfect day—not to mention sugar overload from Kate's apple pie. Suddenly, Jordan's phone beeped.

"I thought this was a dead zone," said Kate.

"I guess not," Jordan responded, "I just got a message."

Beep, beep, beep, beep. More messages continued to roll in on Jordan's phone. She sat up straight, "Geez, I just got like five messages, I hope nothing is wrong." She flipped open her phone case and read one of them. Her mood soured immediately.

"Is everything okay?" asked Nance.

Jordan did not respond as she read message after message then snapped the phone case shut and threw it on the seat in disgust. She visibly withdrew, angrily staring out into the distance.

Kate looked at her in the rear-view mirror. "What's going on, Jordan?" she asked.

"Rodney," Jordan answered flatly.

"What about Rodney?" Kate asked.

"He's getting married."

"What! When?" asked Annie and Nance, completely in shock.

"Today."

"You're kidding," responded Kate, bringing the Jeep to a halt.

"To who?" asked Annie. She unbuckled her seatbelt and turned around to face Jordan.

"Marilee Belmont."

"*Marilee Belmont*," Nance responded with alarm. "Isn't she one of your clients?"

"Yes," answered Jordan, her eyes narrowing. "Rodney and I met her at one of his masquerade balls for charity, exactly one month before we broke up," she added with tight lips. "She was dressed as Little Bo Peep."

"This is crazy," said Annie.

"Well, she sounds like a bimbo," said Nance, "from what I already know about her."

"Yeah, like a bimbo," Annie agreed.

"Really?" Jordan responded curtly. "How does that

make me look?"

Annie blinked, not prepared for the angry response.

Beep, beep, beep, Jordan's phone sounded again. Everyone looked at the phone, but no one dared to say anything. It was obvious Jordan was not in a happy place. Each beep was like a hot nail being hammered into her brain. Kate put the Jeep in drive and they silently continued towards home.

After a few minutes, Kate, the bravest, was the first to break the silence. She offered her heartfelt sympathy, "I'm sorry, Jordan."

"No big deal," shrugged Jordan, though the tone of her voice and the anger on her face showed her *true* feelings. It was obvious to her, Rodney had wasted no time getting to the altar with Marilee.

The phone beeped several more times.

"Nothin' like friends anxious to share the good news," said Jordan sarcastically.

"Don't open them, Jordan," said Kate.

"Yeah, don't open them," Annie agreed.

"Rodney is such a jerk," said Nance.

"Yeah, a jerk," Annie concurred.

"You're better off without him, Jordan," said Kate.

"Well, that must be easy for you to say, Kate," Jordan sniped.

"What?" Kate responded in surprise.

"Your life has always been so perfect," Jordan answered smugly.

Kate stopped the Jeep again and looked at Jordan in the rearview mirror. "You're kidding, right?"

Annie unbuckled her seatbelt and again turned around

to see Jordan's face. *She can't be serious,* she thought.

"Not everyone is privy to that kind of luxury," shot Jordan.

"Bull-shit!" said Kate.

Annie, alarmed, looked over at Kate then re-buckled her seatbelt. She knew for Kate to use a bad word meant she was *really* getting pissed.

"You know, Jordan, just because I don't whine and bitch about everything like you do, doesn't mean I don't have problems," Kate shot back.

"*Oh, really,* like what?" inquired Jordan, reeking with sarcasm.

"Jordan," Nance intervened, uncomfortable with the direction their conversation had taken.

"Oh, what do you know, Nance?" snapped Jordan.

Nance scowled back, squeezing herself as far away from Jordan as she could in the confines of the Jeep.

"Like a couple of months ago," said Kate, "when I had my own brush with cancer."

"What?" quickly came the overwhelming responses. "*Cancer? When? You never told us about this!"*

Kate immediately winced and looked over at Annie. The pain she saw on her face said everything.

"Annie . . . ."

Annie again undid her seatbelt, tears welling up in her eyes.

"Annie—I'm fine. I didn't even need surgery; they just zapped me a few times with radiation."

"Let me out of the Jeep," demanded Annie.

"Annie, I didn't tell you because it was no big deal and I didn't want to upset you."

"*Stop the car!*" yelled Annie.

Kate brought the Jeep to a halt and Annie hopped out.

"Annie," said Jordan, "get back in the Jeep."

"C'mon, Annie," pleaded Nance, "the storm is coming in."

Annie ignored them and trudged ahead on the trail.

"Annie, you can't walk home," Kate called out. "I promise we'll talk about this when we get back to the cabin."

Annie did not respond, she just continued walking, tears now running down her face. Kate put the Jeep in gear and slowly followed alongside her, begging her to get back in. When Annie saw an overgrown trail veer off to the right, she took it, hoping they would not be able to follow her.

"Annie," Kate again called out, "we're not supposed to take the Jeep off the designated road." She turned the Jeep onto the overgrown trail anyways and shot an angry look at Jordan.

Ten minutes went by before they came upon a large branch blocking the trail. Annie easily hopped it and continued walking, but Kate was forced to drive the Jeep around it. Without warning, the girls screamed as both left side wheels dropped into an unseen ditch, stranding them. Kate switched gears in an attempt to free the Jeep, but with each attempt the tires only dug in deeper. Everyone carefully vacated the Jeep. Annie, muttering something in defiance, came back to help. Together they assessed the situation.

"We need a piece of wood for leverage," said Kate. Everyone, feeling stressed and nervous, quietly fanned out.

Fifteen minutes later they all arrived back at the Jeep with various scraps of wood, mostly branches, all of which were either too small or too flimsy. Having no other options they decided to try anyway. Using one of the stronger pieces, Jordan dug under the trapped tires and everyone helped wedge what they could beneath them. When ready, Kate asked Annie to start the Jeep while she, Jordan and Nance positioned themselves to push from behind. They rocked the Jeep several times in neutral, then, on the count of three, Annie dropped it into gear hoping to use the momentum. The wheels quickly broke all the branches and spun uselessly, coating Kate, Jordan and Nance with the rich dark soil that in most cases would be considered an asset to the area. Yelling and accusations ensued.

"I can't believe you drove into this ditch," Jordan shot at Kate as she futilely tried to wipe the damp dirt off her jeans.

"Well what was I supposed to do Jordan, just let Annie walk off into the wilderness?" Kate yelled back.

"You didn't put the wood under it right, Jordan," Annie accused, jumping down from the Jeep.

"Well why did you have to walk off like that?" Jordan yelled back.

"Oh, my, now we'll never make it back in time," Nance fretted, looking at her watch. "It's past four now."

"*Great.* The storm is already moving in," Kate grumbled, noting the dark clouds looming above.

"Oh, that's just perfect," added Jordan.

"*Okay!*" exclaimed Annie, oddly finding herself the voice of reason. "Jordan, do you still have a signal on your phone?"

"No."

"It's getting dark quickly," Nance said nervously, "surely Grant will come looking for us."

"*Look,*" said Annie, pointing toward a thin line of

smoke rising in the distance. "Maybe it's a cabin. It looks like this trail might lead to it."

"A cabin? Way up here? I doubt it," said Kate.

"Maybe they have a telephone," said Nance.

"Yeah right, a telephone," Jordan scoffed.

Nance scowled back at her.

With no other options, they grabbed their limited gear out of the Jeep and in cold silence began trudging up the trail. Luckily they had all brought jackets because the air was cooling considerably. Before long, a hard rain began to fall.

Finally, twenty or so minutes later, they came upon a small rustic cabin tucked among tall firs. Not charmingly rustic like the lodge, rustic like—*really old*. They shivered on the porch as Kate politely knocked several times on the door. When no one answered, they peeked in the windows and could see a fire burning, beckoning them in, but there was not a person in sight. A too-close lightning crack and a boom of thunder was the only inspiration they needed to ignore their manners and simultaneously try to squeeze through the unlocked door.

Inside, the fireplace instantly drew them in with its warmth and for several minutes they huddled around it, warming their faces and hands. Recovering, Kate and Jordan slipped out of their jackets and slowly began to take in their surroundings. Constructed of heavy wood logs, the interior walls were darkened a rich brown with age. Consisting of only one room, the cabin was sparsely furnished. There was a single bed along one wall and a minimal kitchen with a small window on another. In the center of the room was a kitchen table made of wood and four ladder-back chairs. A second taller table, hand-crafted from tree limbs stood against another wall. Old iron pots and pans hung above the kitchen sink. Running water was questionable. There certainly was no electric, considering the location and the two small lanterns that flickered on each of the tables.

Jordan's eye was drawn to a stack of books on the floor by the bed. Curiosity got the better of her and she picked one up. "Harvard Law?" she read with surprise.

Kate's attention was drawn to an old, framed photo on the tall table. "This is weird," she said, her comment drawing Jordan over. Annie and Nance were oblivious, still glued to the warmth of the fire.

"What?" asked Jordan.

"Look at this picture," said Kate.

Jordan picked it up and looked at the old sepia print. "Yeah?" she questioned.

"Remember that time when we were kids and I told a story about an old scar-faced Indian."

"Right."

"That's him."

"What do you mean that's him," responded Jordan, "I thought you made him up."

"I did . . . sort of. I mean the story just came to me, but I saw it clearly in my mind as if it had really happened." She paused in thought then continued. "The best way for me to describe it is . . . it was like a movie playing in my head, I just read the script. And look, he fits the description exactly, the scar, the patch, even the eagle feather hanging from his braids," said Kate. She picked up an old newspaper clipping from a messy pile that lay next to a large leather-bound book.

"Maybe you just thought you made it up," said Jordan. "Are you sure you never met him?"

"How could I?" responded Kate, holding up one of the clippings. "This is his obituary. It says here he died before I was even born. See, same photo." She handed the clipping to Jordan.

"This *is* weird," said Jordan with a shiver. She looked around, *What else are we going to find.*

Suddenly—Annie gasped, causing Kate and Jordan to spin around. Her mouth agape, Annie was pointing up above the fireplace mantel. Kate and Jordan quickly joined her and Nance where they still stood in front of the fire. Looking up, they were astonished to see, dulled and burnished with age—a shield. And not just any shield, it was *the* shield, identical to the one on the hand of the Great Spirit carving on the mountain. At its center was a dove with its wings spread outward in flight and on the breast of the dove was a heart.

"*It's real*," said Annie in awe.

Kate, Jordan and Nance, too, were spellbound. They stared up at it, taking in its subtle beauty. Three different metals glowed softly in the flickering light. There was the silver-grey of the shield, the gold of the dove and the gentle pink of the heart. A stamped border around its edge also glowed of gold.

"Ho-ly cow," said Nance, not believing what she was looking at.

Annie slowly reached her hand up to touch it, but a loud burst of thunder caused them all to scream and she quickly withdrew her hand. Already on edge, the girls looked at each other and nervously laughed. Annie again reached out her hand to touch the shield. Thoughts were running through her head, *Did it really hold powers? Should she even touch it; what if it is sacred?* Her hand trembled visibly as she extended it. The others, also having their own thoughts, watched wide-eyed.

BOOM! The girls screamed, grabbing on to each other in fear. The cabin door had crashed open and a gust of wind blew out the lamp on the kitchen table, darkening the room.

"Who's in here?" a man's voice questioned, its tone deep and threatening. Lightning cracked and flickered, briefly illuminating the doorway where a dark-cloaked figure stood, his face concealed under the shadow of a wide-brimmed hat.

The girls cowered. "Our-our car broke down . . . ," Kate nervously began, pulling her friends closer. Another loud boom of thunder quickly silenced her.

The ominous figure stepped toward them into the room and the girls shuffled back in fear, quickly realizing there was nowhere to go; the only door was blocked by the angry stranger. Time felt as if it was standing still as they waited to see what the man was going to do next. He turned his back to them and removed his full-length coat. Still dripping from the rain, he speared it on a peg near the door. He removed his hat—pinning it there as well.

When the man turned to face them, Kate instinctively took mental notes. *About six feet tall with a medium build. Jet black ponytail. Handsome, with familiar dark eyes, obviously of Indian descent.* She estimated he was in his mid-thirties.

To the girls' surprise, the stranger smiled. "I'm sorry, I don't get many visitors up here," he said. "My name is Jonathan Black," he added, bowing his head slightly.

The girls took a collective breath. True, one should not judge a book by its cover, but at least the initial panic was over. Kate explained about the Jeep.

Jonathan relit the lantern on the kitchen table and

motioned for them to sit. Seeing the girls were cold, he offered them warm blankets and cups of hot tea. They gladly accepted. Kate, Jordan and Nance took seats at the table while Annie sat down on the stone hearth. They watched as Jonathan set small white cups on the table then took a copper teakettle from the old iron stove and filled them with tea. He passed them around then sat down to join them.

Kate did the intros and they commiserated about the weather, but soon, curiosity took over and the girls began to ask questions.

"Are you an attorney?" asked Jordan. "I noticed the Harvard Law textbook."

"I am," Jonathan answered.

"Do you live here year-round?" asked Annie, cupping her tea with her hands for warmth.

"No," Jonathan responded. "I live in a town about an hour away from here, where my practice is. I come up here as often as I can to study, unwind, reconnect."

"Do you have a telephone?" asked Nance.

Jordan rolled her eyes.

"No, sorry," Jonathan answered. "You won't get a signal up here either, but I'm sure Grant is out looking for you."

"You *know* Grant," Kate was pleased to hear.

"Yes. He is like a brother to me."

"Jonathan, may I ask you about the old photo?" Kate ventured, nodding toward the subject that was *really* monopolizing her thoughts.

"Yes," Jonathan smiled, "That is a picture of my great-great-great-grandfather. He went by the name Eagle Sam." Rising from the table he picked up the picture and handed it to Kate who passed it around for all to see. "He was a great man," Jonathan continued. "He passed away a long time ago. I never got a chance to meet him of course, but I have heard so many wonderful stories about his life."

Jonathan picked up the large leather-bound book along with a handful of the newspaper clippings. He paused and looked around, "This was his cabin," he said proudly. "It is over a hundred years old."

"Was he the Chief?" asked Annie. "The one carved into the side of the mountain?"

"Nooo, but he was one of his closest advisors," answered Jonathan. "When the tribe was dismantled, there was a lot of confusion and many families were separated. The Chief appointed my great-great-great-grandfather to watch after the children. It was the Chief's belief that the spirits of children lit the path to happiness and one day they would make everything right again. Eagle Sam fought hard for them, instilling them with courage and insisting on an education, both for their safety and for their future."

Jonathan set the book down on the kitchen table and passed around some of the clippings. "Look at these newspaper articles; I've been collecting them for years."

Kate read one out loud. "Child Miraculously Found Alive," the headline read. "Three-year-old Tyler James," she continued, "was thought to have drowned Monday when he fell from a moving boat on a family fishing excursion. Amazingly he was found later that day on a distant shore. Tyler was dry, happy and showing no signs of distress. Doctors gave him a clean bill of health and he is at home with his family. September, 10th, 1945."

Jordan read the next one aloud. "Jamie Pearce Found.

Six-year-old Jamie Pearce who had been missing for five days was found alive yesterday, two miles from his family's campsite. John and Tess Pearce, experienced backpackers, woke up early last Tuesday and were shocked to find Jamie was not in their tent. After frantically searching for him with no success, they quickly agreed Tess should hike out to get help. A full scale search was immediately launched, but after four days the family was beginning to lose hope. Friday, Tess reluctantly returned to their home in Maine to man the phones and do whatever she could to facilitate the search from there while John maintained their campsite, hoping Jamie would somehow find his way back. Daybreak Saturday, John was awoken by what he could only describe as a flash of black and white outside his tent door and a piercing scream."

The girls looked at each other, their eye's wide. That sounded very familiar. Annie wanted to speak but instead stopped herself, tuning in as Jordan continued reading the article.

"When he emerged from his tent," Jordan read, "an eagle perched in a nearby tree flew away then perched again in a tree about thirty feet away. He grabbed his backpack, instinctively knowing he was to follow it. According to John, the eagle continued to encourage him until they emerged in a small clearing. There, he found Jamie dirty and hungry but showing no other signs of harm. July 17th, 1962."

"Child Survives Fall—Eight-Year-Old Recovers," read Kate, sorting through the clippings. "Wow, they go on and on."

"And look at all the years they span," Jonathan pointed out.

"1936, 1965, 1948—*2012*," read Kate. "There are

hundreds of clippings here. And almost every one of them mentions an eagle in one form or another," she noted, stunned by this revelation.

"We believe we had an encounter with your great-great-great-grandfather's spirit," Jordan revealed. "Tell him Kate."

"*Really?* What happened?" Jonathan asked, leaning forward with great interest. "And please, great-grandfather is fine. The long version can be a bit of a tongue twister," he smiled.

"Well, it started with a story," Kate began. "It seems your great-grandfather came to me and told me about the shield and its powers."

"Ahh, the shield," Jonathan smiled, "so you're the ones that let the cat out of the bag." His expression quickly changed. "You know people come from all over the world to see the carving and its shield. I trust you will help to keep *this* one a secret," he nodded toward the *real* one, hanging over the fireplace.

"Yes, yes, of course," they all agreed. "This place never existed."

"Annie might not be alive today if it were not for your great-grandfather," said Nance, she had been quietly listening up until now.

"All I remember," said Annie, "is I was about to fall from the ledge where the carving sits . . . and there was a flutter of black and white . . . and a scream—an eagle's scream."

"That flutter of black and white, and the eagle's scream," Jonathan noted, excitedly sorting through the articles, "it's mentioned over and over."

Just then, headlights flashed through the cabin windows and the sound of a vehicle came to a halt outside. "Grant has found you," said Jonathan, rising from the table. He stopped and turned to the girls. "There is one thing you do not know about the shield," he said. He stepped toward it where it hung over the fireplace and spread his arms wide, opening his palms. "The outspread wings of the dove, they signify unity. Without it, the tribe had nothing."

Thc girls sheepishly looked at each other, then away. It was too painful; the bitter words from earlier in the day still stung.

Outside, Grant and Colby jumped out of their vehicle, one of the other rentals, and ran through the cold rain up onto the porch. Jonathan greeted them at the door. They spoke briefly then Grant stepped into the room. "A bit off the trail, girls?" he asked, obviously agitated.

The girls winced. They rose and thanked Jonathan for his kindness then one by one ran through the rain to the Jeep. Grant, not knowing what to expect had loaded all kinds of rescue gear into the vehicle. That meant all four girls had to be uncomfortably crammed into the back. Nance sat in the back seat with Jordan and Kate wedged in between. Annie crunched up in the small available area behind them.

Grant grumbled to Colby as he slammed his door shut. "I told you Jeep rentals were a bad idea."

The long, bumpy ride home was excruciating and painfully quiet to say the least. Back at the cabin, the girls immediately retired to their separate bedrooms. What had started out as a perfect day had gone up in smoke.

That night, Jordan had a dream. She was standing once again at Mirror Lake, skipping stones. In the distance, she could see Kate further down by the shore. Jordan angrily threw a stone at her. But she regretted it immediately because even in her dream, she knew Kate was not the cause of her anger. As the stone flew through the air she followed it with her eyes. Just before it hit Kate, the stone split in two midair also striking a second person—Annie.

Nance had a dream, too. A much longer and detailed one. Hers started with the old scar-faced Indian. They were in the forest and she felt no fear as she approached him. He smiled, bowed his head slightly and swept out his arm in a gesture to welcome and to guide her. Ahead of her was a winding path lit by the warmth of tiny glowing lights. It stretched for miles over hills and into valleys—as far as her eyes could see. When she listened closely she could hear the voices and laughter of children. *Could this be the path to happiness?* Nance wondered as she began to follow it. The earth felt soft beneath her feet and as she passed the first light, a small child revealed itself. It was a little boy, joyfully zooming about with his toy airplane. She continued walking and the next light came alive as she neared it. This time it was a little girl in a painter's smock. She was thoughtfully poised at an artist's easel, contemplating her next stroke of vibrant color. Across from her was another little girl happily twirling in a pink tutu. Her calico kitten was playfully spinning with her. The next child, a boy, wore a white doctor's coat. He had a stethoscope pressed against the chest of a playful pup intent on licking his face. "Now stay still, Sport," said the little boy, trying to be serious. "Look at me, Nance!" a girl's voice called out. Nance spun around to see who had called her by name. It was young Kate, dangling upside down from a nearby tree. She must have been about eight or nine years old. Nance enthusiastically waved back at her. Compelled to continue on her way, children appeared again and again—a little boy playing a guitar—a little girl in an apron, stirring a bowl of batter. *Click . . . click-click-click.* Nance looked to her right, attracted by the sound. There was young Annie, bent over photographing a tiny flower. Upon seeing Nance, Annie stood up, laughed and waved. Young Jordan was next, happily swinging on a rope that hung from a tree. She grinned at Nance and pointed to the other side of the path. There, was yet another little girl, looking into a mirror and giggling as she rolled her long dark hair onto big pink curlers. She wore a purple sea serpent life preserver around her waist. It was herself.

Neither Kate nor Annie had slept well and both were up in the wee hours of the morning. Looking out the kitchen window together, they were glad to see the rains had stopped. The only evidence left behind were shallow pools of mud. The bond between Kate and Annie established over many years ran deep, so discussion about the previous day came easily and gently.

"You didn't call because you think I am weak," expressed Annie.

"That's not true," responded Kate.

"You know, I took care of my parents for 14 years," said Annie, "you can't do that if you are weak. I fought their battles daily and got the best care I could find for them."

"I know, Annie," said Kate, "and you did a great job. I saw everything you went through with them. I don't think you're weak—really."

"Well why didn't you tell me?" asked Annie. "I could have been there for you, like you have been there for me all these years."

"I just didn't want to make a bigger deal out of it than it was," Kate answered. "I would have let you know had it been more serious. I have my own way of dealing with things; you should know that by now."

Annie nodded. She understood and trusted her friend was telling the truth. That was all it took for them to clear the air. However, it would not clear so easily with the rest of the crew.

Jordan stumbled into the kitchen where they sat and grumbled a barely audible, "Good morning." She poured a cup of coffee and continued out onto the porch.

Nance shuffled in next, her mood uncharacteristically subdued. She also poured a cup of coffee and Kate and Annie watched *her* step onto the porch. Noticing Jordan there, she proceeded to the opposite end, plopped down into a chair and buried herself in a quilt.

"I'm not going to be able to take another day like this," Kate said to Annie, "much less the rest of our vacation."

"Me, neither," said Annie. "What are we going to do?"

"Let's just go out there and be ourselves," said Kate. "I'm not holding a grudge; I know Jordan was just having a bad day."

"Okay."

Taking their coffees with them, they joined Nance and Jordan on the porch. Kate and Annie attempted to break the ice with the usual morning chatter but found both Nance and Jordan unresponsive, still sulking from the day before. Eventually, talk came to a complete standstill.

Within minutes, Annie declared she could take the silence no longer and stomped off the porch. *This* caught

Jordan and Nance's attention though neither made any effort to stop her. However, when Annie slipped butt first into a puddle, Kate saw both of them restrain a giggle.

Concerned for Annie, Kate ran down the steps to see if she was okay. She knelt down next to her, teetering on her toes to avoid the thick sludge, almost losing her balance.

A mischievous look came across Annie's face. She reached out with one finger and gently nudged. This was all it took for Kate to plop onto *her* rear in the mud.

This time Nance and Jordan could not help but burst out laughing.

"You brat," Kate said to Annie. Annoyed by the laughter coming from the porch-side peanut gallery, she leaned in and whispered, "Play along."

Annie caught her drift.

Kate put both hands behind her and wailed, *"Oww, my back."*

Annie looked down and noticed Kate's hands were discreetly gathering mud. She raised her eyebrows to confirm the message she thought she was getting.

Kate nodded slightly and murmured, "Don't hit the quilts." She moaned again, "*Owww—oooo.*"

"Are you okay?" Nance stood up, concerned. She and Jordan set their coffees down and rushed towards Kate.

Splat. Kate hit Jordan's pajama shirt with a handful of mud. Annie simultaneously hit Nance with hers, watching with glee as the gooey mess splattered up onto Nance's chin. Now it was Kate and Annie's turn to laugh. They scrambled to get up, expecting a full retaliation.

Nance looked at Jordan then at Kate and Annie in disbelief. "*Really?*" she asked.

Jordan, already *in it*, picked up her own pile of mud and glopped it on Nance's shoulder.

"Oh, no you didn't," said Nance, pushing Jordan down into a puddle.

Everyone grabbed handfuls of mud and it began flying everywhere amidst screams and laughter.

Splat—gush—glop.

Minutes later, when Grant and the Swedes came along on their morning hike, the girls were so plastered with mud you could not tell who was whom.

"I implore you gentleman, just keep on walking," Grant advised, keeping his distance.

Splat. Someone hit Grant on the back with a mud ball. He stopped abruptly. The Swedes looked nervous, unsure of what would happen next. Grant raised one eyebrow, composed himself and without looking back continued walking away.

Splat. Jordan hit him with another.

"*Okay that's it!*" Grant yelled, lunging toward a puddle for a handful of pay-back.

The girls screamed and scrambled behind each other for cover.

It took both Olaf and Karl to restrain Grant and the men finally continued on their way. Grant, his fist held high in the air, called out a warning, "Revenge is sweet ladies, revenge is sweet."

Spent with laughter and energy, the girls pulled themselves together and headed for the cabin. "Oh, no," said Kate, "outdoor shower—I don't care how cold the water is."

NINE
All Growed Up

We did not change as we grew older, we just became more clearly ourselves.
Lynn Hall

"I *love* boxing!" said Jordan excitedly as she bounced around Nance like a new puppy. They were on the path back to Kate's cabin after a rousing afternoon at Betty's.

Nance, doing a slow jog, responded with considerably less enthusiasm, "Uh-huh."

"What a great stress reliever," Jordan continued, "I can't wait to do it again."

"Great," said Nance, *just great.*

As they approached the cabin, Kate and Annie stepped down from the porch to greet them. "How was it?" asked Kate. It was so good to see Jordan and Nance's friendship back on track.

"*Fantastic!*" raved Jordan. "I think we should all do it together."

"Really?" Kate asked.

From behind Jordan, Nance was motioning a big, silent, *"No!"* Jordan had shown *way* too much enthusiasm when punching the bag. Even Betty had been impressed.

"Don't you think, Nance?" Jordan asked, turning to face her.

"Oh, uh, yes," Nance answered.

"Annie and I were thinking about dinner at the lodge tonight. Are you guys hungry?" asked Kate.

"Sounds great," responded Jordan, bounding up the steps and through the door. "I just need a few minutes."

"Me, too," said Nance, coming up the steps.

"What's up?" Kate discreetly asked.

Nance responded with a wide-eyed look and mouthed the word, "*Cra-zy.*"

Kate and Annie got the message. They knew it was only a matter of time before all Jordan's pent up anger came out. This was a good thing—maybe.

At the lodge, they opted to eat at the Old Tyme Diner. It was always fun to sit at the counter and swap stories with kindred travelers. And of course, no dinner was complete without a parfait glassful of the diner's homemade ice cream. Tonight's flavor was Blueberry Swirl. Afterward, they all ordered coffees *to go* and settled into a cozy nook by the fireplace, the inviting sounds of the fire again a welcome friend.

When Annie saw Grant come up the lodge stairwell, she noticed Jordan's eyes were following him as he crossed the room and entered the Bistro. It was obvious to Annie that Jordan felt something for Grant. She wanted to tell her that Krista was involved with Colby, but before she had a chance, Jordan got up and scurried away. She saw her duck into one of the two high-back chairs facing the window.

"Hello, Jordan."

"Oh! Judy—gosh you scared me to death," said Jordan.

Judy noticed Jordan peek around the chair and asked, "Are you hiding from someone?"

"No . . . well . . . yes," she admitted in a low voice.

After a brief pause, Judy set down her book and asked, "How long have you been attracted to Grant?"

"What? Oh, no, I'm not attracted to Grant," said

Jordan. But she could see Judy was giving her a you-can't-fool-me look and she sighed. "The last thing I need in my life is a man," she declared, her brow furrowing.

"Okay," Judy responded calmly.

"You know, Judy, I can say I've gotten *way* more out of owning my own business than I ever have from a relationship," Jordan added.

"And this makes you angry?" Judy questioned.

"Shouldn't it?" Jordan stated more than asked.

"Well, not really, if you are speaking of the confidence, self-esteem and satisfaction that come with a sense of accomplishment," said Judy. "Were you expecting to get that from another person?"

"All I know is, when I apply myself at work I get results. I can't say the same for my relationships," said Jordan.

"Okay," Judy responded.

"Plus," Jordan continued, "I was devastated when my last relationship ended. I don't want to feel that kind of pain again."

"Well . . . there are definitely no guarantees," said Judy.

Jordan was quiet for a moment then posed a question, "Let me ask you this, Judy . . . if I did decide—*and I'm not saying I will,* but if I did decide I want to try a relationship again, how will I know if a guy is normal?"

Judy chuckled. "First of all Jordan, there is no such thing as normal. *Everyone* comes with their very own *as-is* tag. But," she continued, "I have found most men will tell you who they are. Unfortunately, many women tend to ignore what they say. Did you have any clues to this in the beginning of your last relationship?"

Jordan thought for a minute then said, "Well . . . now that you mention it, I remember on my first date with Rodney I asked him why he had not been in a long-term relationship. His response made me cringe. He said that it was because he was selfish and that he did not like the emotional garbage that came with relationships."

"Wow," responded Judy. Not many revelations made her cringe at this age, but this one sure did.

Jordan sensed this and suddenly the reality of those words made her feel sick to her stomach.

"Sorry," said Judy. "I'm not being judgmental. So what brought the relationship to an end?" she asked.

"As time went by, my feelings for him were getting stronger," answered Jordan, "but even though he was attentive, I could tell he was not in love with me."

"He may indeed have loved you as much as he was *able* to love someone, but he was obviously incapable of a deeper commitment," observed Judy.

"Maybe so, but it was tormenting me and I wanted out," said Jordan, "but fear kept me trapped; I was too scared to run and I was too scared to stay. It was awful."

"Fear of what?" asked Judy.

"Fear of being alone, fear of the unknown," answered Jordan.

"What did you do?" Judy asked.

"Well, he called one evening like he did every evening, only on this particular night he was out of town. Although it was a huge struggle for me to formulate the words, I told him that I was falling in love with him, which was true. He seemed happy about it. At the end of the call he said he would talk to me the next day as usual, but then . . . he never called."

"Ever?" asked Judy.

"Ever," frowned Jordan.

"Did you try to call him?"

"No. You see . . . I knew if he heard the word *love* he would run," said Jordan, "and that's exactly what he did."

"That must have been difficult," said Judy.

"Very."

Judy reflected for a moment then said, "Well, Jordan, as I said there are no guarantees you won't get hurt again if you enter into a new relationship. But I can tell you, if you look objectively at the person you are getting involved with, you can make smarter choices. Listen to him when he tells you who he is. Get to know him before you make a major commitment. How does he live his life? Are there any extremes or red flags? Does he love adventure? Great! Just make sure he doesn't rob banks. A sense of humor? Wonderful! As long as it is not at the expense of others."

Jordan nodded her head.

"And more important," Judy added, "is the life he lives compatible with how you want to live yours?"

Jordan sat for a moment soaking in what Judy said. "Thanks, Judy, that makes a lot of sense." Feeling lighter, Jordan rose from the chair and extended her hand, "The girls are probably wondering where I am. See you later?"

"Of course," Judy smiled and momentarily took her hand. As Jordan walked away she settled back in to read her book.

"Hey," said Jordan as she approached the girls, still sitting by the fireplace. "Sorry I disappeared like that, I was talking to Judy."

"No problem," said Kate. "We were just heading out

on the deck. Coming?"

"Okay," said Jordan. She glanced quickly about the lodge and noticed Grant speaking to some guests near the stairwell. Their eyes met and he smiled hesitantly. Jordan looked back at the girls and opened her mouth to speak.

Kate beat her to the punch, "Go . . . we'll be outside."

Jordan smiled appreciatively and turned, only to find Grant was no longer there.

"He went downstairs," said Annie with a smile.

"Thanks, Annie," said Jordan.

At the base of the stairs, Jordan stopped and looked around the busy lobby, but, no Grant. She checked the News Stand, but he was not in there either. Before leaving she reached in the cooler for bottled water and approached the counter to pay. Amazingly, she recognized the elderly gentleman working the register.

"Aren't you Mr. Jenkins?" she asked.

"Why, yes," he answered with a smile. "Do I know you?" he asked, peering through his bifocals.

"I used to come here as a child," answered Jordan. "I remember you. Have you been working here all this time?" she asked.

"Yes, I have," he responded. "The Kingsley's have been very good to me. We're like family here," he added with a twinkle in his eyes.

"That's really nice," said Jordan. "I was looking for Grant, have you seen him recently?"

"You just missed him," he answered, pointing toward the lodge entrance.

"Thank you," said Jordan, turning to go.

"Fine fella that Grant," Mr. Jenkins called out.

Jordan turned around and grinned, "Yes—thank you."

Outside she found Grant leaning against one of the stone pillars. He was gazing up at the night sky through the open canopy of tall pines.

"Hey," said Jordan as she approached him.

Grant looked at her and smiled, "Hey."

"Peace offering," said Jordan as she handed him one of her bottled waters.

He took the bottle from her hand, "Thank you." He looked back up at the sky. "Look at all those stars," he commented. "After all these years it still blows my mind."

Jordan looked up and admired them, too. "Beautiful." After a moment, she began, "Grant . . . I wanted to say I'm sorry for the way I've acted lately. Please don't take it personally."

"Okay," Grant responded. He looked at her and waited for her to say something more, but she didn't. "Listen, I'm working on some pottery pieces tomorrow, would you like to come by?"

"Yes, I'd love to," Jordan answered. She felt a surge of excitement about it, but then, she remembered Krista. "Are you sure your girlfriend won't mind?"

"Girlfriend?" Grant asked. "What girlfriend?"

"Krista."

"*Krista?*"

"Yes, you two seem . . . well . . . close," said Jordan.

"We *are* close," responded Grant, "she's my cousin and soon to be married to Colby."

"*Oh,*" Jordan's face flushed with embarrassment.

Grant grinned at her, "You have no idea, do you?"

"About what?" asked Jordan.

"I had such a major crush on you when we were kids."

Jordan blushed. "I hope I'm not a disappointment," she said quietly, looking down at the ground.

Grant lifted her chin and looked into her eyes, "Not one bit."

"Grant," Colby called from the lodge entrance, "they need you at the registration desk."

"Okay," Grant acknowledged. "Duty calls, my dear," he said. "Ten o'clock tomorrow morning good for you?"

"Sure," responded Jordan.

"Great. See you then."

See you then, she thought, watching him go.

* * * * *

The next morning, Kate and Annie were still wrapped up in quilts on the porch when Jordan once again flew past them and down the steps. "Morning," she called out as she trotted away.

"Where are you going?" Kate asked.

Jordan turned to face them, a huge smile on her face, "Grant's giving me pottery lessons."

"Oh, is that what they call it these days?" Kate teased.

"Very funny," said Jordan.

"I could use some pottery lessons," Annie called out.

Jordan laughed and continued on her way.

Kate looked seriously at Annie, "I think we need an intervention; she's way too happy lately."

"Morning," Nance said cheerfully, flying out the door and down the steps. "I'm off to Betty's."

"Look," Annie mused, "they all growed up."

"'Bout time," said Kate.

Annie snuggled back into her chair and took a sip of her coffee. Though a tad chilly, it was a beautiful sunny day and the lake was perfectly calm.

Kate looked at Annie and asked, "Kayaking?"

"Uh . . . ye-ah," answered Annie, hopping up from her chair.

They quickly packed a few essentials, dragged their kayaks down to the shore and shoved off. Their favorite route took them past the lodge along the shore of the lake to a waterfall that cascaded off a steep granite cliff. It would take roughly three hours to complete the trip at a leisurely pace.

The weather continued to cooperate perfectly as pure white clouds floated in startling contrast across a deep blue sky. When they came around the bend of the lake, the larger mountains came into view. No matter how many times they experienced that first glimpse of the mountains, they always found it breathtaking.

Gliding effortlessly along in their kayaks, the girls passed the willows where Nance and Betty first met, their long sweeping branches moved by the smallest whispers of wind. Sunlight filtering through their tall branches dappled the water with light.

Nearby, an osprey perched on an old tree limb, spread its wings and lifted off. It returned moments later at breakneck speed, diving into the water and snagging a fish. Then, shaking the water from its wings in midair, it returned to his original perch to dine.

Leaving the more populated area of the lodge and cabins behind, Kate and Annie could feel the forest become more intimate and more wildlife began to appear. When they paddled past their swimming hole, a small red fox appeared and took interest. He followed them for a good while along the shore and then just as quickly disappeared. A few minutes later they spotted a bull moose foraging the edible roots below the surface of the water. Keeping their distance, they steadied their kayaks and watched in awe. It was not every trip they were this fortunate, but the rut would be beginning soon and large bulls were becoming more visible. When he lifted his head, water cascaded from his massive antlers. Chewing away, he vaguely acknowledged them then went back to the business at hand. This is why Kate and Annie came here. Nature, with its way of melting time and troubles away, washed the windows of their souls. They were not visitors here; they were a part of it.

They continued to paddle north past a stand of tall birch trees already turning a deep golden yellow. The water reflecting on their bright white trunks gave them an ethereal glow—light begat light.

The route began to narrow at their destination where a waterfall plummeted from fifty feet above. It bounced off several large boulders before uniting with the lake. The water pushed their kayaks hard as they maneuvered into one of the many swirling eddies created by the flow. They lingered there and enjoyed the welcoming fine mist that fell upon their faces.

An eagle, keeping close tabs on them, spread its great wings and took off from a nearby perch. Annie pointed and watched as it soared ever higher above them. She imagined its bird's-eye-view of the area. From her own experience, she knew that a river fed this waterfall after winding its way through a rock strewn meadow. The meadow, a favorite hiking area for birders and photographers, increasingly attracted botanists doing fieldwork due to its endless list of indigenous plants. Along the river's shore were designated camping areas hosting those looking for outdoor fun and adventure. She imagined on a beautiful day like today, the river would be full of fly fishermen and picnic tables would be occupied with hungry campers. The granite cliffs loomed beyond, offering climbing routes for both novice and experienced climbers. She marveled at the thought, that nature, in its infinite vastness and variety, offered so many opportunities to tailor one's experience into one that has a personal meaning; to be enjoyed in one's own way. *At the very least, it's a cheap psychiatrist,* she mused. No matter how negative a path her thoughts or memories might take her, nature always beckoned her back.

"Annie," Kate called out again.

Annie turned to face her. The first time, lost in thought, she had not heard Kate. Not to mention the roar of the waterfall cascading nearby.

"Are you ready to head back?" asked Kate.

"Yes," Annie answered, "ready when you are."

They maneuvered their kayaks to the edge of the eddy, enjoying the slingshot effect this gave them as they re-entered the mainstream. With the waterfall behind them, they would barely have to use the oars until they merged completely with the main body of the lake. They were quiet as they continued on their way. The only sound was the steady *dip-swish* of their oars. They did not need to speak; nature had already spoken volumes.

* * * * *

"Get him Viktor!" his brothers called out as he dodged

jabs from Olaf's boxing glove.

"Karl, maybe this wasn't such a good idea," Nance said nervously from their ringside perch. "I don't want anyone to get hurt."

"No worries, Nance. Olaf is all talk," Karl assured.

"Oooo," Nance winced, watching Viktor take another blow. She glanced at Betty who was taking her coaching job quite seriously. She even looked the part dressed in a sporty black-and-white tracksuit and red high-top sneakers. A whistle hung around her neck which she used when she wanted to call off a match.

"Left jab—block," Betty shouted to Viktor who was definitely the underdog of the match. "Move in on him," she instructed, exuberantly hopping to and fro.

The match continued for a while longer until Viktor took a rather hard hit to the right side of his padded helmet. He stumbled, dazed by the unexpected blow.

Betty blew the whistle.

"Olaf—not so hard," Karl reprimanded.

Olaf, unfazed by the comment, continued bouncing about, keeping his energy up for his next conquest.

Niles untied Viktor's gloves and Viktor angrily threw one at Olaf. Storming out of the ring, he muttered something in Swedish. Olaf, having successfully dodged the glove, teased him then turned back around to meet his next challenger. Expecting to find Mikael standing there, he laughed when he looked down to find Betty squaring off, her red-gloved dukes raised menacingly up at him. Mikael quickly hit the bell, signaling the start of the match. This caught Olaf off guard and Betty took full advantage. She gave him several swift punches in the stomach and he doubled over to the delight of his brothers. Olaf quickly recovered only to find Betty poised for her next punch. He hesitated; he couldn't retaliate against an eighty-three-year-old woman. Instead he made light of the situation. He playfully placed his gloved hand on Betty's helmet. This kept her just far enough away that her spirited swings could not reach him.

Olaf's actions only served to aggravate Betty and she stepped back from his grip to plan her next move. "Oh, the hell with it," she said and promptly kicked him in the shin.

"Ow, ow, ow," yelped Olaf, holding up his leg in pain, the same leg with the still sore toe.

Betty pretended to spit and left the ring wearing a satisfied grin. The brothers broke into laughter.

Olaf, looking to redeem himself, boldly challenged the one he knew to be his toughest competitor—Karl.

"No, Olaf," said Karl, "I don't want to fight you." He knew Olaf all too well when he was in this kind of mood—*especially* when a pretty woman was present.

Nance looked nervously over as she untied Betty's gloves.

For several minutes, Olaf danced around the ring and continued to taunt Karl. Finally, Karl, though shaking his head in disagreement, put on the gloves and helmet.

Mikael rang the bell and the two men squared off. They circled round and round, each one trying to psyche the other out. Olaf, grinning with confidence, threw the first punch at Karl and missed. They circled each other again, glaring, glove to glove, eye to eye. Olaf threw another punch and again—missed.

From the sidelines, the younger brothers rooted, "Teach him a lesson, Karl. Wipe that grin off his face!"

Nance bit her nails as she watched from her perch. Betty watched with more enthusiasm, nothing wrong in her book with a little friendly competition.

Olaf was about to throw another punch, but Karl swung first and caught him on the chin with a right jab. Olaf promptly dropped to the ground.

Betty blew the whistle.

It took a moment for Olaf to recuperate and he teetered when he stood up. Karl and his brothers gathered around him and made sure that he was okay. Olaf shrugged, chalking it up to luck. He was good-natured about it knowing that at times he could be his own worst enemy. Nance sensed that the camaraderie between the brothers was far more important than who had won or lost. She liked that.

Betty called it a day and after the boys left she invited Nance in for a cup of tea. Nance accepted her offer and followed her into the cabin.

"Karl is sweet on you," Betty commented as she poured two cups of Earl Grey.

"Do you think?" Nance asked, liking the thought. "I can't help but think I should be more entertaining."

"You're doing just fine," Betty assured, joining Nance at the table. "*He's* enjoying entertaining *you*."

"Maybe I need some good jokes," said Nance.

"Ha! Don't waste your time. A man will only think you have a sense of humor if *you* laugh at *his* jokes. A man needs a job to be happy, Nance, why take that away from him? Did you see that big grin on his face when he brought you out a glass of iced tea? It was as if he had grown the tea leaves himself. Besides, how are you going to get to know a man if you don't let him *do* for you?"

"I don't know," Nance responded, "I'm not really used to a man *doing* for me. It's usually me *doing* for them."

"How's that working out for you?" asked Betty.

"Not so good," Nance frowned.

"Look . . . you've talked about wanting to be a *new you*," said Betty, "today is as good a day as any to start. Become the person you want to be; do what you love and I promise everything else will fall into place. When you meet the right man, let him be the icing on the cake."

"Only problem is, Betty," said Nance, "I'm not sure who the *new me* is going to be."

"All the more reason to take it slow, Nance," said Betty. "For now, just enjoy the ride."

Nance sipped her tea thoughtfully. "Thanks, Betty."

"For what?"

"For being such a great friend."

"Awww," Betty smiled. She reached across the table and patted Nance's hand. "You're most welcome."

* * * * *

"Morning," Jordan greeted as she walked through the open door of Grant's studio. Ever since the night before, she had greatly anticipated this time with Grant. She felt both excited and nervous. The flutters of butterflies in her stomach were testimony to that.

"Good morning, Sunshine," Grant grinned.

"Am I too early?" Jordan asked, removing her jacket.

"Nope. Perfect timing, I was just beginning to glaze this, if I must say so myself—*spectacular* vase."

Jordan dropped her jacket on a chair and approached

the workbench. "Wow, that is beautiful," she agreed, admiring the tall cayenne-colored vase that stood on a turntable. Its shape was simple, but Jordan knew it was Grant's use of colorful glazes that would bring it to life.

"Coffee?" he asked, lifting a thermos.

"Sure." Jordan watched as Grant poured the steaming coffee into a mug then added just the right amount of cream and sugar. *He remembered*, she thought. As he handed her the coffee, her butterflies took wing and she rambled, "I hope I'm not intruding. I've always been fascinated by your work. I probably go to all your exhibits in New York." Immediately she felt silly. *I sounded like a schoolgirl*, she thought.

"Well come on over," said Grant as he rolled up his shirtsleeves, "you've got a backstage pass." He pulled a stool over for Jordan near the workbench and she settled in.

Though it was chilly out that morning, the studio felt warm and cozy even with the door open. A small wood burning stove on one wall contributed to that. Jordan took a sip of her coffee and watched as Grant moved about the studio. "Mmmm, delicious," she commented. He turned and smiled. She awkwardly motioned at her coffee. He chuckled and went about mixing the glazes.

"I don't want to overmix the colors," he commented as he poured from several different containers into small glass bowls.

It amazed Jordan to watch Grant's big strong hands translate into such creativity. As he worked, she found her eyes following his muscular arms up to his broad shoulders. *And don't you look dangerously handsome today*, she thought. Her mind drifted, visualizing once again the sight of him without his shirt. She had to force herself to refocus on the glazes, but when he leaned over to search a lower shelf for another bowl she could not help but notice his perfectly filled out jeans. *Geez,* she thought, averting her eyes, *get your mind out of the gutter.*

Grant returned to the workbench and Jordan continued to watch with great interest as he dipped his brush into a bowl of deep blue glaze then confidently set the brush to the rim of the vase. It was fascinating to watch as the liquid slowly dripped and flowed along the curves of the vase. He then picked up a second bowl of glaze, this time an earthy green. Again he set the brush to the rim of the vase and she watched as the green glaze melded with the blue but mostly stayed true to its own color.

Curious, Jordan asked, "How is it the green color maintains its own integrity?"

"Uh . . . ," Grant gave her a puzzled look, "I hate to tell you this but I am not as intelligent as I appear."

Jordan laughed.

When a third color was added, a warm glittery gold, Grant expertly tilted and turned the vase, causing the colors to swirl beautifully. *Almost sensuously*, thought Jordan. She found herself becoming increasingly aware of Grant's presence next to her as he continued his work. He was so close she could practically feel the warmth of his body. He smelled good, too, a smell that awoke something deep inside of her. When his long hair fell forward, she instinctively wanted to reach up and brush it back but chose to restrain herself from what had become in her mind, an intimate gesture. *Snap out of it,* she silently reprimanded herself again. She wriggled on her stool and regained her composure, but as she continued to watch she began to feel very nervous. It had been a long time since she allowed herself to enjoy the physical presence of a man.

Grant glanced over at Jordan. He could sense her uneasiness. Unsure of what had triggered it, he offered her the paintbrush. "Here, give it a shot."

"I-I can't," Jordan shook her head, "my hand is not steady enough."

"Sure you can," said Grant, gently pulling her up from the stool. He stood behind her and placed his hand over hers to help steady the brush against the rim of the vase. "Just turn the vase very slowly," he said helpfully, his lips now very close to Jordan's ear. "Let the glaze follow its own path."

"Okay," Jordan responded.

Together they placed the tip of the brush on the rim and she watched as the gold glaze dripped luxuriously down the curvature of the vase. It was captivating and again she found it impossible for her thoughts not to wander. She could feel the warmth of Grant's skin as his strong forearm pressed against her arm and how nicely his hand enveloped hers. Suddenly, she became keenly aware of her body responding to Grant. It unnerved her and she abruptly pushed away from the workbench, knocking over the stool. Grant barely caught the brush as he stepped back in complete surprise.

"I . . . I've got to go," Jordan stammered and began searching the room for her jacket.

"What is your problem?" Grant asked, again frustrated by Jordan's fluctuating moods. He watched as she darted about the room.

"It's none of your business," said Jordan, feeling her emotions rise.

"Look," Grant responded, his emotions rising, too, "I

don't know who hurt you, but I am not that guy."

Jordan yelled back, "You don't understand!"

"Try me," challenged Grant, setting the brush down.

"Okay," Jordan glared, "what is the worst thing that could happen to you when you tell someone you love them?"

"I don't know," Grant shrugged.

"He never even called me back!" yelled Jordan as tears began to stream down her cheeks.

Grant stood there, stunned at first, but his emotions were now in play, too. "Do you think you're the only one that's ever been hurt in a relationship?" he asked. "I had my heart broken a couple of years ago and when she left she took my damn dog with her. Sure, I was angry for a while, but I decided I wasn't going to let it ruin my life or keep me from giving the *right* person a chance."

Jordan, momentarily taken aback, stared at Grant. Softened by his words, she looked down at the floor and in a much quieter voice said, "And that's not all."

"What?" asked Grant, still on edge.

"I," said Jordan, cautiously, "I'm beginning to have feelings for you."

"What did you say?" asked Grant, unsure that he heard what he thought he had heard.

"I'm beginning to have feelings for you," Jordan repeated, slightly louder. "And it's terrifying me!" She looked up at Grant, her face full of anguish, preparing for the worst.

Grant rubbed his chin, feigning deep contemplation. He did hear what he thought he had heard. "Ummm . . . I'll get back to you on that."

"You jerk!" Jordan exclaimed. She pushed Grant aside and stormed toward the door.

"*I was kidding*," responded Grant, trying to block her way.

"Where is my jacket?" Jordan asked angrily.

"Calm down . . . here's your jacket," said Grant, picking it up off the chair.

When Jordan stepped toward it, he grabbed her, pulling her close. She tried to push him away, but the more she resisted the tighter he held her. Soon, laughter stole her strength and she relaxed into the comfort of his enveloping arms. She surrendered to her emotions and rested her forehead against his chest, her tension melting away. When she looked up into his smiling face he pressed his soft lips sweetly against hers. *Oh, yes,* she thought, drifting. *If you can't stop love from happening—why fight it?*

* * * * *

Nance and Jordan both arrived back at the cabin around two and found the "Gone kayaking" note on the table from Kate and Annie.

"You want some coffee, Nance?" Jordan asked.

"Sure," Nance answered and watched as Jordan happily fluttered about the kitchen. The invite had surprised her. After all, the last time they were alone together was the airplane trip and they did not exactly *kumbaya*.

"Cookie or muffin?" Jordan asked.

"Cookie," Nance responded, taking a seat at the kitchen table.

Jordan took two large freshly-baked chocolate chip cookies from the jar. Cradling them in napkins, she handed one to Nance. As she stirred cream and sugar into the steaming cups of coffee she began to hum.

Nance eyed her suspiciously. *Why is she so happy?*

"Let's sit on the porch and watch for Kate and Annie," Jordan suggested.

"Okay," said Nance, following her out to the porch. They settled into the comfortable old chairs.

"Isn't it a beautiful day?" Jordan smiled.

"Oh, yes," said Nance, dreamily looking out at the lake. Her cheeks blushed with thoughts of Karl.

Jordan eyed her suspiciously.

Nance looked back at her with squinted eyes.

"*Did you have sex?*" Jordan asked accusingly.

"*No,*" Nance responded in defense. "Did you?"

"*No*," said Jordan.

Silence.

"Can't say I wouldn't like to," Jordan admitted and they both began to laugh.

"I'm with you on that one," Nance agreed.

They quietly sipped their coffees, then, after a moment, Nance became serious. "Jordan, can we talk about something?" she asked.

"Anything," said Jordan, setting down her coffee. She folded her hands in her lap and gave Nance her full attention.

"I know in recent times we have had some disagreements," Nance began.

"Nance," Jordan interrupted, "I'm sorry, I know I've said some mean things lately. I wasn't angry at you, I was just . . . well . . . angry."

Nance nodded, "It's okay, I knew it wasn't personal."

"I hope so," said Jordan. "You're my best bud."

Nance smiled and continued. "Do you remember when

I was volunteering at that consignment store benefiting the homeless?"

"Yes."

"Well, there was this lady that consigned her clothing who was never happy with the amount of money she made. Every month she came in to check her account and even if it was a big payout, she would be nasty to me. It was very upsetting and I had to bite my tongue at the abuse. Then one day her husband brought in *all* of her clothing for the shop to sell."

"All of it?" Jordan questioned.

"Yes," Nance answered. "Her husband told me she had killed herself."

"Oh, wow, really?"

"Yes. It was then I realized that she must have been miserable," Nance continued, "I just happen to be the person in her sights that day. I know it's not always personal."

"Right," said Jordan, nodding her head.

"But that's not really what I want to talk about," said Nance. "What I want to talk about is, it's great that we have both met wonderful men, but I think we are both very vulnerable right now."

"I agree," said Jordan. "I've been giving it a lot of thought, too."

"We can't continue making the same mistakes over and over," said Nance.

"Maybe we need a game plan," suggested Jordan. Too bad there's not a Penis God Support Group."

Nance laughed, "I was just picturing the hors d'oeuvres."

Jordan laughed, "Just think, we could have annual

hotdog roasts."

"Yeah, and give out Big Wienie awards," chuckled Nance.

"Boy we could write the handbook on this subject," said Jordan.

"Yes, we could," Nance agreed. "But seriously, maybe we could help each other keep on track."

"I think that's a great idea," said Jordan.

"It will take real honesty," said Nance. "No glossing over."

"That's for sure," said Jordan.

"Even if it hurts to hear the truth," said Nance.

"Even if it hurts," said Jordan. "Hey, isn't that what best friends are for?"

"High five," said Nance, putting her hand forward.

"High five," said Jordan. She settled back into her chair and took a bite of her cookie. She was finally beginning to let go of her painful past and her anger. But with it came clarity and a truth she felt the desire to express. She admitted to Nance, "I would be lying if I said I did not want a man in my life."

"Me, too," said Nance. "It's natural, embedded in who we are—the whole continuation of the species thing."

"Right," Jordan nodded then stated. "I'm kinda done with that last part."

"Me, too," Nance chuckled.

"But," Jordan continued, "we have to be strong enough to choose life alone rather than settle for an abusive or unhappy relationship."

"That's right," agreed Nance, "eyes wide open."

"And know thyself," Jordan added. "Understand what

is acceptable for one person might not be acceptable for another."

"True," said Nance. "No judgment."

"We should encourage each other to become who we want to be, regardless of whether or not we have a man in our life."

"Sounds good to me," Nance responded. She thought for a moment then revealed, "You know, I've always felt pretty good in my own skin until I started to date Randall. He would constantly point out what he perceived to be my imperfections and I started to feel insecure about myself."

"What gave him the right to judge?" Jordan questioned.

"*Really,*" Nance concurred. "You know he was far from perfect. I probably never told you this, as a pilot he was cool as a cucumber, but outside his job he had absolutely no coping skills."

"No, you never told me that," Jordan responded.

"Yeah, when he got nervous or upset he'd start burping uncontrollably," said Nance.

"Really?"

"Really."

"Gee," said Jordan, "suddenly the whiner sounds like a good catch."

They laughed. Then with a smile, Nance said, "I love you girlfriend."

"I love you, too, Nance."

TEN
I Like Myself in Blue

In the midst of winter I learned that there was in me an invincible summer.
Albert Camus

For all of the girls, time had passed much too quickly at Kate's cabin on the lake. Although they had purposely filled many days with activities there was still plenty of time spent lazing on the porch enjoying each other's company or simply reading a good book. At night they would play cards or head up to the lodge to dine and warm themselves by the fireplace. They always welcomed chats with newfound friends or to listen to the winsome melodies of visiting musicians.

Mischievous Olaf continued to supply plenty of comedic relief. One night, as the girls were enjoying sunset at the lodge, he ran past in pursuit of a baby raccoon. He was wearing only one slipper and the raccoon was quickly gaining distance with the other. When Karl happened to capture a video of Olaf barely dodging the antlers of an angry bull moose, the lodge decided to use the film as a tutorial to demonstrate why people should never approach wild animals.

One afternoon, Jordan and Nance were sitting at the kitchen table when Kate came in with a small bag of groceries. Nothing much would be needed to fill the pantry now that their trip was nearing its end.

"Where's Annie?" Kate asked.

"I don't know," responded Jordan, "I thought she was with you."

"So did I," said Nance.

"No. She went off to take some pictures around ten,

it's almost two now," said Kate, concerned. "Did she come back for lunch?"

"No," Nance answered, looking surprised.

"It's not like her to miss a meal," said Jordan.

"No, it isn't," Kate agreed.

"There she is," said Nance, craning to look out the window. In the bright afternoon sun they could see Annie sitting down by the lake, leaning against a tree. "She looks kind of sad; I don't think Ben called her yesterday."

"He calls her every day," said Kate. "Are you sure?"

"Let's go check on her," said Jordan, rising from her chair.

As they approached Annie they could see she was deep in thought, staring out at the lake. She did not notice the girls arrive. Kate spoke first, "Annie, are you okay?"

Startled, Annie looked up, "Yeah." She seemed surprised by the question.

"How long have you been sitting here?" Kate asked.

"Since noonish I guess," Annie answered. She acted wary—like she was hiding something.

Kate looked at her suspiciously. "Did you hear from Ben today?" she asked.

"Uh-huh," Annie replied. "He sent chocolates," she added then pulled a half-eaten box of candy from behind her back.

"Godiva," Kate noted. "Were you even going to share those?"

"Well . . . sure," said Annie, handing her the box.

Kate frowned. "I see all the *dark* chocolates are gone."

"I have a stomachache," Annie grimaced, hoping for sympathy.

"Good—you deserve it," said Kate. She helped Annie get up and thought, *You're just like having another child at times.* "You probably should lie down for a while," she told her. "Don't forget, the lodge party is tonight."

"Okay," said Annie, holding her belly as she walked toward the cabin, "and I *was* planning on sharing."

"Did you notice she emphasized the word *was?*" asked Jordan.

Annie smiled weakly.

Back at the cabin, Annie retired to her room and Nance began to fret about what she would wear to the lodge that night. "I forgot about the party," she said. "I didn't bring anything fancy to wear."

"Nance, nobody dresses up," Kate responded, "jeans and flannel shirts are like formal wear here. Just wear something comfortable."

"Okay," Nance replied.

"I'm wearing my black skirt and boots with my denim jacket," said Jordan. "I bought some beautiful turquoise jewelry at the gift shop to wear with them."

Later that day, Nance retired to her room. She really was focused on a fresh beginning for herself and thought tonight would be a good opportunity to present the *new* Nance. She knew that her clothes were fitting more loosely and remembered about the jeans in the bottom of her suitcase. She dug them out and pulled them on. *They fit!* she thought excitedly, admiring them in the full-length mirror. She searched again through her suitcase for something other than a sweatshirt or an old tee to wear but had no luck. However, she did have the new tee shirt that she had bought at the gift shop still in its bag. She pulled it on only to find it looked just the way all the others in her suitcase did—awful. It was too big, drably colored and without a touch of femininity to it. She took it off, neatly folded it and put it back in the gift shop bag. She changed back into her other clothes, picked up her purchase and scurried out the cabin door.

As Nance walked to the lodge, she felt elated about the way her jeans now fit. Her energy was way up, too. The great part was that she had been more active than usual, but in a way that was fun, not tedious.

In the gift shop, Nance handed the bag to the clerk. "I'll take this in a smaller size," she said. "Oh, in blue," she added with a smile. *I like myself in blue.*

"No problem," said the store clerk, a young man, likely a college student on break as so many were at the lodge.

"And," Nance added, looking up, "I'll take that one, too." She pointed to a pretty, soft-pink peasant blouse on the wall. "And these," she said, plucking a delicate pair of pearl dangle earrings off a rack.

As Nance waited for the clerk to total her bill, she noticed a basketful of mini picture viewers. *How fun,* she thought, remembering them from her childhood. She picked one up and peered into its tiny opening. "I love these little picture viewers," she said, spinning it to catch the light.

"That's a pencil sharpener, lady," said the clerk.

"Oh," Nance laughed, setting it back in the basket. "I knew that." After paying, she excitedly hurried back to the cabin and found the girls were already dressed, waiting for her on the porch.

"Are you ready to go, Nance?" asked Kate.

"Go on ahead, I'll just be a few minutes," Nance responded.

"Okay," Kate said. "Don't be long."

"I won't."

As Nance dressed, she pushed her bangs away from her face for the hundredth time and remembered Kate's scissors. A quick rummage through the kitchen drawer turned them up. She hurried into the bathroom, pulled up her hair, twisted it and secured it on top of her head. Then she combed her bangs down and carefully trimmed them to a flattering length.

Back in her bedroom, Nance searched deeply into her purse and pulled out a small makeup bag. A little blush, a dab of lip gloss and mascara was all it took to compliment her prettiness. She pulled on her new jeans and the pretty pink blouse she had bought at the lodge gift shop. When she finished dressing, she stood in front of the full-length mirror and straightened her shoulders. She liked how the peasant blouse fell flatteringly across her breasts then draped lightly over her hips. She smiled; it was good to feel feminine again. She loosened her hair and it dropped in soft dark curls past her shoulders. She pushed it away from her face and slipped on the pearl earrings. After assessing several views in the mirror, she ran her hands down both sides of her full womanly body and thought, *Not bad.* She liked what she saw, but more important, she liked who she was.

* * * * *

Every year the Buckskin Lodge closed in early October as winter edged down from the north. To cap off the end of the busy season, the lodge always threw a big party in the large upstairs hall where both visitors and locals alike were welcome. With a lively band and a free buffet, it was a guaranteed packed house and a good time.

As Nance headed for the lodge, even though it was still light out the stars were already beginning to open their eyes. She inhaled deeply, enjoying the scent of the night air. The sounds of nature, the rustling of leaves, a sprightly chirp, even a distant howl had become familiar to her. Earlier fears had been replaced by a deepened sense of herself and her connection to her surroundings. Many introspective walks and spending time with caring friends had begun to erase the imaginary boundaries she had placed upon herself. This evening, as she walked, she consciously released many of the old confining thoughts. With every step and every liberating exhale she felt lighter and more free.

As Nance ascended the lodge stairwell, she could hear the sounds of the party in full swing as music and laughter filled the air. *Old Nance* would have been intimidated. *New Nance* took a deep breath, smiled and entered the hall, anticipating a fun night with friends. Inside, the full dance floor pulsed as guests of all ages interpreted the lively music. Its vibe was upbeat and jazzy. She searched the room for the girls and laughed when Betty and Mr. Lewis waltzed by, both grinning from ear to ear. From a table across the room, Annie waved and motioned her over.

"*Wow*, look at Nance," said Annie, leaning in to speak to Kate and Jordan. The girls turned to see her heading their way. Nance radiated femininity and grace.

"She looks wonderful," expressed Jordan.

"Yes, truly," Kate agreed.

Nance felt a tinge of nervousness as she crossed the room. She was very aware of the eyes that were upon her. The

Swedes, who were sitting at a nearby table and making their usual jovial ruckus, suddenly became silent. Karl, who had his back to Nance, turned around and saw her as she approached the girls' table. The expression on his face revealed just how stunning he thought she looked.

"Nance, you look beautiful," complimented Annie.

"Thank you," said Nance, striking a cute pose. Then she coyly glanced over at Karl, smiled and nodded.

Karl was mesmerized. Neils nudged him and he managed to respond with a smile and a wave. However Olaf, immediately jumped to his feet and tried to head toward Nance, but Viktor and Mikael pulled him firmly back down into his chair.

"Olaf, leave the poor girl alone," said Viktor, a little too loudly. "Can't you see Karl has eyes for her?"

Karl, embarrassed by the statement, quickly turned back around in his chair. He gave Viktor a stern look.

Nance blushed and pretended not to hear.

Olaf grumbled and shrugged off Viktor's grip. He got up and crossed the room. Soon he was encircled by giggling women, two of whom had been on the river float trip. Animated and chest puffed out, he began telling a wild tale about a killer moose.

"This is such a pretty top," said Kate, reaching up and feeling the soft fabric of Nance's blouse.

"Isn't it?" Nance gushed, admiring the tiny, dark pink flowers embroidered around the edges. "I bought it at the gift shop today. And I'm wearing my *new* jeans," she added proudly, spinning around.

"Looking good," Jordan complimented.

"Your hair," asked Annie, "did you cut it?"

"Just the bangs," Nance answered as she took a seat at the table. "What are you guys drinking?"

"Wine. Colby is walking around filling glasses," said Kate. "Here, we saved one for you—Pinot Grigio."

"Excellent, thank you," said Nance as she took a sip. She looked around at the bustling party. "This is great," she commented.

"Let's get some food," Annie urged. The buffet had been calling her name for some time now.

Before they had a chance to rise from the table, Betty, wearing a pretty, soft-blue dress, came over to say hello. Mr. Lewis was happily in tow. He wore a plaid sport coat with a crisp, light-blue shirt. To Jordan, he looked twenty years younger than the first day she had seen him on The Swan. Tonight he was in high spirits and moved with *much* more ease and vitality. *In fact*, she observed of his attentiveness to Betty, *He looks like he's in love.*

"Hello, Mr. Lewis," said Kate.

"Well I'll be," Mr. Lewis looked around the table and grinned. "If it isn't the Scraped Knee Gang! Let's see, Kate . . . Jordy . . . Nance . . . and Annie," he said as he proudly pointed each one out.

"That's right. Great memory, Mr. Lewis," said Kate, extending her hand.

"You can call me, Ned," he responded as he clasped both of his hands around hers.

"Ned . . . of course," said Nance, glancing Betty's way.

Betty smiled broadly and winked. A new song began to play and Ned whisked her back out onto the dance floor.

"Isn't that sweet," said Nance, watching them go.

Grant snuck up behind Jordan and whispered into her

ear. "Would you like to dance?"

An unmistakable tingle ran up Jordan's spine. She turned around and found Grant looking very dapper in a black blazer, jeans and a white open-collar shirt. He stood there smiling with his hands innocently clasped behind his back.

"I did not know you could dance," said Jordan.

"Well I guess that's a chance you'll have to take," he said, grabbing her hands and pulling her out onto the dance floor.

"Food?" Annie pleaded, looking back and forth from Kate to Nance.

"Food," Kate responded and they all rose from the table.

"The buffet looks wonderful," said Nance. She smiled over at Karl, again sensing his eyes following her across the room.

The buffet table exceeded their expectations; it was a feast to behold. There was every kind of entree one could imagine from barbeque ribs to roast chicken to freshly caught local fish. Side dishes abounded, like crusty macaroni and cheese and green bean casserole still bubbling from the oven. Roasted and sautéed vegetables were offered a la carte or tossed into delectable pasta dishes. Assorted fresh baked breads and rolls were cozy in baskets under white cloth napkins, waiting to be slathered with butter and jam. Homemade soup and chili steamed enticingly inside large crocks. For those who still had room, a dessert table promised sweet rewards.

"Hello, girls," said Judy, speaking loudly over the music. She, too, was indulgently filling a plate with food. To commemorate the festivities, she was wearing an artsy hand-painted blazer. “Having a good time?” she asked.

“Hi, Judy,” Kate responded. “Yes, wonderful. Will you sit with us?”

“Of course,” Judy responded. She waited while the girls made their plates then followed them to their table. Jordan was back and Colby had already refilled their glasses with wine, leaving a couple of spares. Judy gladly accepted one and offered a toast. “To the lodge,” she said appreciatively.

“To the lodge,” the girls concurred, clinking their glasses together.

Annie took a bite of her macaroni and cheese and drifted blissfully. Jordan couldn’t resist and took a forkful when she thought Annie wasn’t looking.

“Hey, get your own,” Annie frowned, pulling the plate close to her.

“I’m really not that hungry,” said Jordan.

“*Someone’s* in love,” teased Nance.

Jordan ignored her, took a sip of her wine and tried to conceal a smile.

“Sooo,” said Nance, looking at Judy. She still had questions about the whole Penis God thing but obviously felt hesitant to ask.

Kate, Jordan and Annie looked at her curiously.

“So,” responded Judy. Unruffled, she looked back at Nance expectantly.

“Can I ask you a question?” Nance proceeded slowly.

“Anything,” Judy responded.

“Well . . . ,” Nance continued, “I understand what you were talking about the other night, but . . . ,” again, she hesitated.

"But, what?" asked Judy. She set down her fork, patted her lips with her napkin and waited for Nance to talk.

Nance looked around and lowered her voice, "But . . . well . . . what about sex?" Unfortunately, Nance's question came out the very moment the band stopped playing. She *had* lowered her voice but still had to be heard over the sound of the music. She might as well have used the loud speaker. A good portion of the room fell silent and curious eyes turned toward her. She cringed, you'd think she was about to give out the winning lottery numbers.

"Excuse us," Judy reprimanded the onlookers, "private conversation here." She shook her head and turned her attention back to Nance.

The girls giggled; something about selective hearing. The band began a new song.

"Sex," said Judy, "is a personal choice. But you have to be aware of the physiological changes that can happen to a woman when she engages. It's definitely a factor for many. Keep in mind, the goal is to be able to make intelligent choices about whom we enter into long-term relationships with. Sex can definitely cloud the decision-making process and give you a false sense of security."

"Yeah, Nance," said Jordan, "beware the Penis God."

"Mmm-mm," Nance agreed.

"I prayed about it," Annie said matter-of-factly.

"You prayed about what?" asked Nance.

"I prayed exactly that—Dear, God, what about sex?"

"Did you get an answer?" Nance asked.

"Immediately," said Annie. "It was clear as a bell."

"What was it?" asked Nance.

"I heard the words in my head, 'Hasn't that got you in

enough trouble?' and I immediately thought, *Yep*."

And they all thought, *Yep*.

"What happens after the Penis God is dead, Judy?" asked Jordan.

"You have learned to accept that men are only human. You cherish the one you love, but you do not put him on an exaggerated pedestal. You understand you must be responsible for your own happiness. Then you can enter into a relationship informed and start to make better decisions about who you choose as your significant other. It is one of the most important decisions you will ever make. Now you are free to love with your eyes wide open, not based on the lies we tell ourselves or baseless dreams of what can be."

They were quiet for a moment then Kate raised her glass, "Cheers to that."

"Cheers," said the others. *Clink—clink*.

The music stopped playing and one of the band members, the fedora wearing lead singer, announced, "We have a real treat tonight. My new friend, Karl, has asked to sing a song from his homeland of Sweden for us."

The room hooted, whistled and clapped. Nance looked at the other girls and shrugged with surprise. She did not know Karl could sing.

The girls watched as Karl walked up to the small stage. He looked very handsome in an un-tucked, pin-striped shirt and jeans. He picked up a guitar and confidently took a seat on a tall stool. He cleared his voice and began to strum a stirring melody on the guitar. When he began to sing, it was in a voice that was completely unexpected; it was clear and strong, yet gentle and moving, much like Karl's personality. As he sang the beautiful Swedish ballad, he often glanced Nance's way.

She did not understand the words, but it did not matter, for like everyone else listening she was completely captivated.

When Karl finished singing, the room filled with appreciative applause. Karl grinned widely, raising his hand and thanking the audience as he rose from the stool.

Olaf teasingly hollered out in a woman's voice, "Karl, I want to have your baby!"

Everyone laughed, including Karl.

Still entranced, Nance watched Karl as he walked across the room to his table. "Men," she said dreamily, "they really are like a box of chocolates."

"You got that right," Jordan agreed, glancing over at Grant.

The band resumed playing a slow song and couples began to emerge, folding in to one another on the dance floor. Karl approached Nance and reached out his hand in a sweet gesture to dance. Nance arose without saying a word and they drifted out onto the floor, locked into each other's eyes.

Annie and Kate smiled at each other and resumed eating what was left on their plates. Jordan had picked up her fork and was eye-balling Annie's plate when Grant came back to the table and once again stole her away. He led her onto the dance floor, pulling her close.

The song had barely finished when out of the blue, Betty yelled, "Hit it boys!"

The band broke into a lively Latin beat. The lead singer belted out in his gritty voice, "*Let's do the Mambo! Shimmy, shimmy Mambo!*"

Betty took the lead and the dance floor came alive as everyone tried to follow her moves. Onlookers were laughing and clapping appreciatively and when the music segued into the Twist, the younger Swedes pulled Annie, Kate and Judy up to join them. By the end of the song, almost everyone was out of their seats and swinging to the music.

Afterwards, exhausted and exhilarated, Karl and Nance burst through the lodge doors onto the deck, anxious to feel the cool evening air. "*That was crazy,*" laughed Nance, leaning against the deck rail to catch her breath.

"*Ya, crazy,*" Karl laughed.

Nance had begun to love hearing the sound of Karl's laugh. It was a deep, honest laugh. To her it was one more thing that epitomized his true character—Karl gave you Karl. The more she got to know him the stronger her feelings for him had grown. Even though it was not in her nature to hold back, up until now she had been quite reserved toward him. They obviously enjoyed each other's company, but she did not take lightly the mistakes she had made in the past. So far she had not noticed any red flags, except—*hello,* he lived in Sweden. The thought saddened her and she turned to look out at the lake.

Karl, sensitive to her emotions, noticed her sudden quietness. "Are you okay?" he asked.

"Yes . . . fine," Nance answered, her tone subdued.

"Are you warm enough?" Karl asked. "I'll get my jacket for you," he offered, already moving toward the door.

"No," Nance stopped him, "I'm okay. Thank you."

He respected her continued silence and stopped asking questions, but he was there for her if she wanted to talk. Together they quietly looked out upon the lake. A fine mist began to settle and the moon cocooned them in its silvery light.

After a few minutes, Karl, no longer able to be silent,

turned to Nance and said softly, "Come to Sweden in the summer."

"Oh . . . no . . . ," the *old* Nance immediately answered, "I don't like to trav--." Just then, Betty caught her eye through the tall lodge window. Dancing past with Ned, she was grinning and giving her a big thumbs-up. Nance turned back to Karl. She saw his eyes were full of emotion. She reached down and took his big hands in hers and said, "I'd love to."

Karl let out a loud "*Whoop!*" then excitedly picked Nance up and spun her around. She laughed and when he set her down he bent over and kissed her softly on the lips. He then jubilantly spun her around again. When he released her, she wobbled momentarily but she was laughing—it was all good.

After the lodge party ended, the girls could not help but giggle as they walked back to the cabin through the darkness. "Look," said Annie, pointing up, "there's a full moon tonight. We have to go up Great Spirit Mountain tomorrow morning."

"Yes, let's do it," Jordan agreed. "It would be a great finale for our trip."

"I'm game," said Nance.

"Okay," said Kate. "The weather should be perfect tomorrow. We can pack our lunches tonight so we can get an early start."

"Yes!" Annie was pleased.

In the morning, thermoses were filled with ice tea and the girls packed their sandwiches and trail mix for the hike. When they were ready to go, Kate noticed Annie did not have her camera with her. This was very unusual and she asked Annie about it.

"I'm leaving the camera home today," Annie answered, looking somewhat disheartened. "It's too heavy. With all the lenses that stuff weighs like twenty pounds."

"I'll carry a piece in my backpack," Kate offered.

"I can carry a piece, too," said Jordan.

"Really?" Annie asked, her face brightening. *"Okay."* She trotted down the hall, grabbed her equipment off the bed and quickly returned.

"Gosh," said Annie as she handed each of the girls a lens, "I *really* appreciate this."

"Like, 'I'll share my dark chocolates with you next time' appreciative?" asked Kate, one eyebrow raised.

Annie smiled guiltily and nodded back at her.

"Everybody ready?" asked Kate, pulling on her backpack.

"Ready."

The girls followed their usual route along the edge of the lake. First they passed the boathouse with its brightly colored rental boats bobbing ever-so-slightly in the soft breeze. Above, the lodge, backlit by soft morning light was just beginning to stir. The morning air had an invigorating feel to it, once again reminding them the seasonal change was coming. On the lake trail there was an abundance of chipmunks and squirrels gathering autumn's bounty of seeds and nuts. A lone jay flitted from tree to tree, briefly following the girls as they walked. He chattered loudly, seeming to scold them for their frivolous use of time. "Hurry, hurry," he cried, "hurry, hurry." As if to warn them that Old Man Winter was on his way.

From the base of the mountain, it only took the girls about thirty minutes to reach the rock outcropping where the carving of the Great Spirit sat. With their newfound knowledge, the carving and the shield had even more meaning to them now. They marveled at it, as if seeing it for the first time. Annie approached it first and instinctively placed the palm of her hand on the shield.

"The old Indian still looks pretty good," commented Jordan, touching the cool granite.

"Yes, it does," Nance agreed. "The shield is starting to show some wear though."

"Yeah," said Kate, looking at Annie. "*Someone* spread a rumor about an old Indian and the Legend of the Shield."

"You started it," Annie frowned. "We should be making royaltics off all the tee shirts they sell in the gift shop."

"Really," Kate agreed. "Not to mention all the gift items."

"Really, though I'm not sure if it's a rumor anymore," Annie added thoughtfully.

"*Oh*," Kate suddenly remembered. She turned to Jordan and Nance, "Remind me to show you the old book Ed found at the flea market when we get back to the cabin."

"Okay," said Jordan.

"Man, am I hungry," said Annie.

"Oh, big surprise there," said Kate, pulling her backpack off.

"Anybody want a power bar?" Nance asked, pulling several from her pocket. "They're awesome." Everyone gave her an odd look and declined.

They settled into what had been their usual picnic spot when they were children; a comfortable place close to the edge where they could safely dangle their legs. They unpacked their sandwiches and opened their thermoses of cold tea. Below them, the sweeping view of the valley was a refreshing site to Jordan and Nance.

"It looks different than I remember," commented Nance.

Kate pointed out why. In recent years the river's course had been permanently altered by an overactive beaver. He was nicknamed 'The Terminator' for the effect his ferocious dam building had had on the waters flow.

"Nance and I have been thinking," Jordan spoke, "we know it's usually just you and Annie on these trips, but would we be intruding if we joined you on occasion? We don't want our friendships to take a back seat anymore," she added, "this place, these times . . .. we haven't had this much fun and felt so renewed in a long time."

"Of course," Kate answered. "We would love it. Every girl needs a good jammie hang."

"Great," Nance responded. "I also thought it would be nice to rent one of the cabins next summer and bring my kids. It would be a shame not to introduce them to the beauty of this place. I can't believe I have not done it sooner."

"It's like we've been walking around in some kind of fog," Jordan added. She and Nance looked hopefully at Annie who had been quiet, listening attentively.

"I'm in," Annie chirped.

"Wonderful," Jordan grinned.

Quietly the girls savored their sandwiches. Kate had made her tarragon chicken salad with slivered almonds. It was nestled on a croissant and complimented with a side of seedless grapes. Each savory bite was enhanced by the wonderful view of the valley.

After lunch, Annie got up and fiddled with her camera,

taking several photos of the girls and the landscape.

"What was your favorite part of the trip?" Kate asked Jordan and Nance collectively.

"Oh, it was definitely the Jeep ride wouldn't you say, Nance?" Jordan asked.

"Oh," Nance laughed, "most definitely."

"Best of luck Marilee Belmont," said Jordan. The reality of it didn't hurt anymore.

"It won't be easy for her," said Kate. "Rodney's going to be a hard man to love after the glow wears off."

"Yeah, but he was sho' easy to look at," said Jordan.

"Hey," said Annie, rejoining them, "that would make a great country western song."

"How so?" asked Kate.

"He was easy to look at but a ha-ard man to love," Annie crooned.

Kate, Nance and Jordan laughed.

After a pause, Kate, too, began to sing, "When he walked into a room, he knew just what to do. Tan and tall and handsome, he made the girls all swoon."

The girls all laughed again.

Then Nance sang, "His hair was always perfect . . . his pearly whites so bright."

"His butt was nice and perky so his jeans they fit just right," Jordan rhymed.

They laughed again then Annie belted out, "Oh, he was a good-lookin' man."

They finished the song together, "Easy to look at but a ha-ard man to love."

The girls stayed on the mountain long into the afternoon and the sun began to tinge the horizon amber. They wanted to soak in every last moment of the day, knowing their trip would soon end. As they finally began their descent, each of them once again stopped to touch the shield on the hand of the Indian carving for good measure. Annie, the last to do so, spun around at the sound of an eagle's screech. She searched the sky in earnest, but nothing was there. She smiled and turned toward home.

* * * * *

The shades and colors of autumn were quickly becoming more evident in the landscape around Buckskin Lake. Soon, deep reds, golds and oranges would weave together with the eternal green of the firs, once again creating one of nature's most beautiful tapestries.

Today was the last day of vacation and Kate sat alone on the cabin porch, reflecting on the days gone by. This rustic cabin of weathered wood and river rock harbored so many years of happy memories. She was grateful to have it and to be able to share it with her family and friends. She thought back to the days of her childhood when she sat in this very chair, chatting away as her mother lovingly hand-stitched one of the many quilts that to this day brought so much comfort. Only the strongest thread and the softest of fabrics would do. She also remembered evenings spent watching her father's hands as he expertly tied intricate fishing flies at the kitchen table. Fascinated, she watched as he would carefully select a feather from his extensive collection, looking for the perfect blend of color and movement to guarantee the catch. There were countless days of canoeing and hiking with her father on and around Buckskin Lake. The air was constantly filled with chatter, mostly *hers*, that only stopped long enough for them to devour the delicious sandwiches and gulp down the fresh lemonade her mother had packed. There were long walks with her mother, too. They would pick plump blueberries from the many patches that lined the upper trail. What wasn't devoured along the way was baked into muffins, bursting with the flavor only fresh-picked berries could provide. For breakfast, her mother would bake them into silver dollar pancakes on an old, seasoned iron skillet that perfectly crisped the edges. Pure maple syrup from local farms was always at hand.

Kate smiled and took a sip of her hot tea. Those days with her parents were gone now, tucked away as cherished memories, never to be replaced but refreshed by *new* days filled with the effervescent laughter of her grandchildren. She pulled her quilt up around her shoulders, it was October now and the soft breezes of September were turning into gusts of cold air. Out on the lake, she could see Jordan and Grant scooting near the shore in his little sailboat, the "Itildo." Jordan was reclined in his arms as he maneuvered about through hundreds of flitting white-winged flies. Down by the shore, Annie was being Annie. She was enraptured with a small yellow flower growing out of an old tree stump. Kate shook her head in amusement; it was always funny to watch Annie twist in all sorts of weird positions while trying to capture a photo with her camera. Not far from her, Nance was basking in the glow of desirability as Karl and Olaf argued over who was the best man to teach her to fly fish. Her hair was pulled back in an attractive up-sweep and a cascade of pretty dark curls fell around her face. She wore a two-tone blue fitted tee over her jeans. Gone was the frumpy clothing that she hid behind at the beginning of the trip.

Kate sat back contentedly in her chair. It was good to see her friends happy and know in some small way she had been a part of it. Out on the lake, a gust of wind suddenly billowed Itildo's sail, setting it on a new course. It made Kate wonder, *When does a new voyage begin? Is it when we leave for some exotic port or is it when we finally decide to leave the painful past behind and embark on a new journey, as Jordan had?* She looked affectionately at Nance. *Or is it when we stand up for ourselves and say, 'This is me and I am proud of who I am,' and we honor ourselves by letting someone into our life that will truly love us just as we are. Or is it when we are struck by illness,* she looked lovingly at Annie, *and life as we know it changes forever? Whatever that turning point is*, her thoughts continued, *all we can really do is board our ships with courage, crew it with people who care and support us, then trust the winds will come and fill our sails again. How many times we begin a new journey does not matter, the key is to bravely embrace the challenge and anticipate that something good will come—to keep searching the horizon for that silver lining. Never stop looking. Never stop hoping.*

* * * * *

The airport was its usual sea of activity as Kate pulled the Suburban to the curb. On board was Nance and Annie. Grant was bringing Jordan in one of the lodge vans not far behind them. The girls knew this day of departure would be bittersweet. Though they hated to say goodbye, they had solace in knowing they had plans for many more good times ahead.

The girls hopped from the Suburban just in time to see Betty walk by. She was followed by Colby who was carrying what appeared to be a surfboard in a hot-pink floral carrying case.

"Betty," Nance called out, "where are you going?"

"Hawaii," Betty called back, a big grin on her face. "Surf on the north shore is rad this time of year."

Not far behind, Colby was followed by Mr. Lewis. He was wearing a dapper straw hat and sporting a splashy tropical shirt. He, too, had a big grin on his face and tipped his hat as he strolled by.

The girls were still shaking their heads in amusement when Grant and Jordan pulled up. Grant helped Jordan from the van then opened the side door to retrieve her luggage. He began to reach for them but abruptly stopped, recalling their last airport encounter. He turned to Jordan and teasingly asked, "May I help you with your luggage?"

"Yes," Jordan responded, feigning annoyance.

Grant proceeded to unload Jordan's luggage, then toted hers along with Nance's inside the busy airport lobby. The girls followed him inside the terminal. After situating them at the ticket counter, Grant disappeared then came back and surprised Jordan with the cayenne-colored vase they had worked on together.

"It turned out so beautiful," Jordan beamed. She looked up into Grant's eyes, "So, I'll see you in two weeks?"

"You betcha," Grant grinned then spontaneously gave her a big kiss.

Jordan, smiling, watched him go. She was pleased when he stopped and spun around to give her one last wave. She blew him a kiss and waved back, watching until he disappeared into the bustle of the airport.

"Oh, no," said Nance, color draining from her face.

"Nance," a man's voice called out from across the airport.

Nance turned her back to the man, hoping he would not approach, but it was too late.

"Nance, is that you?" asked the man dressed in a pilot's uniform. He was fiftyish, average height and somewhat pudgy around the waistline. For some reason Annie immediately visualized a squirrel.

Nance sighed and turned around. "Hello, Randall," she said with little enthusiasm.

"You look *great*, babe," he commented as he rudely checked her out.

"You remember Jordan," Nance said flatly, "and this is Kate and Annie."

Randall greeted Kate and Annie but deftly avoided contact with Jordan.

"So what's up, Nance," he asked, blatantly enamored with her new look.

Nance shifted uncomfortably. "I've been busy," she responded.

"Uh, what do you say we get together next week?" Randall asked, emboldened by the misguided assumptions of an egotist. "I'll even let you cook me one of your delicious roast beef dinners."

Jordan looked at Nance and bit her tongue. No matter how Nance responded, it was *her* call. It quickly disheartened her when she saw Nance's face brighten as she began to smile. *Oh, please no*, thought Jordan, *you've come so far*.

Randall confidently grinned back at Nance, expecting her usual response. Suddenly, he became aware that Nance was not looking at him—she was looking *above* him. Sensing a looming presence, he spun around and came face to face with Karl's big chest.

"Randall . . . this is Karl," said Nance with a polite yet stern smile.

Karl peered down at him with an equally stern smile on his face.

Randall burped. He burped again. He nervously looked at his watch and mumbled something about a flight to catch. Randall—continuing to burp as he scurried away—got the message.

"I guess Betty's right," Nance chuckled, "sometimes a frog *is* just a frog."

"You let him off *way* to easy," said Jordan.

Karl stepped toward Nance and embraced her. "Are you okay?" he asked.

"Yes, I'm fine, thank you. I thought you had an early flight?" she asked.

"Olaf," responded Karl, nodding toward his brother. Sporting a fresh cast on his arm, Olaf was engaging a pretty female attendant at the ticket counter. His other brothers were crashed out on the floor using their backpacks as pillows.

"What happened?" Nance asked.

"Long story," responded Karl.

The loudspeaker sounded, "Now boarding flight 320."

"I'm sorry, that's our flight." said Nance. She glanced over at Jordan, sensing her friend's discomfort with the Randall encounter. Turning back to Karl, she asked, "Can you do something for me?"

"Anything," Karl answered.

Nance took a pen from her purse and scribbled something on a piece of paper. She handed it to Karl. He looked at it then back at her and grinned. He gave her a quick kiss and with a wave to the others headed off.

Jordan, still freaking out, asked Nance, "What would you have done if Karl had not come along? Would you have said yes?"

"No, of course not, Jordan," Nance reassured her. "I'm the *new* Nance, remember? I'm not going back to my old ways." She knew that in time, Jordan would trust her on this subject and vice versa. And she was pretty sure that was the last she'd hear from Randall.

At the security gate, the four girls all hugged each other and said their good-byes. As Jordan and Nance continued on, curiosity got the best of Jordan and she asked Nance about the note she had handed to Karl. Before Nance could answer, the loudspeaker sounded again.

"Paging . . . Uh," the woman's voice hesitated. There was murmuring and confusion in the background.

"Paging . . . ," the woman said again, suppressing an obvious giggle. It was triggered by a tall handsome Swede named Karl, grinning at her from the other side of the counter.

"Paging Captain Jack Ass."

Somewhere in the Manchester-Boston Regional Airport, Randall burped.

* * * * *

On a crisp winter day in Middleton, New Hampshire, Jimmy's delivery truck shuttered to an abrupt halt in its usual spot in front of Stella's Beauty Salon. He quickly gathered his packages and stepped down from the truck, the sound of freshly fallen snow crunching beneath his shoes.

As usual, several women, including feisty old Dorothy Miller, took notice of the handsome delivery man from Stella's large plate-glass window.

Next door, in the upstairs apartment of The Big Pink Donut, Tammy was busy sketching vintage dress designs for her portfolio. Intentionally situated by the window, she, too, leaned forward from her chair to catch a view of Jimmy.

"Woo-ooo!" the familiar rusty red pickup went by and the three young girls hooted.

Jimmy smiled and waved back. He was beginning to sense a pattern here. Suddenly, out of nowhere, Ida Mae Perkins was directly in his path and he nearly tripped over her. "Morning, Mrs. Perkins," he said, stepping warily around her.

Dorothy Miller, obviously annoyed and still gawking from Stella's window, shot a disapproving look at Ida Mae.

"Morning, Jimmy," Ida Mae greeted. She turned and looked back at him as he went on his way. Then, with a mischievous grin, she looked up at Dorothy Miller and winked.

THE END

Love and Purple Sea Serpents

What would the world be, once bereft
of wet and of wildness?
Let them be left, O let them be left, wildness and wet,
long live the weeds and wilderness yet.
Gerard Manley Hopkins

Made in the USA
Lexington, KY
03 November 2019

56413183R00187